LADIES' DAY

LADIES' DAY

Lisa Williams Kline

CamCat
Books

CamCat Publishing, LLC
Fort Collins, Colorado 80524
camcatpublishing.com

This is a work of fiction. Names, characters, places, and incidents are either products of the author's imagination or are used fictitiously.

Hardcover ISBN 9780744309157
Paperback ISBN 9780744309188
Large-Print Paperback ISBN 9780744309195
eBook ISBN 9780744309270
Audiobook ISBN 9780744309287

Library of Congress Control Number: 2022949449

Book and cover design by Maryann Appel

5 3 1 2 4

FOR JEFF—

WHO TAUGHT ME TO PLAY GOLF.

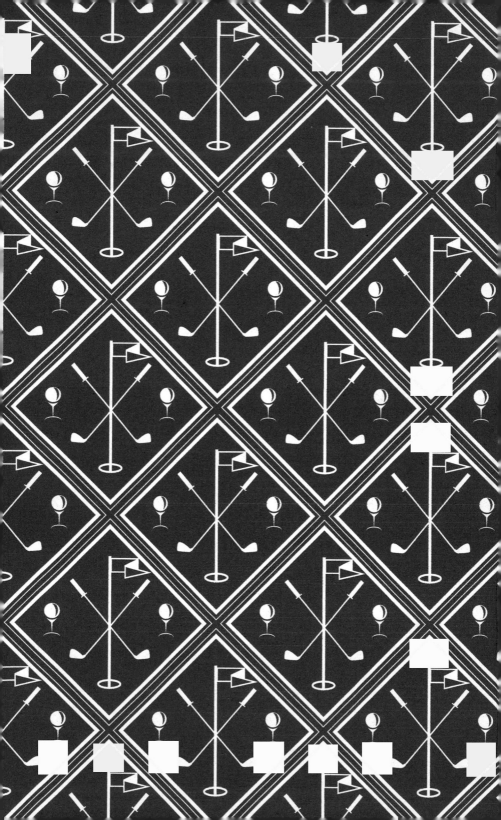

CHAPTER ONE

Beth

B eth went by the university to check her mail, and one of her freshman comp students was waiting for her in the faculty parking lot. Beth hadn't seen her in class for weeks and had, in fact, given up on her. But now here she stood, in jeans and a T-shirt that looked slept in, shifting her weight from one dirty flip-flopped foot to the other.

"Mrs. Sawyer, I know I've missed some classes, but can you give me an incomplete?" One of her pierced ears was infected; the lobe was an angry red.

"You have an F, Tiffany," Beth said mechanically, her heart beginning to pound as she unlocked her Civic door. That haunted look in Tiffany's eyes—it was like Julie's. And the way she resembled a wild cat yearning for escape. Beth had that sinking feeling she always got when a student self-destructed. Every battle she fought with a student reopened the battle she'd lost with Julie.

"Mrs. Sawyer, please." The girl's bloodshot brown eyes welled. "You have to give me another chance. I got kicked out of my apartment and I've been living in my car."

"What about your parents?" Beth studied Tiffany's face. So many of them lied. The lies they told were endlessly brazen and inventive. Not just the grandparents dying and dogs eating homework and computer malfunctions, but wild stories about crazed roommates and bizarre accidents. If only they put half that creativity into their essays.

"I can't go back home. Please, just give me an incomplete. I have to get this grade to keep my financial aid."

A bluish vein pulsed in the girl's thin neck, and her slender fingers trembled slightly. When had she eaten last? Beth's throat tightened, and she was carried back to that day with Julie. A day she yearned to have a chance to relive.

She dug into her purse and pulled out a bar of Hershey's chocolate she had packed for energy during her upcoming golf round and gave it to Tiffany. "How much time do you need?" she asked.

THIRTY MINUTES LATER, Beth sat down on the wooden steps in front of the rundown Silver Lakes pro shop to put on her golf shoes and wait for Margo and Vanessa. A late spring breeze ruffled through the hot pink azalea blossoms, and a few petals fluttered to the ground. Stray dandelions bravely popped through a sidewalk crack next to Beth's foot. While tying her left shoe, Beth spotted another spider vein beside her knee and scrubbed her thumb over it.

She suddenly had to think of sitting on the couch with Julie and Paul when they were little, on Friday afternoons, watching some animated movie, her fingers tracing the fine, damp hair at her children's temples. They would still be in that position when

Mark arrived home. He'd come up behind them and put his warm, capable hands on Beth's shoulders. She remembered it so clearly it could have been yesterday.

That was before.

When life was sweet and simple.

Paul had just told her the night before that Mark was thinking about marrying Ronda, the woman he'd been living with for the past few years. She'd always known that her husband would move on long before she could. She'd been dreading it for years.

Beth gave her head a good shake to force herself back into the present, when Margo pulled her SUV into the lot and stuck her head out the window. "Hey, girl! Ready to bring this course to its knees?"

"Oh, sure," Beth said, grinning. Margo could always make her smile.

Margo, tall, thin, and athletic, with a long thick ponytail she'd let go gray, climbed out and headed around the back of her SUV to unload her clubs, then stuffed her golf glove into her back shorts pocket. "Now, should I accidentally on purpose forget to get a scorecard, or do we feel like higher math today?" Margo, a retired high school gym teacher and several years older than Beth, had kept her Maryland accent even though she'd been living in North Carolina for close to twenty years.

"Oh, let's keep score, we're not that bad." Beth followed Margo into the pro shop to check in.

"Afternoon, ladies!" said Vanessa, joining them inside to complete their usual threesome.

As Vanessa leaned over the counter to grab a scorecard, Beth admired her slim, dark legs and glossy black box-braided hair, both of which made her look younger than her sixty years. "Did you girls notice," said Vanessa, "that the Memberships Available sign by the club entrance has been vandalized?"

"Really?" Beth rolled her eyes.

"Somebody changed the *p* in *memberships* to a *t*, so it now says Membershits Available. Isn't that the most juvenile thing?"

"Teenagers!" growled Margo. "Jean and I used to live on Bonner Lane and teenagers used to keep stealing our street sign because they thought it said Boner Lane. I wanted to say, 'Hellooo! Spell much?'"

Beth laughed. "Have you ever known a time when Silver Lakes *wasn't* having a membership drive?" In their small town of Solomon, there was the Old South Club for the old rich and the Country Day Club for the new rich. And then there was their Silver Lakes—the Groucho Marx of country clubs. People who *weren't* rich and didn't want to belong to any club that would accept them as a member.

"I don't think I could play on one of those fancy courses with putting greens like velvet. Silver Lakes is just my speed," Beth said.

"You would be referring to bumpy greens constantly under repair?" Vanessa shook her head, laughing.

As the three of them headed down the path toward the first tee, Beth patted her left pocket for her lucky ball and her right pocket for the ibuprofen for her joints on the back nine. Her old pull cart squeaked as it bounced along behind her. Sturdy yellow daylilies swayed in an overgrown bed beside the cement walkway, which badly needed power washing.

Margo, Beth's friend and neighbor, with Mark's support, had persuaded her to try golf. It was fun but also required intense concentration. It helped to push the obsessive thoughts out of Beth's mind. Vanessa, who taught composition at the university with Beth, joined. Beth had always envied Vanessa's no-nonsense, upbeat control of a classroom. The three women, none of whom had played before, had taken lessons together. They'd never found a fourth, though they'd invited others to join them at first. Fitting the weekly game around their respective work schedules, they became comfortable as just three. They complemented each other so well. Beth was perfectly content playing straight man to Vanessa and Margo. She had long accepted that she didn't stand out in a crowd, neither with her reserved, quiet personality nor with her appearance—average height, slim build, and light brown hair that she occasionally highlighted to disguise the threads of gray. She loved the laughter caused by Margo's outspoken wit, and she reveled in the attention caused by Vanessa's beauty and confidence. And that's the way it had been, for over fifteen years.

"Well, Silver Lakes isn't as bad as it used to be," Beth said. "Remember when we didn't even have a porta-potty on the course and we had to go in the woods?"

"And instead of a snack bar," Vanessa added, "they had that self-serve steamer with those wrinkled, green weenies?" All three of them made faces and laughed at the memory.

"Come on, let's show this course who's boss," Margo said, teeing up her ball.

"I hear you, girlfriend," said Vanessa.

Beth smiled. Being with Margo and Vanessa had lifted her spirits already.

The friends had a long-standing agreement that serious subjects had to wait until after the round, and so Beth didn't bring up Mark's plans to get married again until they had ventured into the parking lot. "I knew it would happen someday, but it still comes as a shock!"

Margo opened the back of her SUV and sat on the tailgate to take off her golf shoes. "After all the water under the bridge, do you really care?"

"No, I guess I don't really care." Beth put her ibuprofen and lucky ball back in the zippered compartment of her golf bag, knowing she sounded defensive.

"Yes, you do." Vanessa threw her clubs in the back of her little red convertible. "But you shouldn't. That's ancient history."

Margo took off her visor and redid her gray ponytail. She gave Beth a pointed, almost pained look. "You do still care, don't you?

Aww, Beth. Vanessa is right. That's ancient history. Think how hard you've worked . . . how hard we've all worked . . . to put that in the rearview mirror."

Beth looked away.

CHAPTER TWO

❖ ❖ ❖

Beth

Beth and Vanessa were almost out to the first tee for their weekly round when Margo came scooting up on a cart at top speed. "Sorry I'm late, girls!"

Vanessa glanced back at the pro shop and pointed to two carts full of men racing toward them. "Hey, is that Buddy Watkins's group trying to jump in front of us?"

"Oh, they're slow as Methuselah!" Beth said. "Quick, Margo, gun it up there and hit!"

Margo, the only one on a cart, gasped and zipped toward the red tees, still eighty yards away. The golf clubs in the men's bags rattled like sabers as their carts bounced over the gravel path, closing the distance to the women.

"Hey, girls," Buddy shouted, twenty yards away. "When's your tee time?"

"Twelve-forty-one," Vanessa said.

"Ours is twelve-thirty-one." Buddy, red-faced, screeched his cart to a halt and jumped out. "So I guess we're up." He hiked his pants under his protruding stomach and pulled out a driver with a head the size of a Clydesdale's hoof.

"Your tee time is twelve-fifty-one," said Beth, feeling heat rush to her face. "I saw the book. We're up."

Buddy glowered, caught in the lie.

His current behavior was proof of his misogyny. Not that proof was needed. The three friends hated Buddy on principle, because he'd once stopped Vanessa in the hallway of the clubhouse and asked her to get him another beer—even though she was dressed in golf attire.

Beth knew all of Buddy's buddies, except the man sitting in the back cart. He was slim, with salt-and-pepper hair, and seemed entirely too distinguished to be with the rest of those Neanderthals.

"Be reasonable, ladies," Buddy said. "We're on carts and you're walking. We'll get on out of your way and you can have a nice *leisurely* game. Talk all you want." He minced his fingers together like he was tapping the ash from a cigar.

His mocking emphasis on *leisurely* made blood pound in Beth's head.

Buddy Watkins had been known to go into a catatonic state while standing over a putt, and he had the nerve to accuse them of slow play?

"We don't have to go ahead of them, Buddy," said the salt-and-pepper man. "I'm not in that big of a hurry." He smiled. At Beth. She almost turned around to see if there was someone behind her whom he was smiling at.

"Aw, let them go," Vanessa whispered to Beth. "If they're behind us they'll try to hit us with every shot."

Beth stared at Vanessa for a few long seconds, glanced at salt-and-pepper man, then finally shrugged. "Fine."

"Mighty kind of you ladies," said Buddy with a gloating smile. "We'll get right on out of your way. I doubt you'll see our dust for the rest of the afternoon."

Beth waved up at Margo to move aside, then stepped behind the ball cleaner to wait with Vanessa while the men hit. Buddy had a baseball swing but was a competitor who managed to muscle most shots down the fairway.

Beth heaved a sigh. Sometimes she damn near hated every man on earth. At the same time, there was always that deep and almost indescribable connection with Mark that would never be severed. All those years they'd spent with Julie, and the difficult years after she was gone.

But what was with salt-and-pepper guy in the back cart? She could feel him looking at her. It surprised her. Most men, when meeting the three of them, would check out Vanessa, and laugh at Margo's jokes. Men didn't even notice Beth. According to Vanessa, it was because Beth didn't send out signals. "What signals?" Beth had asked. "You know, girl . . . *signals*," Vanessa had said. "Obviously you don't know what they are because you haven't sent out any for fifteen years."

When the gray-haired stranger stood to hit, he had a smooth swing that spoke of a few lessons, but mostly of natural athleticism. He was a thinking player. While he didn't hit his drive as far as Buddy's, the ball was in a better position for his next shot.

Beth joined Vanessa in managing a flinty smile as the men scooted by. She looked away but she was too late to avoid snagging the gaze of the gray-haired man again. He touched his fingers to the brim of his cap. Funny, they hadn't said a word. Signals, she supposed, beginning to feel the heat of a blush.

Good grief, she'd literally felt a physical pull, like being reeled in by a fishing line. Maybe it was the pills. She had just started on estrogen. Within days, the hot flashes and mood swings gloriously disappeared, but Beth also found herself struggling not to stare at men's crotches, and she'd nearly tackled that poor new management trainee at Harris Teeter, with his starched white shirt. Surely all she had to do to stop this foolishness was to quit taking the pills for a few days. Who said there was no upside to getting older?

Beth had told herself for years that her life was full without a man. She had her own house. Her teaching career. A son she saw three times a year. The possibility of a very sweet daughter-in-law, if Paul *ever* married Andrea. Grandchildren, maybe, in the future. And she knew that the reason her marriage had ended had very little to do with her or her ex.

No, Julie's disappearance had done them in.

As she and Vanessa headed down the fairway to meet up with Margo, two well-fed Canadian geese and their long-legged, downy babies waddled along a muddy pond's edge. A couple of yellow butterflies looped by, fluttering around each other in figure eights, then, seconds later, a pair of dragonflies, stuck together, buzzed around Beth's ear. Pairs everywhere.

When Beth and Vanessa arrived, Margo picked up her tee. "I cannot *believe* y'all let them play through."

BETH HAD A HARD time concentrating on the game. On the fifth hole, she hit a terrible shot that went deep into the woods. She waded through the muscled oaks and grasping underbrush to find her ball, but she found her mind wandering back to the unraveling of her marriage. The sun went behind a cloud, and suddenly the air went cold and the leaves on the trees rattled like bones. A vine wrapped around her ankle, and she kicked her foot blindly, her eyes beginning to swim with tears as she tried to shake it off. Her friends seemed so small and so far away.

"C'mon, Beth," Margo yelled. "It's not the Hope Diamond. Just drop one!"

Beth didn't answer and, finally, she found the ball nestled under a healthy-looking patch of poison ivy. Beth could hardly see the ball for her tears. She'd gotten pretty good at losing things. Golf balls. Daughters. Husbands. She launched a low screamer and the ball skidded out of the poison ivy, solidly bonked the trunk of the oak tree, and ricocheted into the rough ten yards behind her original location.

"I can't concentrate," she told Margo. "I should just quit."

"If there's one thing I know, woman, you're not a quitter," Margo said.

THERE WERE NO silver lakes at Silver Lakes Country Club, although there were several muddy, scum-covered ponds badly in need of dredging. When they reached the seventeenth tee, a par three over one of the ponds, Buddy's group was still on the green. Like a buzzard, Buddy circled his putt, peering from every angle.

"Jesus H. Christ." Margo leaned against her cart, blowing air through her cheeks. "They've been there long enough to take out a mortgage." She rummaged in her bag to pull out a short tee. A printout fluttered out of the pocket.

Beth jumped to pick it up.

"No!" Margo reached for the flyer. "Let me have that! You're not supposed to see that!"

Beth, surprised, began to hand the printout back to Margo, but couldn't help but glimpse a photo of a tall, solid girl with shoulder length chestnut hair. The resemblance was inescapable.

Margo tried to snatch the printout back, but Beth pulled away. "No, Beth!"

Beth turned her back to Margo to read the caption. "Local Teen Phenom Sky Sawyer to Play in US Girls Junior Qualifying Event in Winston-Salem."

She looked like Julie, but yet, she didn't. She was serious, determined, nothing impulsive or dangerous about her. Where Julie's eyes had always flickered with mischief and secrets, this girl's eyes, beneath her visor, looked out across the fairway with disarming honesty, determination, and lack of guile. "Sky Sawyer? Oh my God."

Beth flashed to a memory of Julie announcing that should she ever have a daughter she'd name her Sky. And Beth and Mark had laughed; the choice had seemed so, well, like a teenager.

"Okay, fine, you've seen it. Freaks you out, doesn't it? I mean, the name and the resemblance. What are the odds?" Margo raked a hand through her gray hair and jammed on a flowered sun visor. "Vanessa and I kind of had words over it. We wanted to tell you, but thought we'd be jumping back on that crazy merry-go-round again. I told her, 'Let's just not say anything.' But, last night I thought about it, and woman, you deserve to know. I was going to show you after the round."

Beth scanned the article. Sky Sawyer was a fifteen-year-old freshman at Solomon High, a small school south of Statesville. She had moved to the area a few years ago, taken up golf, and had quickly begun to score well against the country club girls who had started at a much younger age. In exchange for lessons, she worked at the driving range at Solomon Municipal. "I cannot believe this."

Vanessa waved a long-fingered and manicured hand at Beth. "She's fifteen, Beth," she said. "About the right age."

"Could be coincidence," Margo said.

"An incredible coincidence. But she could be her—" Beth couldn't finish the thought. Was it possible? No. She couldn't believe how easy it was for her to get her hopes up. After the private investigator, thousands of dollars, hours of therapy for both herself and Mark, after fifteen years of false clues and dashed hopes, this was the closest thing to a lead in a long, long time. Beth pulled out her three wood and took a practice swing, but her brain was a jumble and her hands were shaking. She forgot to check to see if the men had cleared the green. And she must have had more adrenaline than she thought. Her shot soared over the pond and took the green on the fly.

"Fore!" Beth should never have yelled. Buddy Watkins straightened up and glared. Just as Mr. Salt-and-Pepper turned to look, he grabbed his side and doubled over. Beth's ball had hit him right in the ribcage.

"Oh my God, you did a Gerald Ford!" Vanessa said, gasping.

After a jumbled moment of confusion, they agreed that Beth should take Margo's cart and go down and see if the man was okay. Margo offered to go with her, but Beth thought that could be more incendiary than helpful. Beth jumped in, feeling like an idiot as she bounced down the asphalt path and thundered over the small wooden bridge to the turnaround beside the green. By the time she pulled up beside the other two carts, the man was hunched over with his hands on his knees, surrounded by his buddies.

"I'm so sorry," Beth called as she tried to push through. "Are you hurt?"

Buddy's face was florid as he poked at the air in front of Beth's nose with his index finger. "Were you trying to kill somebody?"

"In all fairness, Buddy," said Salt-and-Pepper Man, rubbing his ribcage, "I could have read the Sunday *New York Times* while you were standing over that four-footer."

Beth felt a flush of appreciation for the man's support, especially since he was the one she'd hit. She stepped closer. "Seriously, maybe you should get that looked at."

"It's okay, I'll be fine. Just a little bruise." The man hobbled back to his cart.

"If you end up having to go to the doctor, I'll take care of the bill," Beth said. She checked her pockets, already knowing she hadn't brought any business cards, and finally scribbled with the stubby golf pencil on the scorecard folded in her pocket. "Here's my name and number. I'm so sorry," she said again.

"It was a nice shot," he said with a grin, wincing slightly. "Rib . . . I mean pin high." He looked at the scorecard. "You have a decent round going here. You sure you want to give me the scorecard?"

"With the amount of time I've spent in the woods today, I don't think I'm going on tour any time soon."

"So who is?" He laughed. He had nice, even teeth, with one crooked incisor on the right side. Lively, deep-set brown eyes with crow's feet around them. A person who laughed a lot. Again, the pull, like a magnet. Good God, maybe she ought to ask her doctor if cutting back on that estrogen dosage would help her gain back her equilibrium.

"Do you have any ice? Try putting ice on it," she ended up saying, a little breathlessly. And as quickly as she could escape, she rode the cart back up the hill toward her friends.

"You survived!" Margo said, shielding her eyes against the sun. "Did you get your ball?"

"Shit. In all the confusion, I forgot."

Beth looked back just in time to see Buddy Watkins pluck her ball from the green, glance at their group on the tee, and toss the ball into the pond. Then he got in his cart and headed for eighteen.

"That son of a bitch!" Margo said.

"We ought to report him to the golf committee!" said Vanessa, crossing her arms in frustration.

"That's okay, I don't need that ball, because I'm definitely quitting now." Beth climbed out of the cart. She just couldn't concentrate. All she could think about was Sky Sawyer.

CHAPTER THREE

Beth

Beth settled onto Margo's floral couch with a glass of Pinot Noir next to Vanessa as Margo fired up a playlist on her phone. Melissa Etheridge's voice enveloped the room. Margo's two cats lay on the rug, watching her every move, waiting for snacks.

"Do we have to listen to that white music?" Vanessa complained good-naturedly, drumming her purple-decorated nails on her wineglass and crossing her long, dark legs. "Bruno Mars, John Legend, something."

Margo changed the music to Tracy Chapman, which met with Vanessa's approval, and sat down with her wine. She propped one ankle on the other knee, removed her flowered golf visor, threaded her fingers through the sweat-soaked gray hair at her temples, and redid her ponytail.

"So, Beth, how about that guy you hit? Think he'll call and ask you to pay up?"

"God, I hope not. That was incredibly embarrassing. I hope he wasn't seriously hurt. I don't think he was, do you?"

"No, Beth, she means *pay up*." Vanessa used air quotes.

"Ask you out." Margo nodded. "I saw him checking you out."

"You saw him checking me out?" Beth felt a flush creep up her neck.

"Absolutely, what, am I blind?"

For years Beth had tried not to be envious of Margo's *sureness*. She always knew her position on everything and wasn't afraid to tell anyone what she thought. There were no gray or murky shadow areas for Margo. There was right and there was wrong. Good and bad.

True and untrue.

Not so with Beth.

"Oh, I'm not interested in dating." She tried to wave off the topic. "I don't want to talk about that. I want to talk about Sky Sawyer."

"Okay, but first, I want to tell you, somebody was talking about him at the homeowners' association meeting last night. He's Buddy's brother-in-law. His wife died about two years ago. He lives in Maryland, his oldest son just started college orientation at Davidson and he's thinking of moving down here. His name's Barry something. Barry Redmond?" Margo winked and pointed an accusing finger. "Tell me you were fantasizing how he'd look without his shirt. Come on. You were, don't lie."

Beth tried not to laugh but was unsuccessful. "You've poisoned my mind, Margo. I would never think stuff like that on my own."

Beth and Vanessa often kidded that everyone had love problems but Margo. She'd had one awful marriage to a man, and a son, and then had found Jean and never looked back. Margo had long struggled with her sexual orientation and resisted inklings that she was gay, but then, when she finally met Jean, she realized, "Hey, guess what? I am! And proud of it."

"Here's the important question—did you give him your number?"

"I did. But just in case he needs me to pay for a doctor's visit. I told you, I'm not interested in dating."

"Beth! You can't tell me you didn't find him attractive."

"Well, I did think he was attractive. For ten years I thought men were annoying pains in the asses—"

"No argument here!"

"—and now I find them attractive again. Maybe it's the estrogen. But I've tried dating, and it didn't work. I mean, remember that guy who serenaded me with those out-of-tune electric guitar solos and kept blowing out the power?"

"I'll never forget that guy who tried to turn our double date into a Cutco sales presentation." Vanessa laughed.

"Or what about that guy who invited me to dinner and wore plaid cargo shorts and fixed Hamburger Helper? I kept hoping that he'd turn out to be a really brilliant and funny guy, but I just couldn't get past the shorts and the menu." Beth rolled her eyes.

"Maybe you should just settle for a couple of C batteries. Probably a helluva lot less trouble." Margo downed her wine.

They laughed.

"Seriously, I think you should go out with Barry Redmond and thoroughly check out his injuries," Vanessa added.

"I'll think about it." Beth took a swig of wine, then sucked in a deep breath and plunged in before she changed her mind. "Okay, so now can I talk about Sky Sawyer? Will you girls go with me to that girls' event in Winston-Salem—it's on the weekend."

"To see that girl play? Sky Sawyer?"

"Yes. I'd like to get a good look at her. Maybe even meet her." Just saying those words out loud made her throat suddenly feel raw.

"I knew you'd want to go," Margo said. "Count me in."

"Sure," said Vanessa. "Of course I'll be there."

"I know it's a stretch, but what if she is her daughter?" Beth looked at her friends as if to implore them to make it so. "What if she is?"

"It boggles the mind." Vanessa smiled as she reached out and touched Beth's hand to reassure her.

"Gosh, for so long, I thought Julie might be . . ."

"I know," Margo said quickly, before she had a chance to say the word.

It was exhausting, wanting something as badly as Beth had wanted to find Julie. Sometimes she thought the yearning had gone away; she'd find herself completely enjoying something, and then she'd suddenly remember that Julie was gone, and she'd feel the joy rush away like water from a broken dam. It was curious how life could do this to a person. How you could believe that you'd survived something and then a single grainy newspaper photo could both inspire you with hope and plunge you to despair in a matter of seconds.

"Vanessa and I knew you'd obsess."

"Lord, did we know you'd obsess."

"I really don't want to, though. It's so painful. But I can't help it."

"I know. You've got to find out. It has to be done. I know that." Margo poured everyone another inch of wine. "I just wish you didn't have to go through it, that's all."

"Right." Vanessa nodded, drumming her nails on the stem of her wineglass. "I mean, you don't even know if Julie ever had a daughter. Maybe it won't be her, maybe it's just a coincidence, and you'll have gotten your hopes up for nothing."

Beth nodded, unable to speak. She let Tracy Chapman's gravelly and haunting voice wrap around her, and feared she was going to cry.

"You know, you think you get over something . . . "

"There are things we never get over."

Vanessa added, "Seriously, we get it."

Margo's phone rang, and while she answered, Beth picked up the photo of Sky Sawyer, went to the kitchen, and put her wineglass in the dishwasher. She could tell from Margo's voice that the call was from Jean, on her way home from work. A business letter, signed by Jean, lay on the counter next to the phone. It was a letter of resignation from her law firm.

"Hey," Beth said to Margo when she hung up. "Not being nosey, but is Jean changing jobs?"

Margo waved at the letter dismissively. "Every summer Jean has an existential crisis and starts thinking, 'Is this all there is?' Then she writes a resignation letter. It's a seasonal thing. Most people are depressed in the winter, Jean is in the summer, don't ask me why. I just sign her up for guitar lessons or take her to a Melissa Etheridge concert and she perks right up. She never goes through with it."

"A tad too blasé, don't you think? Aren't you concerned? You don't want her to be miserable at her job," Vanessa said. Vanessa's husband, Justin, as a cameraman on the local eleven o'clock news, was never home at night and almost never got vacation.

"Of course I don't. I was just kidding, but after fifteen years together, you get to know a person. In the end, she loves her job. Sometimes Jean's needs are simple."

"Come on, is anyone simple?" In the years since Julie had left, Beth had wondered *Is that all there is?* a dozen times a day.

The huge ache at the center of her being had just become part of her.

"It's getting late." Beth looked at her watch. "I've got big plans to go home and curl up in front of the TV with a Lean Cuisine. Gosh, at some point I should probably call Mark."

The two cats, splayed in the last patch of sun on the dining room floor beside the bay window, leaped to their feet, their silky tails weaving through the air.

"Well, I wouldn't call him until you're sure." Margo and Vanessa exchanged looks Beth did not miss as they all headed for the front door. She knew Margo and Vanessa didn't like the idea of Beth contacting Mark.

And she knew she was going to contact him anyway.

CHAPTER FOUR

Beth

I n the twilight, Beth's house waited, dark and quiet. She put on Barenaked Ladies to try to keep her mood from plunging to despair. She made herself a cup of tea. Neither helped. So she just faced up to it and put on an old Bonnie Raitt playlist that dripped with slide guitar, self-pity, and blues. As she listened to Bonnie sing "I Can't Make You Love Me," she pondered the truth of that statement.

Beth had stopped trying to make Mark love her after Julie ran away. They'd moved here to the suburbs of Charlotte twenty years ago because it was where *he'd* wanted to live. Mark, who'd grown up in a lower-middle-class neighborhood in Winston-Salem, had seen living here as a beacon of success in his optometry practice. They'd led an idyllic life. At least that's what Beth thought. Then, Julie disappeared. They'd worked with the police for a few months. While the police searched for her, they did not do so with the fervor and vigor Beth would have liked. Assuming Julie was a runaway, her case was not a priority. Beth was all too happy to believe that Julie had run away and hadn't become victim to a crime—kidnapping or, worse, murder—but she was disappointed and frustrated in the detectives' jaded attitude. Maybe she didn't want to be found, they'd say. She could be anywhere, they'd say, miles from their jurisdiction. Don't worry too much, she'll show up when she's ready, they'd say. That was by far the most infuriating comment.

So, when someone claimed they'd seen her at Cherry Grove Beach, Beth and Mark didn't even notify the police but went down there themselves to check in the nightclubs, under piers and bridges, in abandoned homes. Once, when she'd run away before, they'd found her like that with a boy. After a month, the police told them they had run out of leads. Good riddance, Beth had thought, and they'd hired a private investigator, who, after several months, was not able to come up with anything, either.

So, they were on their own—scouring social media, calling Julie's friends to ask if they'd heard anything, searching the neighborhoods she'd frequent for the slightest clue. At first every day. Then once a week. Then once a month. Then, after about three years, Mark gave up. Beth was devastated. She could never give up on her daughter, didn't know how. She couldn't focus on anything except looking for Julie. She knew she'd crossed a line when one of Julie's friends blocked her number after years of regular text messages, asking the same question, "Have you heard from Julie?" She also knew she'd be losing Mark if she kept going, but there wasn't a thing she could do about it.

For so many years, her thoughts were repetitive, like an earworm, over and over. *Why had Julie run away? Where was she? Was she alive? What would she do if Beth found her? Would she ever come home?* Beth had even had to take medication to free herself from the repetitive thoughts.

She'd had thousands of sleepless nights. She'd lost Mark. She'd lost friends. People sympathize for a while, but eventually, life goes on. Beth didn't think anyone really meant to abandon her, but only Margo and Vanessa, really, had stuck by her side.

After Beth and Mark divorced, she'd stayed in the neighborhood because she'd wanted Julie to be able to find her if she ever tried to come back. She'd even kept Mark's name and increased her social media presence so Julie could find her. Even now, fifteen years later, she maintained an online presence. She'd told herself, and everyone else, she'd moved past it all. She'd redecorated Julie's room. She'd been through years of counseling, she'd thrown herself into teaching, and she'd gone through the motions of dating a few men.

All this time, had she been kidding herself? Had she never truly given up that hope? Was there still that huge emptiness at the heart of who she was? The force of her longing was as powerful as a surprise wave at the beach throwing her onto the sand.

Her all-encompassing love for her children had surprised her. After she and Mark got married, she'd worked long hours in the training department of a corporation, helping Mark pay off his school loans and establish his practice. Julie and Paul were at daycare until Paul was a year old, when the babysitter reported seeing Paul's first steps. That's when she realized that nothing mattered more to her than her children.

With heart-stopping speed, she'd given up the corporate job and began teaching adjunct at the college level to spend more time with them, to be there when they'd go through their fleeting and irretrievable firsts.

Then, after Julie was gone, Paul an adult, and her marriage over, she took on a full load of classes. It had become her new passion, her new family, her new everything. She had a knack, it seemed, for inspiring students to examine their lives and write about it. She'd spend entire weekends grading compositions, writing long encouraging notes to every student. She was aware that she needed her students much more than they needed her. And that in asking them to examine their lives in their essays, she was avoiding looking at her own.

Beth walked upstairs to the bedroom she'd turned into an office, checked her university email, and found three more late student essays. She also found, to her relief, that Tiffany had submitted all of her late work. Sometimes these students did reward her faith in them. She started printing the essays and assignments, then went to the kitchen and dialed Paul's office number, glancing at the clock. Three o'clock California time.

"Hi, sweetie. Did I call at a bad time?"

"Hey, Mom. Uh, no, I've got a couple minutes. What's up?"

She could hear the staccato rhythm of his fingers on the keyboard as he spoke to her, and thought about his piano lessons, and how much he had hated them. His bony butt squirming on the piano stool, his small knees bouncing, beat-up from scrapping on the basketball court. While Julie looked like Mark, Paul looked like Beth. Wiry, slight, with curly light-brown hair. He'd unfortunately inherited her myopic brown eyes as well.

He now worked for a software company developing specialized internal search appliances. She'd visited once, and there was a foosball table around the corner from his cubicle, and sometimes when she talked to him, she could hear the slam of the rubber ball into the goal slot. It sounded no different from his college dorm. The cafeteria featured cuisine from all over the world and outdoor tables with umbrellas like a French bistro. People kept stuffed animals on their desks.

"Oh, I just played golf with the girls," she said. "Is it nice out there?"

"It's nice out here every day, Mom." She wished he would stop typing while he talked to her. "What's up?"

Beth hesitated.

He probably didn't really want to know. "How's Andrea?"

"Whoa, now there's a subtle conversational misdirect. She's fine."

"That's good." Beth took a breath, ready to tell him.

"Not getting married, Mom."

"I wasn't even thinking that."

"Yes, you were. I could feel you thinking it transcontinentally."

"Paul, I was not!" She tried to talk over his infectious laugh. "How's work?"

"Ex-cellent. Just got a bonus."

"That's fantastic! What for?"

He was working on an employee information system for internal corporate use. His musical young voice unraveled into her ear, and she tuned out and just let herself float in the pleasure of the sound. "It's like a corporate version of we will find you, we will hunt you down, you cannot run, you cannot hide," he finished.

Beth hesitated, then asked the first question that came to her head. "Could you use something like that to track down Julie?"

Paul sighed. "Mom."

"Well, could you?"

Paul abruptly changed the subject. "So, what's up?"

"Paul, there's this young girl. She's a golfer. She looks like Julie and her last name is Sawyer. And guess what her first name is?"

"What?" Now the typing stopped.

"Sky." Silence on the other end.

"Paul, are you still there? Do you remember Julie saying that's what she'd name a daughter?"

"Yeah." His voice sounded scratchy.

"So...?"

"I'm thinking." She could picture him, hunched over his desk in his jeans and T-shirt. His serious freckled face, rounded when he was a boy, now planed, with a vessel in one temple nearly always pulsing. "Sawyer is a pretty common name."

"Not that common."

"I mean, this is not even really a lead, Mom."

"Yes, it is. More than anything in several years."

"You don't know anything about this girl."

"I know that what I read fits."

Paul was quiet for a while. "Have you talked to her?"

"No, not yet. I'm going to watch her in a tournament."

"I'm just . . . maybe I am freaking out a little. Does Dad know?"

"Not yet."

"Don't tell him. Not unless you find out more about this girl."

Beth was silent.

"Did you hear me, Mom?"

After she and Paul hung up, Beth studied the photo of Sky Sawyer again, touched her finger to the girl's earnest face. The dirge-like guitar progressions of "Love has No Pride" began, and then Bonnie sang about calling out someone's name, and falling down on her knees, her world-weary voice made exquisitely and achingly beautiful with its longing. Beth laid the article on her counter. She had a flash vision of the swing of Julie's dark hair as she climbed into her car that last time, and a throbbing rose in her throat.

CHAPTER FIVE

Sky

"**O**kay, so Silas and I tee off right behind these two hot-shots—you know the type, guys with pastel polo shirts and custom-made Ping clubs. They take thirty practice swings on every hole." Sky let her arm hang out the car window as they chugged up the highway in her dad's red work truck with the Moving Up in the World logo on the doors, on their way to the last tournament of the year with her high school team. She loved telling her dad these war stories from the golf course.

"Yeah, yeah." Her dad laughed, glancing over at Sky, sweat shining on his face.

"And so on the second hole we hit these monster drives so we're practically right on top of them. One of the guys waves us through, and Silas says, 'Sure, but we could all play together if you want.' So they hesitate, you know, because they don't want to play with a girl, so Silas says, 'She won't hold us up,' and they finally say 'Okay.'"

"That was their first mistake," her dad crowed, with a cackle, as he pulled through the stone entrance of a fancy neighborhood.

"And this is my favorite part. I bend down to tee up from the men's tee, and one of the guys points and says, 'Wrong tee, the ladies' tees are way up there.' I said, casually, 'I think I'll hit from here today.'"

Her dad grinned, glancing at her again. "And . . .?"

"And I bombed one thirty yards past them!"

"That's my girl!" He gave her a high five.

"And they were standing there with their mouths hanging open. So by the fourth hole, one of the guys, as usual, couldn't resist a bet. He bet Silas that he couldn't get it closer to the hole. Silas swipes his club across the grass, and says, 'Oh, I better not. My folks wouldn't like that.' And then the other guy says, right on cue, 'No big money. Just a dollar, how's that?' Then I said, 'Silas, you know what your dad said about betting on the golf course.' And that pretty much iced it. When Silas's dad came out to the course and met us on the eighteenth fairway, still in his shirt and tie from the office, he says to these guys, 'Hope my boy and his friend Sky didn't take too much of your money.'"

Sky savored this moment. She reached into her back pocket and unfolded four twenties and waved them in front of her dad's face.

Her dad threw back his head and roared with laughter. She loved being able to make him do that.

As he swung into the club entrance, both of them fell silent. A line of tall oak trees stood at the end of the driving range, and the sun, behind them, lit their top leaves on fire. Gleaming pyramids of pristine balls were stacked in each position on the range, and the putting green was like green velvet. The rounded white-columned porch of the clubhouse overlooked the pond by the eighteenth green.

"Look at that pond, Sky," her dad said. "It looks like somebody poured melted gold over the top, I swear."

Sky nodded. "Wow." Sarcastically, she added, "I bet I'll fit right in."

"Listen, baby girl, you can *play*. So, you're damn right you fit in." He gave her another high five. "Good luck, Sky. Call me when you need me to pick you up."

Sky waved good-bye and raced to the ladies' locker room and threw cold water on her face. Her dad couldn't watch her play because he had a roofing job, but she was secretly glad he couldn't stay. She wandered, popping her knuckles, through the maze of lockers, showers, stalls, even the posh card room. This locker room was as big as her whole apartment. Someone had lit a scented candle and the sweet waxy odor permeated the rooms, as if the walls themselves were made of wax, as if everyone and everything here was historic. Polished caramel-colored wood shone on the locker doors, and gold plaques with ladies' names engraved on them gleamed. Sky rubbed her thumbnail over a couple of them. Frances Wilkinson. Carolyn Abbey. Wilhelmina Harris.

The Ladies' Room at Solomon Municipal, which Sky jokingly called her home course—as if anyone would claim it—had mildewed indoor-outdoor carpet, cinder-block walls, four warped rusty metal lockers that didn't close, and one loose, ancient toilet stall that always backed up. The only thing that looked even slightly well cared for was the flowered plastic case for the toilet plunger.

Sky rifled through a basket on the marble countertop that held free lotion, shampoo, hairspray, and foot cream. She unscrewed the cap and smelled the foot cream. Peppermint.

In the sitting area, she examined a miniature bonsai tree with bright stuffed birds perched on twisted limbs. A plaque read, "Royal Run Birdie Tree." Each of the little birds had somebody's name embroidered on it. Wilhelmina Harris #12. Wilhelmina Harris must've had a birdie on the twelfth hole in a tournament. *You go, Wilhelmina. You own #12, Wilhelmina.*

The other girls on the team would laugh their asses off. Jordan, the number two player on the Solomon team, laughed at the green and pink skirts the ladies wore, and the little engraved golfer pins and key chains they carried. She did hilarious imitations of the studied way these old ladies addressed the ball, first bending their knees, then straightening their elbows, and then poking their butts out and doing about ten waggles, and finally swinging the club like a slow-motion pendulum on a grandfather clock. Jordan would use this snobby, nasal tone and put her hand on her hip and say, "Willie, you are just going to *love* that shot."

But Jordan could hang out at a club like this and make fun of it for the rest of her life. Her dad was a golf pro and her family had connections. Around Jordan and the other girls, Sky pretended to have just as much contempt for the fancy clubs as they did.

Now, as she rubbed the exotic hand lotion on the back of one hand, she heard someone vomiting in a bathroom stall. Her own stomach tightened, and hot saliva filled her mouth.

"Need some help?" she asked through the marble door. The toilet flushed.

The door opened, and, to Sky's shock, Jordan came out, wiping her mouth with a wad of toilet paper. Jordan had been number one on the team until Sky joined. Sky had thought there might be some hard feelings, but it seemed as though Jordan wanted to ally herself with Sky. She had made friendly overtures.

"Hey, are you okay?" Maybe Jordan had an eating disorder. They were rampant at school. Though Sky was aware of the drugs and the rainbow parties and the various other disorders and excesses among her peers, she had tunnel vision. She played golf. She wasn't interested in what the other girls talked about. She wasn't included in the social life of any clique. She didn't have a mother who networked with the other moms. She didn't care.

"Don't look at me like that."

"Like what?"

"I'm not bulimic, I just do this before every tournament," Jordan said in a hoarse voice. "Nerves, that's all." Jordan went to the sink and splashed water on her face, staring at herself. "I look like shit," she said.

"Yeah, you kinda do." Sky didn't try to lie. Jordan's face was pasty, and she had prune-colored circles under her eyes. "Want some water?" From the refrigerator under the sink, she gave Jordan a small, cool bottle.

Jordan held the bottle against one slate-colored cheek, then the other, taking shaky breaths. "Thanks. I'm going to be okay."

Sky nodded. She wished she hadn't heard Jordan barfing. She'd been nervous, but not *that* nervous. Like being pulled into a whirlpool or vortex. She stepped back. "Ready to go out on the range?"

"In a minute." Jordan brushed her teeth with her finger, then gargled with the free mouthwash. She put her hands over her face and just stood there.

"Okay, well, see you out there." Sky turned and went outside into the sun.

Sky knew she'd just been insensitive and uncaring. She probably should have hugged Jordan or something. But better to let Jordan pull herself together and not get sucked in. Sky needed to focus on her game.

She didn't see the other two girls on her team, so she found a spot on the range and took a slow practice swing with her nine iron. She tried to push Jordan's nerves out of her mind, but a tremble twitched up her wrist and forearm, and she stepped away from her ball. The other girls who were lined along the practice range acted like they belonged here. The way they moved oozed confidence.

Sky took a few deep breaths, copying the smooth, focused way the other girls swung. It was true, nobody needed to know she felt like a fish out of water. She could play, so she belonged on the course.

The air buzzed with the sounds of birds, frogs, and late-season bees. By the lake's edge glided a black-faced swan, its alabaster neck arched like the handle on a pitcher of iced tea.

"That swan is mean as a fucking snake." One of the girls in blue—"Katherine Anne Boyd" was embroidered on her golf bag— spoke up. Katherine Anne was built like a gazelle, with long tanned legs, calculating eyes, and spiky dark hair.

"No shit!" said a tiny girl whom Sky guessed was Korean. Her bag said "Jenny Park." "Remember, last year during regionals, Jamie Watlington hit her second shot near the water, and when she went down to look for it, that sucker charged her and tried to bite her in the ass." Both girls laughed. Their shirts were an identical shade of royal blue, and they sported blue nylon golf bags not only with their names embroidered in cursive but also insignias reading, "North Carolina Girls' High School State Champions." Sky's entire bag and set of clubs probably cost less than their putters.

Sky's team wore light yellow. She'd saved her money from working at the range to buy the right kind of shorts—khaki, low rise, fitted, with the right logo. She took out her seven iron, hit some warm-up shots, and continued to eavesdrop on the girls' conversation behind her.

"Once last year at regionals, I hit one in a trap near a water hazard and this ginormous alligator is lying in there," added Katherine Anne. "I go over and he starts roaring like a lion. Scared the *pee* out of me."

"Yeah! Someone told us they do that when they see a hot female alligator. Look at it this way, Katie, he was flirting." Jenny weighed about eighty pounds. Sky then watched as she cranked up and, using upper arms about the circumference of spaghetti noodles, smashed a drive about two hundred twenty yards.

"Yeah, right. Just what I want—tongue from an alligator." And Katherine Anne proceeded to hit a drive that looked like it was shot from a cannon, passing the two-hundred-fifty flag and rolling to a stop at about two hundred seventy. She flicked her eyes over at Sky as if she were looking at a bug.

Sky pulled out her driver and cranked out a drive that rolled to a stop only five yards short of Katherine Anne's. When the girls' eyes bored into her back, a tickle of gooseflesh raced over her scalp.

She busied herself with choosing tees and balls, pretending blood wasn't thundering like an express train to every extremity. She had so much adrenaline, her kneecaps were shaking.

Sky shouldered her bag then wrapped her hair tie one loop tighter around her ponytail and headed over to meet the girls' golf coach, Ellie Harper, as she pulled up and glided beside her on an electric cart. "Don't look now, but see that woman in the navy shorts?"

Sky looked over.

Coach Harper rolled her eyes and grinned. "I said don't look now!"

"Oh! Sorry." Sky stared straight ahead.

"That's the women's golf coach from Clemson University."

"No way," Sky said, glancing back again at the woman's casual, unhurried stride. Her stomach muscles tightened.

"Way," said Coach Harper. "Remember, don't think score. Worry about one shot at a time."

Sky nodded, kept her head down, listened to the clink of the clubs on her back as she headed for the tee.

"On number sixteen, there's a blind water hazard in front of the green," said Coach Harper, looking at the course map. "You're not gonna want to hit driver on that hole, else you'll be smack in the drink, okay?"

"Yes, ma'am."

IT WAS A SHOTGUN start, and Coach Harper told Sky her first hole was number eleven. As she headed out over the course and approached it, an uphill par four with a wide fairway, Sky looked up and saw the tall spike-haired girl from the championship team, Katherine Anne, in her royal blue, casually chipping beside the ladies' tee box. Beside her, a curvy African American girl in a pink T-shirt that said "South Iredell" took a powerful practice swing. The coach in the navy-blue shorts waited by the tee.

She'd barely stepped onto the tee box when Katherine Anne flipped a tee and won the first drive, and the girl from South Iredell, who introduced herself as Tanya, won second. Sky stepped back and leaned on her clubs, scanning the horizon and taking shallow breaths to try and focus.

This was good. The other girls hitting first would give her shots to match or beat. She sniffed the exotic free lotion from the fancy ladies' room on the back of her hand.

Katherine Anne's drive was huge—over two hundred fifty— and landed about six inches off the fairway in some scratchy rough. "Katie, oh yeah!" A man and woman in a cart halfway down the fairway cheered. Her parents, no doubt. An impeccably dressed couple—probably Tanya's parents—clapped with civilized support.

Sky stepped up and leaned to sink her tee. She straightened, took a practice swing, aware, from the corner of her eye, of the other girls' parents. And the coach in the navy blue shorts.

She reassured herself, *Nobody can hear your heart but you.*

She swung and hit it cleanly.

It rolled to a stop ten yards short of Katherine Anne's, but in the center of the fairway, in a slightly better position. Time slowed, and for a few long fearful seconds she thought no one would clap for her.

Fine. *Eat shit and die!*

But they did—a smattering of soft, polite applause.

She breathed and stole a glance at the Clemson coach. She was writing something on a notepad, expressionless. Sky shouldered her bag and headed down the fairway.

The other girls' clubs clinked rhythmically in their bags as they strode ahead of Sky. She watched Katherine Anne's mom leap from her golf cart and race, her middle-aged boobs bouncing, to the middle of the fairway to hand her daughter a water bottle. How ridiculous! Thank God she didn't have an embarrassing mother like that.

She imagined herself in the future, coming off the eighteenth green and seeing her mother waiting there. She'd win a lot of prize money and buy her a house. And her mother would kiss the top of her head a thousand times and say how sorry she was that she'd left Sky behind. Once, a long time ago, Dad had said, a girl's mother had come back after years of being gone when the girl wrote a song for her and sang it on *American Idol*. It could happen.

By the sixteenth hole, Sky was in a pretty good zone. Cicadas thrummed in the grass beside the tee, and her brain buzzed pleasantly. Her focus had narrowed to a long, thin tunnel. Katherine Anne, still with the honors, hit a conservative tee shot down the middle with a long iron.

Sky didn't know why Katherine Anne hadn't gone for it. She pulled out her driver, felt a powerful buzz, and bombed a huge drive over the rise. She'd almost driven the green.

"Gorilla!" Katherine Anne suddenly gave Sky a giant smile. "Too bad there's a blind water hazard out there at the bottom of the hill, Sky. Your ball could be a *teeny* bit wet."

Behind her, Tanya said, "Oops."

Oh shit. This was the hole Coach Harper had warned her about.

Sky wanted to throw her club but knew better, and instead just slammed it into her bag marginally harder than usual.

A half hour later Sky walked off the precisely manicured green of the final hole. She avoided meeting Coach Harper's disappointed eyes as she walked around a trap with white crystals of sand raked in perfect symmetry. She shook hands with Tanya, who had shot a

42 for nine holes. She shook hands with Katherine Anne, who had shot an effortless 36. She herself had shot 39, which was not too bad considering she'd had to take that penalty stroke from the water hazard on number sixteen. Sky watched with almost sick fascination as Katherine Anne's mom wrapped her arms around her daughter's neck with a squeal and her dad squeezed her shoulder and pulled her to him.

And then the Clemson coach in the navy blue shorts stepped up to the happy family and introduced herself.

Sky sighed, grabbed her bag, and trudged toward the clubhouse.

As she walked by the pond at the eighteenth, she gave the alabaster swan a respectful berth. She watched Jordan Miller arc her final drive down the middle of the fairway. Jordan's lean, hawk-faced father blasted down to the green in his cart, screeching to a halt a few feet away from where the Clemson coach was talking with Katherine Anne's parents. He got out of the cart and stood impatiently, waiting for them to finish their conversation, occasionally glaring down the fairway at Jordan. Meanwhile, Jordan hit a poor second shot into a greenside bunker and shouldered her bag as if it weighed a thousand pounds. Sky felt her throat thicken, watching Jordan trudge up the fairway.

"Come on, girl," Sky whispered. "Get it together."

Sky's dad's faded red truck, parked on the far edge of the parking lot, had one door hanging open. He sat in the front seat listening to the sports station in his filthy orange shirt with his Moving Up in the World logo on the pocket. Sky took a deep breath and waved. She followed the manicured cart path, lined with spiky bushes with pink flowers, to the parking lot. Her dad came around the back of the truck, and his hands were shaking when he helped her lift her clubs into the truck bed. "So?" She sat on the bumper, took off her golf shoes, and wished so badly that she could tell him more, that she had her own Cinderella story to give him as a gift.

"Next time," she said.

"That's the spirit." He pulled out of the parking lot, and they left that manicured oasis behind. It wasn't long before they passed Solomon Municipal, the course where Sky had gone to her first golf camp and learned to play.

Sky still vividly remembered that entire week, not just because it was the beginning of golf for her, but also because it was the week she found out about her mom.

She remembered pulling the hand-me-down golf bag out of the truck bed back then and standing in the gravel parking lot nervous about her first day of camp, waiting for her dad to roll down the passenger window, which, as always, stuck halfway down.

He leaned across from the driver's seat. "You're going to knock 'em dead, Sky. Remember, Annika played with the men."

"Okay, Dad."

"Drive for show, putt for dough."

"Okay, Dad."

"Pick you up at four-thirty. If it's over before that, just practice putting until I get back. Good luck, tiger."

"Okay, Dad."

Gravel crunched as he drove away. All her life, her dad had regaled her with the old-time golf legends, about the way Bobby Jones had done it all for love, never taking a penny of compensation. About Francis Ouimet, who came from nothing to beat the great Harry Vardon and Ted Ray. About how Lee Trevino grew up playing municipal, talking trash on the tee and about Seve Ballesteros jingling the change in his pocket. About the honor of calling a penalty on yourself. She knew the rags to riches stories. She knew them all by heart.

But that day, she could hardly make herself speak to him. The night before he had had a few too many and said something that she couldn't wrap her head around.

"Maybe, if you get good enough at golf to get on the news," he'd said, as he flipped the channels from his worn easy chair, "your mom will come back to see you play."

Sky felt the blood leave her face. All her life, her dad had told her that her mother died when she was little. "But . . . I thought . . ." Her voice cracked. It felt like the earth had shifted under her feet.

Her father's thumb on the remote suddenly stopped moving. She stared at him. Long seconds went by as she watched his squarish face grow red. "I just said that," he finally said, "to make it easier."

"What?" Her voice was a whisper.

"She left us."

Why had he told her that? She had been satisfied with her life, perfectly content with the idea of Dad and Sky against the world. Now Sky was obsessed. She hadn't slept a wink that night. Where might she be? Why had she left? What was wrong with Sky that she didn't want to be with her? She wished he'd never said it. Those three words of his, that week of golf camp, "She left us," had changed everything about her life.

CHAPTER SIX

Beth

B eth made a copy of the photo and article about Sky Sawyer for Mark. She felt she had to let him know. She'd just stopped in front of his driveway after her yoga class and was opening the car door to put the article in his mailbox when he ran up, dripping, at the end of what seemed like a long morning run in the rain.

"Oh, I wasn't expecting to see you." She felt a sudden flush. "I was just going to put this in your mailbox. You're running in the rain?"

"I run every day. Besides, it's just drizzling." In the last few years, Mark's, hair had turned grayer, but he still remained the fit and attractive man she'd married. He still had those translucent blue eyes. All her friends used to say eyes and eyelashes like that were totally wasted on a man. But of course they weren't. Dozens of middle-aged women came to Mark's optometry office four or five times a year, whether insurance covered the visits or not, on the pretext of having him look at their increasingly presbyopic eyes.

Beth, who had been almost legally blind since birth, still went to him twice a year herself. Her father had always said that it seemed like a lucky twist of fate that a child as blind as a bat should end up marrying an eye doctor. Mark still gave Beth the family discount, and he gave her free samples of artificial tears, but she also liked sitting in the dark room with him, having him slide the cold metal refractor next to her face. Sometimes his finger touched her cheek as he slid the clicking lenses into place and said, "Which is better? One? Or two?" Such a simple question. Such an impossible answer. At first, making the decision was easy, but as the exam progressed, it became more and more difficult for Beth to decide, and by the end the two views seemed the same. Would they be married today if Julie hadn't run away? Seeing him still produced a feeling of lightheadedness and a twinge in her gut.

"So, what were you going to put in my mailbox?" he said, leaning closer.

Beth's windshield wipers thumped rhythmically, seeming to count the seconds, erasing the spatters of rain the instant they fell. She held the flyer out the window. "This article."

He wiped his palms on the back of his shorts and took the flyer, focusing on the picture of Sky Sawyer. His eyes went glassy, and then he dropped his head, hiding his face. He cleared his throat and stood up. "What about it?"

Beth's car engine thrummed, and small clouds of steam rose from under the hood.

"She looks so much like her, Mark. And her name."

Mark drew a deep sigh, and a look of anguish flashed over his features. Beth knew him so well, she could almost trace the history of their relationship on his face. From the delight of the moment they met—a Tuesday evening in Chapel Hill, listening to Bob Dylan perform—to the visceral anguish of the days after Julie ran away and the exhaustion and defeat of the day three years later when Mark moved out. Mark looked up at the treetops, blinked, and thrust the printout back at her.

"That's your copy. I have another one at home."

"I don't want it." Mark glanced down through the bank of trees in his front yard, then at his house, and a look of alarm seized his face. "Ronda, stop!"

Wham! Beth felt a huge jolt and heard the crunch of metal.

She whipped her head around. Ronda, Mark's fiancée, had backed into Beth's passenger door. Mark slapped his forehead.

"Oh my God! Beth?" Ronda's voice warbled up and down several octaves as she leaped out of her car, holding her alligator briefcase over her head to protect from the rain. "I was late for an appointment and wasn't even looking. Beth, what are you doing here?"

With a pained look, Mark examined the damage. "The back bumper on the Lexus is perfect, it's not damaged at all. But Beth, the door of your Civic is completely crushed."

"Naturally," said Beth, with a helpless shrug.

"Oh my God, I didn't know there was anyone at the top of the driveway," Ronda said.

"The body is smashed up against the tire," Mark added. "I don't think you can drive it."

Beth put her foot on the gas and her car gave a grinding lurch.

"No! Don't try!" Mark said. "Cut the engine. It's going to have to be towed."

"Lord, have mercy," said Ronda.

Beth got out of the car and examined the enormous crater sprawling across both passenger doors. Tank meets aluminum foil.

"Who just sits in a car at the end of someone's driveway? I can't stand out here in the rain. I have an appointment at the museum at ten."

"Here's what you should do," Mark said. "Just drive around through the yard and out onto the cul-de-sac."

"Drive over the grass? As hard as Billy has worked on it?"

"Wait, don't we have to take pictures?" said Beth. "And call our insurance companies?"

"I can't do that in the rain, I'm wearing a silk blouse," Ronda said.

"I can do it," Beth said, looking down at the faded bicycle shorts and baggy sleeveless T-shirt she'd worn to yoga.

"No, no, Beth, get back in your car, you're getting wet." Looking at Ronda he continued, "Just give me the car keys."

Ronda handed him the keys and her cell phone, then minced around Beth's car in her heels, still with her briefcase protecting her hair from the rain, and slid in the driver's side back door. "I'll just sit back here for two minutes while Mark moves my car, so I don't get wet. I have a meeting at the museum about my exhibit." Ronda was a photographer. Empathy that Beth never dreamed Ronda possessed oozed from her photographs. Her photographs of children with gleaming cheeks, wisps of hair whisking their temples, and beautiful rounded skulls that might fit into the palm of your hand brought tears to Beth's eyes. They were exquisite, breathtaking. Now Ronda smiled at Beth and floated her arms around trying to air-dry the tiny drop marks on her peach blouse, then took out a puffy Kleenex, dabbed lightly at the raindrops on her face, and then ran it over the dotted surface of her briefcase. "I hate that this happened."

"You and me both." Beth gave Ronda a quick, mirthless smile.

"But you know, maybe with the insurance money, you could get a newer car." Ronda craned her neck at the odometer. "A hundred and seventy thousand miles! Lord have mercy, Beth, you need a new car anyway. See, there's a silver lining under every cloud, isn't that right?"

"My mechanic says I can drive it up to two hundred thousand," Beth said. "That is, I could have, had you not backed into it."

Beth watched Mark walk around the two cars, taking photos with the camera in Ronda's phone from various angles, repeatedly trying to dry his face with the end of his wet T-shirt.

Mark moved the Lexus before taking a return call from his insurance agent. "I'll write you a check to cover the damages, Beth," he said, when he hung up. "She's advised us not to report it."

"Oh, right, I can't get any more points," Ronda said with a cockeyed smile.

"So, are we done? I've got to run." Ronda wiggled her fingers at Beth and Mark as she slid into the driver's seat of the Lexus. She hesitated. "What did you say you were doing here, Beth?"

"Uh . . . news about Paul."

"Oh, I hope he's getting married. It's high time. Y'all be good, now!" She pulled out onto the main road, and in a few seconds, the big car was gone.

"Come inside and call a tow truck," Mark said. "And once he takes your car, I'll drive you home."

"I can call and wait out here. And the tow truck driver can take me home." She looked at her watch. She still had almost ninety minutes before her class.

"Don't be ridiculous. It's pouring. Please come inside."

Beth hesitated for a second, then grabbed her purse and ran down the wet driveway, into the neatly arranged garage, and up the steps into the kitchen. Ronda was a much more fastidious decorator than Beth. The rich Turkish rug on the living room floor looked casual, but Beth knew it had cost more than her Civic. She self-consciously kicked off her wet flip-flops by the door and tiptoed across the blond hardwood, which was polished to the sheen of a basketball court. The butter-colored leather couch must have been fairly new—she could still smell it. And the walls featured impressionist-style oils —mostly water scenes—from Nantucket, Italy, California wine country, and London. Through the great room's picture window at the back of the house she could see the rain-stippled pond and manicured amoeba shape of the eighteenth green, where small puddles accumulated.

"Played much lately?" Beth asked, standing in front of the window and gazing out.

"Thursdays, my day off, with my regular group. I'm supposed to have a tee time in about an hour. Sadly. But maybe it will clear up."

"I remember when we first moved here your day off was Wednesday. You changed it because Wednesday was Ladies' Day and you couldn't stand the thought of playing with all those women on the course."

Mark grinned for the first time all day. "See? I'm not the chauvinist I once was, am I?" Mark opened a cabinet drawer and took out two kitchen towels. He handed her one and began drying his own face and arms with the other.

Beth smiled. "May I point out that you *still* don't play on Wednesdays? But I agree, age has mellowed you. Somewhat." Looking at the way the skin crinkled around his eyes, she felt a warm pull like a plucked violin string down below her navel. She suddenly became aware that the two of them were alone in his elegant house, both wearing wet exercise clothes. She turned her back to him while she toweled her face and arms dry, looking around at some of Ronda's photos. "So, Ronda's very talented."

"Yes, she is. She's an empathetic person, though at times it may not seem that way. But it shows in her photos." Mark gave Beth an enigmatic smile.

"I'm glad you've found someone." Beth wasn't lying. In spite of it all, she still felt for him. "When do you think you'll get married?" Her heart pounded as she asked.

Mark shook his head. "Not right away. Courtney needs to graduate first. Ronda's ex is paying."

Beth nodded. Her stomach gave a sharp twist. Quickly, she turned away and looked out the picture window behind her. "I'd forgotten you all had such a great view of number eighteen. That hole always stresses me out. All those people sitting on the back porch of the clubhouse in those creaking rocking chairs, drinking their mint juleps and waiting—like highway rubberneckers—for you to completely destroy your approach shot."

"Actually, I think most of them are drinking beer." Mark laid his phone on the terra-cotta-colored countertop and typed "Towing Services" into the search line. "I have sat up here and watched many a player drop it in the drink, throw clubs, fall to their knees in disgust."

"The golf gods will punish you for your flippant airs, sir."

"Oh, they already have," Mark answered.

"People do love watching someone else's tragedy." Beth immediately regretted saying it.

Mark raised his eyes to her. "Well, they loved watching ours."

Beth watched him scroll through the list of towing services, and felt heat rise to her cheeks. "Oh, I have Triple A, no need to look anything up." She busied herself taking out her cell phone and AAA card. Mark slid his phone away.

While Beth waited for someone to answer, silence fell between them as she spooled back to the memories. And she was sure he did, too. Memories of the times after Julie, when people called, brought food, and asked for news. But then, after a while, it became too awkward, too painful, too cumbersome, and people had stopped. Then gray soulless months, too many to remember, like dominoes falling into oblivion.

Triple A said to look for them in twenty minutes. She grimaced, closed her phone, and glanced at her watch. "I've got a class in a little over an hour."

"You know," he said, "you gotta get used to people watching you play if you want to be any good."

"I don't care if I'm good."

"Yes, you do!" Mark laughed. "You can't lie to me—I've known you for thirty-five years. You do care. You care very much."

Beth waved a dismissive hand. "Maybe I do, so what? The older I get, the more I think that with golf, as with anything, what's important is the fact you're out there trying to do it. And whether you're a decent sport. Not whether you win or lose."

"I agree," he said. "It's the striving that matters. Not giving up."

"You gave up," she said before she could stop herself.

"I guess so. I was trying to be realistic. It was time to move on. I wanted to go on living."

The air seemed to stop circulating. They were trapped in a block of ice.

She drew a deep painful breath. Here in the house Mark shared with Ronda, she felt self-conscious now. She'd been inside only a few times—once when Paul graduated from college and Ronda had insisted that Mark's larger house, overlooking the pond, was the place to host Paul's graduation party. Paul had liked it better, too, so Beth had been agreeable, dressed up, and brought a centerpiece, her mother, and a brave face.

Beth leaned on the counter, pulled out and looked at the now rain-smudged printout. "Did you notice how much she looks like Julie—the cheekbones, the way her hair parts, that little widow's peak? That hopeful sweet look on her face."

"Newspaper photos are terrible. You have no idea if the girl looks remotely like this. In fact, you really have no idea who this is. You're going solely by a fuzzy newspaper photo and the last name. A last name that isn't uncommon. You know that."

"Do you remember that when she was about twelve, Julie tried to go to the courthouse and change her name? And we brought her home, and she sat in the back seat with her arms crossed over her chest, and she said, 'Summer. My name is Summer.'"

"She had a secret identity at age twelve."

"I still have no idea why she did that. Julie was puzzling. And frustrating sometimes." Beth smoothed her fingers over the photo.

"But remember all her imitations, Mark?" Beth smiled as she looked up at him. "Elvis, Bob Dylan—she was the most amazing dead-on mimic."

Mark grinned. "She was."

"I sort of already feel a connection to this girl, Mark." Beth felt a sudden burning in her eyes. Her nose began to run and she swiped it with the back of her hand like a first grader. "I can run home. I've got to get to my class." She picked up the printout and then put it down again. "This is yours." Keeping her head down, she headed blindly for the door.

"Beth, come on."

Her toes got tangled as she put on her flip-flops and she almost fell down the garage stairs. She caught herself on the hood of one of the cars parked in the garage.

Mark, behind her, took her elbow. "Courtney just left for her junior year abroad. Her car will sit in the garage all year. Why don't you drive it until you get the body work done?"

Beth looked at his fingers around her elbow, and after a beat he released her and stepped away. "I'll get the keys." He went up the steps two at a time and brought back the key to Courtney's vintage midnight blue Volvo convertible with a dent on the left fender.

Hesitantly, she took the squarish key.

CHAPTER SEVEN

Beth

Beth spent hours researching Sky, hunched over her computer in her office, printing up every article that even mentioned her name. Sky seemed to have lived in the area for about four years, and she'd learned to play at a fairly rundown course called Solomon Municipal. One article mentioned that she'd formerly lived in the Chicago area. Beth, feeling only slightly like a snoop, found Sky's apartment building located in a modest neighborhood, on Google maps. Would it be ridiculous to drive by? She called Paul and he said exactly what she knew he would say.

"Yes, Mom, it *would* be ridiculous to drive by! You really don't know anything about this girl. Get a grip!"

She tried. After all, it was painful to open the wounds of these memories. She focused on her daily routine. Teaching her classes. Yoga. Golf with Vanessa and Margo. Counting the days until they went to the tournament in Winston-Salem.

"YOU'RE STALKING HER," Margo accused Beth after she described her online efforts to learn more about Sky.

"No, I'm doing research. There's a difference," Beth insisted.

"And Vanessa! What the hell has gotten into her?"

They were in Margo's SUV on their way to Vanessa's because she had backed out of this week's round, saying she wasn't going to play anymore. Ever. Margo squealed into Vanessa's driveway, and they both went up on the porch and banged on her door.

"Vanessa!" Beth called through the screen door. "Let's go! While we're young!"

"We're not," said Vanessa, calling from the front hall.

Now Margo chimed in. "We need you out there, girl."

Vanessa stepped outside with her arms crossed, shaking her head. She was dressed in silky microfiber loungewear. Definitely not golf attire. "I've made up my mind, ladies," Vanessa croaked. "I've officially retired from golf."

"What? We've been a group for fifteen years. You can't just quit! We need to get there and check in so Buddy Watkins doesn't jump in front of us again."

"That's another thing. I'm tired of fighting the Buddy Watkinses of the world. I'm just tired of it, girls. Tired of fighting. What's the point of being out there?"

"The point of being out there is . . . being out there," Margo boomed. "Goddammit, Vanessa, put on your shorts. Daylight's burnin'."

"Come on, I'll get your clubs and put them in my trunk." Beth headed for Vanessa's garage.

"I said no. I mean it, ladies. Come by, have a drink, tell me every detail about your game when you're done." Vanessa went back inside. Her willowy frame was a smoky shadow behind the screen door.

"You're still coming with us to the tournament to watch Sky?" Beth asked.

"I'll still come to that, of course. But I no longer golf."

THAT DAY BETH and Margo trudged around the course with minimal enthusiasm. The heat made them cranky and tired. The fairways were full of divots and their shots seemed to find every one. The group in front of them was too slow and the group behind them was too fast. On nearly every hole, the greens crew for some reason was mysteriously raking the traps or driving past them at top speeds on green mowers the size of biplanes.

"What is this, a convention? You'd think we were playing topless," Margo complained.

"I just don't get it," Beth said, as she chipped dispiritedly into a trap she'd hitherto managed to avoid. "Vanessa hasn't broken ninety since the millennium. So, why now? What's changed?" In the back of her mind, like a bank of thunderheads piling on the horizon, was a sense of foreboding, a sense that Vanessa was giving up on some aspect of life. "You think there's trouble with Michaela?"

Michaela, Vanessa's daughter and only child, was a year younger than Julie; in fact, she and Julie had been friends in high school. Michaela had lived with Vanessa and Justin on and off through her twenties. She was a high achiever and perfectionist who had won numerous leadership awards as well as a scholarship to Duke to study political science. But Vanessa and Michaela had a rocky relationship that tended to build to a blowup, and then they'd go a few months without speaking before finally having an emotional clearing of the air.

"I don't know. Last time I asked her, they seemed to be getting along great." Margo shook her head, addressed an easy chip shot, and skulled a line drive completely over the green. It finally skidded to a stop at an impossible lie behind a dogwood thirty yards beyond. "Dammit!" she said to the world at large. Margo bent and picked up her ball. "My ball's in my pocket," she said to Beth. "It's been hit too many times on this hole and needs a rest."

Beth, meanwhile, scooped under her ball, and it popped into the air and came down in the trap again, only this time snuggled against the lip. *Shit!* She'd need a garden trowel to make that shot. She blasted out of the trap, and the ball flew the green and landed on the men's next tee. "I'm picking up, too."

"TWELVE-THIRTY, SAME as usual, next week," Margo said to Charles, the assistant pro, after they finished their dismal round.

"Uh . . ." Charles pretended to look at the book, but Beth could tell by the shifty look in his eyes that something was up. "Next Wednesday we're having a charity tournament. The Winston-Salem Men's Club. Shotgun start at noon. Can you play in the morning?"

"Charles, what are you talking about?" said Margo. "Wednesday is Ladies' Day!"

"That's right," Beth said. "A men's tournament can't be scheduled on Ladies' Day."

Charles scratched a place beside his eye and cleared his throat. "Didn't you ladies read your newsletter? The golf committee voted to eliminate Ladies' Day."

"Why? Women are still restricted from playing on Saturday and Sunday mornings," Beth said.

"But you can still tee off after noon. So technically, you're allowed to play every day."

"How can the golf committee make a decision like that without the members voting on it?" said Margo.

Charles held up his hands. "I'm just the messenger, ladies. I just do what I'm told."

"Horse hockey!" said Margo.

"Take it up with the golf committee," said Charles, stepping away from the schedule book, crossing his arms across his Izod-clad chest, and staring at his feet.

"Fine, we will," said Beth. "Who's the chairman?"

Charles cleared his throat.

"Don't tell me," Beth said. "Buddy Watkins, isn't it?"

"Uh . . . I believe so." Charles pulled on his ear and rocked back and forth.

"This is what happens when citizens don't take their responsibilities seriously. We allow complete buffoons to rise to leadership roles," said Margo as they stomped out to the parking lot. "Why didn't we make sure a few women sat on the golf committee?"

"Margo, would you volunteer to be on the golf committee?"

"I'd rather stick needles in my eyes."

"And I'd rather eat a bug. But God, I could kick myself!" said Beth. "You know, I'm sure they think we view this as a step forward. When women reach equality, we don't need Ladies' Day any longer."

"Like saying affirmative action is obsolete."

"Exactly," Beth said. "First Vanessa quits. And now Ladies' Day is gone. I feel like a part of my life has passed away."

"Not to mention the fact that we played like shit," Margo added, throwing her clubs in her trunk.

A few minutes later, after Margo had dropped her off, Beth sat on the back porch clapping her golf shoes together to dislodge the grass, and her cell phone, which was lying on the counter in the kitchen, rang. It continued to ring as she fumbled madly with her keys and raced inside, sliding on the tile in her golf socks.

"Hello?" she said, sure the person would have hung up by now.

"Hello," said an unfamiliar male voice. "Is this Beth Sawyer?"

She looked at the caller ID and didn't recognize the number. "Yes," she said cautiously.

The man cleared his throat. "This is Barry Redmond, the man you hit with the golf ball last week. I just called to tell you not to worry, I've lived to tell the tale, and just, well, wanted to let you know that there's no harm done."

Oh, God!

"So, well! You're all right, then? No broken ribs?"

"Nope. Just a bruise. It's pretty ugly, black and purple. But no harm done. So I thought I'd call and put your mind to rest. Since you seemed worried."

"Oh! I was," she said. "Can I at least cover the doctor visit?"

There was a short silence. He cleared his throat. "I have a proposal for you."

"O-kay." She hesitated. "Shoot."

"My co-pay took care of the doc. Go to dinner with me Friday night instead."

She cradled the phone, looked down at her legs. They'd become flabbier, especially her thighs, which, once firm, seemed in just the past year to have devolved to the consistency of refrigerated chicken broth. Would the estrogen pills fix that, too? "Two days from now?"

"Yes. Is this a bad week for you?"

"Oh, no, it's fine, I don't know why I said that." Beads of sweat had popped out on her temples.

"No, I meant, maybe you're busy." He seemed to be losing steam. And no wonder, since she sounded like someone from another planet.

"Barry, I would love to go to dinner. What kind of food do you like?"

"Anywhere you want is fine with me."

She struggled to come up with some place interesting, and there seemed to be so much noise in her brain that she couldn't. With everything so up in the air with Sky Sawyer, she was too tense. She shouldn't do this. She should just say no. "How about the Mixed Grill at the clubhouse?"

They agreed on six thirty after work. Beth hung up and fanned her burning face with her unopened MasterCard bill.

"MOM?" BETH PUSHED the kitchen door open with her hip and put the grocery bags on the empty counter. Her mom's fat Chihuahua, Chi-Chi, raced around her calves, yapping. Her mom, in one of two matching blue microsuede recliners, watched a taped episode of *All Creatures Great and Small* in the falling dusk. The other recliner had been Beth's dad's; he'd passed away a little over five years ago.

"I'm setting the table," Beth said.

"There's one more scene after this."

By the time Beth had scooped the manicotti onto two plates, James Herriot had delivered a live calf and it stood on spindly legs.

"I love that show!" Her mother stood and held up her hands in appreciation. Carla Swenson's skin was amazingly smooth for a woman in her mid-seventies, and she was proud of her thick curly white hair. She stepped to the piano, skimmed her fingers across the keys in a playful arpeggio, and came to the table. She was dressed in color-coordinated loungewear.

"So, this is from Amedio's?" her mom said.

"Yes."

"I like their food, but you can't hear in there."

"I know. That's why I got takeout." Amedio's wasn't too loud; Beth's mom was going deaf and refused to get hearing aids.

"Plus it's too cold. They keep the air conditioning way up high."

"I know. Here's parmesan cheese," Beth said. "And I brought you a movie. Diane Keaton." Her mother liked anything with Diane Keaton.

Her mom examined the manicotti Beth put in front of her as if it might grow pincers and lop off her nose. "What kind of cheese did they use in this?"

"Whatever they usually use." Beth sat down, handed her mother a napkin, and put her own in her lap. "This is Diane Keaton's latest. It's a dysfunctional family story, and it got good reviews. It's cleverly written."

"I don't know if I'll like this cheese."

"It's the same as always, Mom."

Her mother took a very tiny bite. She tapped her smart phone, which was on the table. "Six thousand steps today," she said. "At the mall. But another one of our girls, Sally Griffith, has wimped out on me. She's stopped walking." Beth's mother kept a busy life. She walked at the mall three times a week, played cards with friends once a week, attended community theater productions, took art lessons, and went to lectures on history and current fiction at the library. Beth had encouraged her mother to walk regularly after reading about the benefits—physical, emotional, and mental. Her mother had been sedentary when she was younger, so Beth considered it a kind of victory that she'd been able to get her mother to make walking a regular part of her routine. "Why did she stop?"

"Well, she turned seventy-five." Her mom took a sip of coffee. "Beth, my coffee's not hot." Beth got up and put the coffee in the microwave. Her mother liked coffee at a temperature that would have burned the skin on the inside of anyone else's mouth.

When reheating her mother's coffee, Beth noticed a painted watercolor of two apples—one red, one green—lying on the counter. The green apple looked all right, but the red one looked like a pepper. Her mother had taken watercolor classes on and off for many years, but never seemed to get any better. Her mother's example had enabled Beth to try golf. It seemed to be permission to pursue interests in life at which she might not be that good.

"Taking another watercolor class?" Beth asked.

"Yes," her mother said. "Don't say anything. I like the way my brain feels after I do it and that's enough. It doesn't have to be good."

"Absolutely," Beth said.

"Besides, I read somewhere that as you get older, you need to try new things."

"True." Beth gave the reheated coffee to her mom, then sat back down. She cut the firm outside layer of pasta and the rich pearly ricotta cheese oozed from the center of the manicotti. Beth sipped her coffee. She shouldn't be drinking it; it kept her up all night.

Beth had thought that she'd encourage her mom to move out of this deteriorating brick rancher. It was too big for one person. But it was in a nice neighborhood, within walking distance of the thriving downtown area of town, and close to the university. Beth had worried how her mom would take care of the yard after her father's death, but Carla had promptly bought a riding lawn mower, and during the growing season rode in circles on her three-acre lawn twice a week, wearing an enormous sunbonnet.

Her mother finished, and fed her leftovers to Chi-Chi, who was standing on his hind legs dancing for more.

"I have a date Friday night," Beth said. She might as well get it over with.

"Really?" Her mother's pale blue eyes widened with interest, and she smiled. "Good for you! I'd like to see you find yourself another man. What does he do for a living?"

"Uh—I looked up his company online, and you'd be interested because it looks like he might be an engineer."

"Does he play golf? Can he tell a joke?" Beth's dad had been good at both those things.

"Well, he does play golf." Beth decided she didn't need to tell her mom that she'd hit Barry Redmond with a golf shot. "Don't know about telling jokes. If he can, that would make one of us."

"But you've always been such a good audience, Beth," her mother said with a smile.

"And I have some other news," Beth said, handing her mother the article Margo had given her. "There's a high school girl who plays golf whose name is Sky Sawyer. She looks exactly like Julie. There's a girls' qualifying tournament this weekend in Winston-Salem. She's playing. I'm going to go meet her."

The moment she said it, darkness swept down her mother's face like shutters closing. "Why?" she asked carefully.

"I want to meet her. She might be my granddaughter."

Her mom wrapped her hands around her coffee cup. Beth knew her mother was remembering the barely disguised antipathy between herself and Julie. *How can you let her dress like that? How can you let her talk like that? Are you really going to allow her to do that?* Those had been her mother's running comments about her daughter. Beth had since understood but chosen to forget that these comments had not really been criticism of Julie's behavior but of Beth's mothering skills.

"How do you know it's her?"

"I don't, not for sure, I just think it could be possible." Beth told her about the newspaper article and the picture. "The name. And the way she looks. Exactly like Julie, Mom. Exactly."

"Oh, Beth." She heaved a sigh. "You're finally getting your life back. You have a date. Besides," she added in a falsely light tone, "I'm too old to go through it again." She patted Beth's hand.

Beth yanked her hand away. "I'm not asking you to go through it. I'm going through it, not you."

"Honey, you know this about having children. If they go through it, you go through it. I just hate thinking that you could be opening a Pandora's Box trying to meet this girl. First of all, you have a good chance of being wrong. Second, kids that age don't even care about grandparents they've known all their lives. What makes you think she'll care about knowing you? I don't want to see you get hurt."

Beth took a breath and put her napkin on the table. She had now completely lost her appetite. How could her mother say that? How could Sky not need Beth when Beth so badly needed her?

"I got cannoli for dessert," she said, getting up quickly and turning toward the counter to hide her face. "Do you want some?"

THAT NIGHT BETH woke suddenly. Her eyes swept across the dark shapes in her bedroom. The clock by her bed said 3:12 and Mo, her black cat, was sleeping by her head, purring in her ear. She wondered why she'd woken up.

Suddenly she heard a girl's voice in the hall. "Mom?"

She bolted upright, swept Mo to the floor, and ran to the doorway. The hallway stood empty, with gray granulated shadows. Beth stood for a moment, grasping the doorjamb, slightly dizzy from getting up so fast. A blinding light flashed down the empty hallway. Was there a slight shift of the air near her, as if a presence had slipped by her in the hall?

Beth's heart was beating so hard it ached.

Then she realized—it was just a car's headlights passing by on the street.

Beth saw floating black spots, swayed, and slid to the floor. Mo joined her, weaving beneath her arm, nudging her fingers to rub his head. She sat and let Mo comfort her until the car went farther down the street and she was sitting in the dark again.

Beth's heart slowed and her eyes adjusted. She went to the bathroom in the dark, and then, instead of going back to bed, she pushed open the closed door to Julie's old room. For months after Julie had been gone, the room still smelled like her. She let her eyes linger on the familiar dark shapes, thought about the months Julie had come home from high school and gone straight to bed, the way she slept through weekends, the way she'd quit every club and sport and floated into a netherworld of sleep. All the doctors she'd seen, all the different antidepressants, antianxiety, anti-everything medications that had been tried. How helpless Beth and Mark had felt. How sometimes she'd just gone into the room and arranged Julie's matted hair on the pillow, listened to her breathe, and thanked God that at least she was still there in her room, alive. And wondered how in the world they would make it through another day. Until that point, parenting had been like walking on coals, where nothing had prevented Beth and Mark from getting burned but sheer faith. And then they lost even that.

Beth ran her hands over her face and waited for her breathing and heart to slow down. Then, she went downstairs, poured herself a glass of milk, and stood at the entrance to the family room. She scanned the built-in bookshelf, with the pictures of Paul and Andrea. If they did get married and have children, Beth's grandchildren would live three thousand miles away. She'd probably see them twice a year. And of course she'd love them desperately, she knew that already. Amazing how humans were able to maintain their passion for loved ones based on the slenderest of threads, the shortest imaginable time together.

Some people, like her mother, had a gravitational pull that kept people in orbit around them, and never released them. Beth had let both of her children drift away, to the outer reaches of the universe, and had not seemed to be able to summon the will or charisma to pull them back. She had once believed in the old saying, "Allow your children to find their own path, and it will always lead back to you." Now she knew that saying was wrong.

On the bookshelf stood a row of photo albums that Beth hadn't opened in years. After Julie was gone, she'd spent hours poring over them, and sometimes Mark found her sitting in an almost catatonic state when he arrived home from work. She'd short-changed Paul. She could barely remember his last three years of high school, so focused had she been on Julie's loss. She couldn't remember going to his soccer games and didn't help him with any of his college applications. And he, so needing to escape the pain of home, had migrated to the opposite coast. He would have gone to Japan or New Zealand if he could have. And even though they talked twice a week, she sometimes feared that in losing Julie, she'd lost Paul, too.

CHAPTER EIGHT

Sky

On Friday, Silas drove Sky and Bart to the Solomon Municipal golf course in his ancient Jeep for a quick nine holes before dark. They were listening to Lizzo and singing "Truth Hurts" at the top of their lungs. Still singing, Sky pulled her bag with its motley collection of used clubs from the trunk. These casual summer rounds with the Wade brothers were among her favorite times in life.

"Fancy bags, guys," she said. Both boys had brand-new canvas bags; their parents were always buying them new golf equipment and Sky liked to tease them.

Silas and Bart, tall boys with white-blond mops of hair, laughed as they shouldered the new bags. A gold earring flashed in Silas's ear. Sky had always liked that earring.

"Shut up. You know we need all the help we can get to beat you," Bart teased right back. He was the only boy in Sky's ninth-grade

English class who read the books they were assigned rather than downloading Spark Notes. Sky sometimes had trouble concentrating on more difficult texts and once he'd peer-tutored her. She'd felt stupider than he and somehow smarter at the same time. He was a better reader, but compared to hers, his life seemed too sheltered, too trusting. She'd become closer to Silas, who was a junior, two years older, and more adventurous than his younger brother.

"Yeah, shut up, Spiderwoman." Silas had called her that since the first week of golf camp, four years ago. That day, she had been in the ladies' room when they announced the winner of the putting competition. The prize had been a statuette of a golden boy at the top of a beautiful swing and Sky had dearly wanted to win it. She didn't think anyone had made a putt longer than hers. Still in the bathroom, she heard the camp director say into the microphone, "The winner of the putting competition is . . . Sky Sawyer! Is Sky still here?"

"Yes!" she yelled, but somehow the door was stuck. She screamed and pushed against the door until she thought the blood vessels in her head would explode, but it didn't budge. She thought about that golden boy on that white marble stand and pounded on the door, yelling, "I'm still here! Let me out!"

She whirled around. Above the sink was a narrow window about two feet high. Could she fit? She crawled onto the sink, cranked the window open, and popped out the screen, which was infested with dead spiders and strung with layers of whitish sticky webs. She couldn't let herself get stuck here. With a mighty effort, she pushed her head and one leg through to the outside and at last was hanging there against the bricks, with one hand and foot stuck inside, and then she pushed off and fell onto the filthy green metal top of the dumpster. She dropped to the ground and raced around to the snack bar, fury and injustice roaring in her ears.

"Oh, here she is." The camp director smiled at her for the very first time as he bestowed the shining golden boy as well as a slick new box of Titleists into her waiting hands. She'd had cobwebs in her hair, blood running down her shinbone, and a humongous greasy smudge across the entire front of her body.

Later, Silas tried to slide the golden boy out of her hands. After a week in the sun at camp, Silas's hair was bleached as white as swan feathers, but his arms were still pale while hers had darkened to the color of maple syrup.

Sky tightened her fingers around the marble stand. "Why didn't you let me out?"

"I tried to. You'd already crawled out the window. You look excellent in spider webs, by the way." And that's how he'd started calling her Spiderwoman. They'd been tight ever since.

AS THEY UNLOADED their gear that Friday, not far from Solomon Municipal, the dark anvil shapes of a dozen buzzards wheeled around a landfill. Beside the dilapidated cart storage area, Mr. McLean, the starter, an old man with a mottled nose and eyes hooded by a thatch of white brows like an eagle's, sat in a cart, cradling his clipboard. He smiled around his cigar, acknowledging Sky and the boys. She smiled back.

A few feet away from the putting green, Mulligan, the yellow Lab, lay on his side under a tree. Flies and gnats buzzed around his head. He looked dead.

Then, suddenly, like something out of *The Hound of the Baskervilles*—which they'd just read in English class—Mulligan raised his head and stared with rheumy, red-rimmed eyes at Sky, his tail thumped the ground, and he struggled to his feet. Mulligan loved to follow Silas, Bart, and Sky around the course when they played. He'd become attached to Sky that first week of golf camp when she gave him part of her baloney sandwich.

"Mulligan's been waiting for y'all. You can go off the back in about ten minutes," Mr. McLean called to them.

"Cool, we'll putt until then." Silas dropped his bag by the practice green and pulled out his putter. Bart followed suit.

Sky went in the clubhouse to buy some peanut butter crackers and saw a jar that Mr. McLean had set out to collect contributions for Sky to play in the girls' tournament. Everyone knew her dad would have a hard time paying the fees for the tournament. There were a few twenties in there already, and Sky would bet that at least one of them belonged to Mr. McLean himself. Tears came to her eyes to think he'd done that for her. Mr. McLean had also given Sky a part-time job driving the caged cart that picked up balls on the driving range, and that was helping, too. He'd been really kind to her.

Back outside, she said, "Thanks for taking up a collection for me." She didn't let her face show the emotion she felt. Mr. McLean, not an advocate of emotions, either, just nodded, his lips working around the wet end of his cigar.

"Golfers have game faces," her dad had told her. "You have a game face, Sky." That was true. Hiding her emotions was one thing she could do well.

When she'd been put in the lowest reading group in third grade, Sky let nothing show on her face. When girls in the hall made fun of Sky's shoes or clothes, Sky let nothing show on her face. When other girls' mothers came to parent teacher conferences and bragged on their daughters and played with their hair as if it were their own, Sky let nothing show on her face. She didn't really have girlfriends, period, unless you counted Jordan, and that was an uneasy relationship.

Yes, she had a game face.

Sky threw down a couple of balls and swung the putter in a smooth pendulum motion the way she'd seen Lydia Ko do on TV. The putt went in, and she felt good to have made one while Mr.

McLean and the guys were watching. She lined up five balls and hit them all from two feet, then from four feet, then from six feet, and farther. She heard her dad's voice. *Drive for show, putt for dough.*

On summer nights her dad used to take Sky out in the backyard to practice chipping and pitching, and occasionally they'd take turns putting into a plastic cup in the upstairs hallway. The mashed-down carpet there was perfect for putting. Her dad told her to visualize the exact track the ball would follow along the slope of the green.

"Great putters see the line," he said. "It can't be taught. It's a gift, a magical thing."

Now she set herself up for a thirty-footer and willed herself, *See the line.* She imagined a faint curved line leading to the cup. It nearly glowed. Her putter made contact with a satisfying click, and she let her hands follow the ball toward the hole. Her scuffed and yellowed Top Flite rolled along the imaginary line and dropped into the cup with a triumphant rattle, like bones. *Yes!* She crossed the green and plucked her ball from the cup with satisfaction.

Her dad couldn't swing a golf club now. He slept in a chair and took pain pills and told stories. He described himself as a cat with nine lives since he'd fallen off roofs nine times and was still alive. But Sky thought that ninth fall off the roof had been a little worse than he let on.

He had a game face, too.

After Mr. McLean gave them the go-ahead, she and the boys strolled out to the tenth tee. The shadows lengthened, a breeze threaded through the trees and the grass in the rough, and Mulligan ambled behind them. They tossed a tee to see who played first, Silas hit, and Sky liked watching the turn of his narrow shoulders and the graceful arc of the ball. Then Bart shanked one into the right rough.

"Hosel rocket!" Silas said, laughing.

"Shut up." Bart took his mulligan and landed a few yards behind Silas.

Sky teed up. Years of her dad's advice were always with her. *Keep your chin in. Don't overcook it. Turn your shoulders.* She closed her eyes and imagined she was a famous female golfer like Annika Sörenstam or Lorena Ochoa or Se-ri Pak, who had started playing golf late, at age fourteen. She felt the turn of her shoulders, like a key in a lock. Then, a whoosh, and miraculously, she connected with a satisfying smack. The ball hung in the air for long delicious seconds and landed about two hundred and twenty yards out, fifty yards past Bart and ten past Silas.

"Too bad you can't hit it worth a shit," said Silas.

"Seriously," Bart echoed. "Get some game."

She loved the way the brothers joked and teased, and wished she wasn't so serious, that she could come up with one-liners and make people laugh. Once someone had quoted a famous person who said, "It is better to be silent and be thought a fool than to open your mouth and remove all doubt."

They walked the course with Mulligan tagging along like some skeleton with yellow fur stretched over it. Butterflies dive-bombed them and the long grass beside the fairway made a pleasant shushing sound in the breeze while the sun warmed the tops of their heads. She usually beat Bart, and most rounds, she and Silas were evenly matched. Tonight, as the sun dropped below the orange horizon and their shadows stretched out long on the final green, with Mulligan lying by the edge, she beat Silas by one putt, which he acknowledged with good-natured insults.

"C'mon, finish up, I've got to close," Mr. McLean yelled at them from under the tree by the putting green, but Silas talked him into staying open long enough for them to each have a hot dog and a brownie from the snack bar. Silas tried to negotiate a couple of beers, too, but Mr. McLean stood firm.

"You kids are a mess," Mr. McLean said, but they were all laughing, and Sky had never loved anything so much.

CHAPTER NINE

Beth

Beth leaned close to her bathroom mirror as she ran a brush through her hair, trying to make her part more uneven. Gray roots showed less that way. She should've made a hair appointment. But a hair appointment would have made this a big deal. Which it wasn't.

She'd *washed* her hair and showered, right? What more could the man ask for?

What would they talk about? She wouldn't bring up Barry's wife. Beth didn't know how she had died, and it would be awkward and painful to ask. Also, Beth cried easily and if he cried, she probably would, too. So she'd avoid it. Unless he brought it up. She certainly wouldn't bring up Julie. And she wouldn't whisper a thing about the chance of meeting her granddaughter tomorrow. She'd keep that secret, hold it close to her heart. Jeans? No, a sundress. No, her arms were too flabby. She changed two more times and ended with the slinky electric blue top with a V neck and black capris. Too low cut? Too tactile? He might think . . . Oh, she couldn't change again.

She picked up her five-year-old bottle of Chanel and started to spritz herself, then stopped. She almost never wore perfume and wasn't about to start now.

Her stomach was starting to hurt. Maybe she should call and cancel.

Beth, you hit the man with a golf ball. After a first impression like that, you have nowhere to go but up.

As Beth ran a tube of lipstick over her lips, a complete scenario unfolded in her mind. Someone she knew from the club was bound to see them at the Mixed Grill. Within forty-eight hours someone would tell Mark. And since Barry's sister was married to Buddy Watkins, he'd certainly know about the date. Containing this would be like trying to contain nuclear waste.

The phone rang.

"Where are you two going?" It was Margo.

"The Mixed Grill at the clubhouse. That's a mistake, isn't it?"

"What, do you want microphones in your salads?"

"I was thinking the same thing. Any suggestions?"

"I think you should eat in another county."

"I'm going to cancel."

"You sound like you need to take some deep, cleansing breaths."

"I feel like I'm going to throw up."

"Sit down and put your head between your knees. Or, better yet, let him put his head between your knees." Margo chuckled at her own cleverness.

"Margo! For crying out loud, the last time I physically touched another human being was when your grandson sat on my lap a few weeks ago at the Memorial Day picnic. Oh, and I did hug my mom Wednesday night after dinner. I'm going to leap straight from that to full-on sexual contact? I don't think so. Anyway, I can't change the place, it's too late, and we're meeting in ten minutes." She grabbed her purse, felt her heart pound, but, thanks to the estrogen, no hot flash. She fished for her keys. "God, this is worse than a colonoscopy."

"Relax. You'll have a lovely time."

"I hope so. I didn't want to do this. You made me."

"I did not."

Beth had to admit, she had wanted to see Barry Redmond's chest. A feeling she hadn't had in quite a few years. Was that too much to ask?

She climbed into the Volvo convertible, thinking that Barry Redmond would think she was a completely different person than she really was, seeing her drive this car. He would admire it, probably, and she'd have to explain that it was her ex-husband's stepdaughter's car and that she was driving it because her ex-husband's fiancée had backed into her and totaled her car. The whole scenario sounded incestuous. He wouldn't want to get involved with someone seemingly so close to her ex. Solution: She'd park around the side of the building.

The clubhouse at Silver Lakes, in an earlier time, had been a sprawling white clapboard farmhouse with a green roof and shutters. Now additions sprouted at various angles like crab legs. The front porch was wide and white with moth-eaten wicker rocking chairs and creaking floorboards with peeling paint. The screen door squeaked. Someone had told Beth the front hall and club offices had been outfitted with furniture from a closed funeral home, which in Beth's opinion, pardon the pun, cast a pall over the entire assemblage. Clarissa Hopewell, the owner of Silver Lakes, had not put more than a dribble of money into the club since she'd bought it. Rumors had circulated for several years that she was thinking about selling it to a developer.

As Beth stepped inside, she fought a strange premonition that Mark and Ronda would be having a Friday night dinner in the

Mixed Grill and that she and Barry Redmond would be escorted to the table next to theirs. She imagined an awkward, polite interaction after which Barry would never call again.

Barry was waiting at the foot of the white-trimmed staircase, wearing khakis with a neat seam ironed down the front and a polo shirt the color of vanilla custard. His graying hair looked to be slightly damp, curling at his temples as it dried in the humid evening air. His cheeks were smooth and cleanly shaven. He wore wire-rimmed glasses, which he hadn't when playing golf. And he smelled of cologne.

Cologne. This was a big deal to him.

Beth smiled and inhaled, wishing she'd given herself a spritz. She held out her hand, concentrating on not tripping again, and he took it in a firm, rather formal handshake. His palm was dry and warm. Just touching him created a pleasant wave of tingles that traveled up her arm to the hollow of her neck.

She yanked her hand away, as if she'd been burned, and gave herself a mental slap on the cheek. *Good grief, snap out of it, Beth.*

He let her lead the way into the Mixed Grill, and she scanned the room for anyone who might gossip. A foursome of strange men sipped beers at the bar, and two other unknown couples were in deep conversation in high-backed red leather booths. What incredible luck.

As Barry held the chair for Beth, blood pounded in her temples. She felt pleased that she managed to get her heels under the table without mishap and didn't pull the tablecloth into her lap. "You didn't wear glasses to play golf," she said.

"It's not imperative to see when playing golf," he said. "I can always listen for my ball to hit tree trunks."

Beth laughed.

"So," he said then, leaning toward her, unwrapping the white linen napkin, and arranging his silverware. "I'm sure you heard that my wife died two years ago."

"Oh!" Beth, who'd been about to sip from her water glass, dropped it, and a small avalanche of ice ovals and frigid water sluiced into her lap. She jumped to her feet, gasping at the shock.

"I'm sorry! I startled you." Barry stood, too, offering his napkin.

"I wasn't going to bring up your wife unless you did." Beth waved him off, using her napkin to soak up the liquid from her pants. Her thighs were stinging from the cold, reminding her of the feeling she'd get years ago when she stayed out sledding too long with the kids. "But I must admit I didn't expect you to open with that."

"I know, I just figure, let's just get it out of the way right off the bat, that way it's not like the big elephant in the room." She looked up from her laundering duties to search his eyes. They were hazel, with flecks of gold. If there was devastation there, it was deep and hooded. He smiled.

Beth wiped off the chair. She wanted to escape to the ladies' room and pull herself together, but the man had just told her his wife died. Fortunately, her pants were dark and it was only water.

"She'd been sick for a long time," he said, as he sat back down.

Beth found herself about to cry. It was sudden, like documentary shots of ice shelves collapsing in the Arctic. "I'm so sorry," she said, her voice cracking. She concentrated on having good posture, hoping that would prevent incoherent sobbing. "It must have been horrible."

"Yes, it was." He cleared his throat.

Devastating grief rippled across his features, so rapid it could have been a subliminal image, and vanished. She looked away, still afraid of breaking down. "Where's our waiter? I could use a drink."

Barry became apologetic. "I went through this grief counseling, and I was taught that it helps to talk about it."

"Has it? Helped?"

"I don't know. Nothing helps but time, to tell the truth."

They'd just met and here they were both ready to burst into tears. The waiter appeared, salvaging the moment. He was a high school or college boy in a rumpled white shirt and black vest. They all looked like infants to Beth now. "Can I get you something to drink?"

"Yes!" Beth said. "A large glass of Pinot Noir." She stood up. "I think I'll just go to the ladies' room and try to get my pants dry," she told Barry, "if you don't mind."

Barry's eyes were starting to widen with alarm.

She bolted. Inside the mostly pink ladies' room, she turned on the hand dryer and tried to stand so the hot flow of air hit her crotch and thighs.

Her eyes began to sting, and she knew she was about to cry in earnest. She gritted her teeth, trying to stop.

What the hell was she thinking? This date was ridiculous. It made about as much sense as Copenhagen's little mermaid bargaining away her future for a pair of legs. She turned off the dryer, leaned on the counter, and stared at herself in the mirror. One side of her face sagged, almost as if she'd had a stroke. Actually, her entire face was sagging. Not to mention the sinews of her neck and her breasts and there were also her flabby arms and sagging kneecaps, though at least those were safely hidden under her clothing. What a fool! For fifteen years she'd accepted herself and her age and what had happened in her life and now suddenly she'd started taking these little yellow pills and poof! Everything had changed. New expectations—or long-buried old expectations—had surfaced, like the Loch Ness Monster, surprising her with their wet and ugly serpent heads.

A toilet flushed and another woman came out and began washing her hands. Beth stood back from the mirror, pretending she was checking her mascara instead of examining the dilapidated state of her very soul.

"I'm sorry I took so long."

Barry stood as she approached the table and put his hand on the back of her chair to pull it out. He had apparently regained control of himself, as he gestured at a glass of wine and a gleaming blue cone-shaped drink on the table. "I thought you slipped out on me."

"Oh, I'd never do that."

She saw the hopeful, almost panicked gleam of humor in his eyes behind his glasses. She had a tendency to be attracted to sad men, thinking her role in life was to do some little tap dance to bring light to their lives. That had been her role with Mark. But after Julie, it no longer worked. She'd assumed Barry might be like that, too. But, in that instant, she thought maybe Barry wasn't a sad person, despite what had happened in his life.

She sat down, smelling the faint aroma of his cologne as he leaned in, sliding her chair closer to the table.

He held his martini in the air, angled toward her. "I'd like to offer a toast. I've met people in a lot of unexpected ways, but never anyone who hit me with a golf ball on a par three."

"Cheers. Thanks for being a good sport about it." Beth toasted and took a sip. The wine wrung a shiver from her as it washed down her throat. "You could've sued me or something. It seemed like Buddy wanted to."

"Never," said Barry. "Buddy's a big grump but he's really a good-hearted guy, believe it or not."

"I do not believe that." Beth smiled. "So, did you google me? I googled you."

"Did you? Ugh, our company hasn't updated our web site since about 2019."

"Well, I got the gist of it. You're an engineer."

He held up his hand. "Yes, and I've heard all the engineer jokes. Let's see . . . the engineer tells his wife he's with his mistress—and tells his mistress he's with his wife—so he can finally get some work done."

Beth laughed. "Maybe I have heard that one."

He placed his fingers on the stem of his glass and twirled it like a drill. "I like my job. The shorthand of what I do is, I manage oversized heavy hauling projects. Like parts for nuclear power plants, transformers, boilers, condensers, and so on."

"On the website it looked like the company also builds tunnels and bridges."

She thought a minute. "This sounds stupid but . . . how do you build a tunnel, anyway? Without water getting in it?"

"Hang on." Barry crossed to the bar and sat back down with two straws. "One straw is one side of the tunnel, with one end closed. The other straw is the other side, with the other end closed." Barry seemed to be enjoying his demonstration thoroughly. "Put them in the water . . . line them up, seal the outside . . . and open the two ends. Voilà." Barry's demonstration reminded Beth of the way her father used to turn dinner conversations into science demonstrations. "And every engineering situation has its own set of circumstances that makes it an interesting problem. Whether it's the depth of the port, the size of the docking area, the tides, or the temperature of the water. I like solving problems." He smiled, and his face became lean and angular in a way she liked.

"You have to travel a lot."

He nodded, shrugged. "At least two or three days a week." He leaned forward. "And I did google you. You're a teacher. Your website is up to date."

"Yep. I teach composition at the college. Which means I spend most of my time asking students to put away their cell phones and the rest of it checking their papers for plagiarism."

"I bet you're a good teacher."

"Some days." She thought about the students she'd somehow lost, and the ways that each of them seemed to be Julie. "I put in a lot of hours for my salary."

"I'm sure you could make more money."

"I'm sure I could." Beth drew a breath. "I was on the training staff in a huge corporation when I was in my twenties. All of us in the department called our work the Golden Handcuffs. I felt like I lied as part of my job every day. Sure, if I had to, of course I'd do it again. But so far these days, as long as I think I've taught someone something useful, I'm okay." She didn't tell him how often she thought about her students.

She asked about his children, and he then asked about Paul. He didn't ask about Julie, and she wondered if he knew. When their entrees came, he surprised her by asking if she'd like to try his. He cut off a careful square of his lamb and put it on the edge of her plate. She didn't have the heart to tell him she hadn't eaten red meat in about ten years. It hadn't been really on purpose; she'd evolved into a mild form of vegetarianism out of preference.

"Want to try my salmon?" she asked, hesitantly.

"Sure!"

She was taken aback by his enthusiasm, and, feeling self-conscious again as if this were too much sharing for a first date, she put a small piece of the pink flesh on the edge of his plate.

"Do you like Indian food? And Thai? And sushi?" she asked.

"Oh, yeah," he said. "You name it, I've eaten it. What the hell, I'll try anything once. There's a great place in Chicago where I ate kangaroo. And once in Mexico I ate a grasshopper. Tasted kind of like salted sunflower seeds. I had a project in China a couple years ago and ate chicken feet. Found out they'd been shipped from the US because they gobble up all their own. They're considered a delicacy there, and of course we have no use for them."

"That's ironic, isn't it?" Beth took another sip of her wine.

"Let's play golf together next week," Barry said. "And we'll hit from the same tees. We'll hit from the seniors.'"

"Such a gentleman!"

"But we'll play even up, no handicaps, no strokes."

Beth took another sip of her wine. "You're on," she said.

CHAPTER TEN

Sky

Sky propped her bare heels on the dashboard and picked at a wart on her calf as her dad steered their faded red pickup down I-40 in the direction of Winston-Salem. They'd left Solomon when it was still dark, and now the red sun was rising past the skyline, where the highway curved through early morning mist. It was so humid, the air felt as though it was being pumped full of steam. The air conditioning was on full blast, but her hair was still sticking to the back of her neck. She looked over at her dad's sweaty face, pain-wrenched due to his back problems from that fall a few months ago, and didn't know how he was going to do this. Her dad had been talking about being her caddy in this qualifying event for weeks.

He wanted to be there for her. How could she tell him no? She knew Silas would have caddied for her, and he could have driven her here in his Jeep, or she could have even gotten a ride with Jordan's family. But it was a done deal. Her dad was driving her, and he was going to be her caddy. She just hoped his back didn't give out.

Katherine Anne was going to be here. Part of Sky was praying for her to come down with something and another part of her was feeling like a bull in the bucking chute at a rodeo, thinking, *Bring her on*. She could still picture Katherine Anne from last month's tournament on number sixteen, grinning and saying, "Too bad, Sky. Your ball might be a *teeny* bit wet." Sky had to hand it to her; Katherine Anne needled and talked trash on the tee like the boys. She respected that.

Her dad took the downtown exit, stopped at the end of the ramp, and looked both ways. He'd shaved and showered before they left. He had a few scraps of thin dark hair left over his ears, but the rest of his head was bald now. He'd bought a new golf shirt with some orange and yellow stripes on it from the sale rack at Dick's. He looked like a bald bumble bee.

"Let me check the directions," Sky said, reaching for the GPS on her phone.

"Executive decision." Her dad turned right.

When her dad had had a few beers, he could reel off a whole repertoire of stories about her mom. How she loved Kurt Cobain, had memorized all the lyrics to "Smells Like Teen Spirit," "Lithium," "Heart-Shaped Box," and "About a Girl." How crazy she was, how she never needed to sleep or eat, just ran on adrenaline, could drink any man under the table, ride any horse, jump into any quarry, run any pool table, take any dare. Then, after everything, she'd crash and burn. Sleep for days. The other night, over dinner of cold pizza after her golf round with Silas and Bart, Sky had coaxed him into telling some stories about her mom.

"The first time I saw your mother, we were all going tubing, and she came with a guy named Lawrence. Nobody ever called him Larry, it was Lawrence; he wasn't a nickname kind of guy. Your mother was wearing a white bathing suit and even a guy like me knew you didn't wear white bathing suits to go swimming in the river. But she didn't care. That girl was tan, and she had this wild black hair down her back. Just like yours, Sky."

He'd paused in his story to look at her with so much love, Sky suspected he was lost in the past, mistaking her for her mother. Then he shook his head and looked away before he continued, "Somebody that day dared her to spend the night on an island in the middle of the river, and I knew she'd do it."

"And what happened?"

"Well, she said she'd do it and so I said I would, too. And we spent the night on an island in the middle of the river."

Not long ago, she'd scavenged a few pictures from a cigar box in her dad's nightstand. She kept them hidden in a paperback copy of *Tuck Everlasting* under her bed. Every now and then she looked through them and tried to create a mental image of a person from the different poses. Tried to imagine how she walked and the sound of her voice. A person who looked like her and maybe was like her in other ways, too. Now they were driving through the downtown area of Winston, between some bank buildings and hotels. Perched on a hill beside the road were little rundown houses and apartments that were mostly yellow and brown.

"You nervous?" her dad asked.

"Not really." *Yes. God yes.* They were taking only the top six players. When she watched golf on TV, the announcers sometimes said of certain golfers that he or she "is in the hunt," and that meant that they were a contender, just a few shots off the lead and could win. Sky imagined a pack of howling hounds chasing a fox. And sometimes she thought that the leader was the head dog, but other times she thought that the leader was the fox, and how different it would feel to be the fox, everyone else chasing you, racing for your life with your heart ready to burst.

"Last month this one girl, Jordan, barfed in the bathroom before we teed off."

"Everybody barfs before a big day. You'll be great. Just stay cool, swing nice and slow."

"Okay, Dad."

"And listen. Babe Zaharias claimed that you take it away with the muscle just above your shoulder blade on the backswing. So isolate that muscle. Feel it before you swing."

"Okay, Dad." Playing golf was the one thing that allowed her to walk down the halls at school, her head held high, thinking that she was just as good as anybody else. Better. Her gift.

"And remember, one shot at a time. Just take the game one shot at a time."

"Okay, Dad."

Sky punched the button to open the window, and it slid down too slowly, squeaking, then stuck halfway down. Again. Sky put her arm out the narrow opening and let the wind push against it, making it float like a wave.

It had been just her and her dad for so long, but now Sky could barely tolerate the chafing of that, and recently found herself lying to him, even about little things that didn't matter. The air skimmed over the upper surface of her arm, rippling the hairs there, and she had a flash memory of skipping out of work at the range early yesterday with Silas, and of him touching her arm as they rode in his ancient gray Jeep to the quarry, of him standing on the warm rocks high above the bottle-green, bottomless water, and saying, "Hey, Spiderwoman, I dare you to dive from here." The surface was completely still, glasslike, and she looked down and saw a dark reflection of herself perched on the edge, and knew that Silas didn't mean it, but that her mother would do it in a second on a dare. Would she? The hairs on the back of her neck rose.

"You're going to knock them dead, Sky," her dad said.

"Okay, Dad." Sky put on her sunglasses so that her dad could not see the fear in her eyes. Silas had taken her to his house a few times. It was on a lake, two stories with huge porches that ran the entire length of the house, a swimming pool in the backyard, and even an outdoor firepit. Silas's parents were nice to her. His mother called her honey, and just a few weeks ago, on Sky's fifteenth birthday, Silas gave her a hot-pink V-neck shirt, and she just knew his mother had helped him pick it out, and that made her like it even more. His father was wearing one of those flowered silk shirts that cost about a hundred dollars and was drinking a big bowl-shaped glass of red wine, and he told her she had a nice swing. Silas's parents wanted to invite her dad, but she hadn't told him. Instead she'd lied and said he had to work.

"So, maybe Mom will read about me being in this qualifying tournament and she'll be here." Sky pulled her hair off her neck and fanned the back of it with her hair. "Like the story you told so many times about the *American Idol* singer."

"Well, maybe she will." Sky had looked up the scenes from the old *American Idol* show on YouTube and couldn't tear her eyes from her phone screen when they showed pictures of the girl when she was little. Sky didn't look at all like her, but still drank in her cheerful heart-shaped face and skinny little arms. If that girl on *American Idol* could make her mom come back, why couldn't Sky? And the girl's mom would never have come back if she just stayed ordinary, kept working as a skating waitress at Sonic.

Just last week, Sky made Silas go to that very Sonic and they'd ordered something and tried to talk to the skating waitress who brought their burgers and fries. Had she heard of the girl from *American Idol*?

"You know, that was ages ago, and people said she worked here for, like, three weeks. She made it sound on TV like she worked here forever." The girl had seemed annoyed and skated away.

"Maybe Mom's in prison," Sky said to her dad now. "We should check."

Her dad didn't answer, just drove.

"Maybe she has amnesia and can't remember that I'm her daughter."

Her dad slammed on the brakes and Sky's heels slid up the truck dashboard and her toes jammed on the windshield. "Sky! Enough!" Sweat popped out in the hollow space above his upper lip.

"Okay, then, why'd you tell me she's still alive and might come back if I try hard enough?" Sky set her jaw and moved away from him as close to the car door as she could. Tears trembled just inside her lashes, but she blinked hard and wouldn't let them out. They drove in tense silence the rest of the way through the town. The rising sun plunged through the windshield. Her head started to pound like crazy.

"Sorry." Her dad squinted at the phone for the directions, dropped it on the console, turned left, and ended up in a ritzy neighborhood with old white-columned homes, winding stone walks, and whispering oak trees spreading their branches over the slate roofs of the houses like giant guardian angels. Sky stared out the window into a screened side porch with a mesmerizing ceiling fan where a wispy girl sat on a white wicker couch reading a book.

Her dad's fleshy white fingers shook on the steering wheel as he let the car inch forward, and then the country club was right there and so was the golf course, with big bushes with white flowers by the gate. A graceful white-columned clubhouse overlooked fairways lined with more gigantic spreading oaks.

Sky shivered even though sweat crawled down her ribcage like a centipede. Lately when Sky's mind went to golf, she couldn't conjure that electric feeling of excitement she used to have. Instead, tension settled in behind her eyes, like rope knots twisting tighter and tighter. Because it seemed more and more that golf was the only answer to every question. And she'd started to feel like it wasn't fun anymore but a survival skill. How would she ever set foot in a house like Silas's again without golf? And was she even good enough? She'd thought so, she'd been so confident until she played against Katherine Anne Boyd.

"We're here," her dad said.

Bile flickered up the back of her throat like a snake tongue. If she had to barf before the match, at least it would be in a nice locker room.

CHAPTER ELEVEN

Beth

Beth craned her neck out the front passenger window of Margo's SUV as they curved around the circular gardenia-lined entrance to the country club. "Good lord, are we in the wrong place? Where are the crowds?"

"This is a girls' event, remember?" said Margo. "Nobody comes to watch girls."

"Ah, smell those gardenias," Vanessa sang from the back seat.

The heavy sweet fragrance of the alabaster blossoms, so perfect they seemed to be made of wax, wafted on soft midmorning air through the open car window.

Scrolling online trying to read up on menopause, Beth had learned that gardenia blossoms had been used by ancient Chinese herbalists to alleviate some of the symptoms. Normally Beth loved the aroma, but this morning she was so tense it seemed cloying, and she felt slightly nauseated.

Beth scanned the half-empty parking lot as Margo pulled into a space. Two teenaged girls carrying Titleist golf bags, their clubs clattering like fencing foils, headed for the putting green. Beth's heart thudded in anticipation, but both girls were short, one with a frizzy red ponytail, the other with cropped brown hair. Not Sky.

What would Beth do if she saw Sky? If she saw Julie? Would she have the courage to approach them? What would she say? Maybe coming here was a mistake, as her mother had said. She realized she was clenching her fists so tightly there were red crescent-shaped marks on her palms from her nails. Her stomach roiled. After a long moment, she climbed out of the car.

"I used to play basketball in middle school," said Beth, as she climbed from the back seat. "When we took the court, the only people there were our parents and the cheerleaders, who had to be. They'd sit on the sidelines braiding each other's hair. Then, the bleachers got packed for the boys' game."

"Shit, something like that could put you on a psychiatrist's couch for years," said Margo as she slammed the driver's door. She jammed a sun visor onto her head and began slathering her arms with number 45 SPF sun block.

"I didn't know you played basketball." Vanessa unfolded her long, dark legs from the back seat. "I did, too! All through high school."

Beth told them how she won the girls' free throw championship in sixth grade. "But then I got my period, started noticing boys, and dropped off the team," she said. "So much for basketball."

"What a waste!" Margo waved her hand dismissively. "I played volleyball." With her lanky frame, Margo was built like a volleyball player.

The three of them followed a young golfer and her parents around the back of the clubhouse. Beth noted with a stab of sentimentality that the girl's father was carrying her golf bag. Who would be carrying Sky's bag? That boy Julie ran away with, Russell something or other? Ray, yes that had been his last name. She'd never had trouble recalling that name, but she was so anxious she couldn't think straight. But no, he wouldn't be there. If he was still in the picture, Sky's last name would be Ray, wouldn't it? Her last name was Sawyer, though, Julie's maiden name. Maybe Julie was a single mom?

They passed the club's outdoor restaurant, with its black wrought-iron chairs and striped umbrellas and checked tablecloths mimicking a French street bistro.

A dark-haired girl in a yellow top ran by barefooted, carrying a putter. Was that her? She wove through a knot of people standing by the course map and Beth lost her.

"Beth, tell us if you see her," Vanessa said as they followed a polished stone walkway to a large kidney-shaped green, where six or seven girls practiced putting.

"I may not *know* her when I see her."

"I bet you will," said Margo.

"I agree," said Vanessa. "I just think it will be karma. Lord, I'm so nervous you'd think this was *my* granddaughter. I've got sweaty palms."

They'd agreed on the way over that even if they found Sky, Beth shouldn't even consider introducing herself until after Sky putted out on eighteen. She might shake Sky's concentration.

Beth breathed deeply and focused on the half dozen girls warming up on the putting green. They wore stretchy low-rise skirts or capris and colorful fitted sleeveless shirts. They had smooth tanned legs. Glowing, muscled arms. Sleek caps with oval brims and shiny braids or ponytails slipped through the back. The old unspoken assumption that all female golfers were lesbians had completely changed how young women dressed for the game, and female sexuality had been heavily injected into the marketing of the sport—like everywhere else these days—and these girls were poster children for that. Surprisingly, almost all the girls were barefoot, their polished young toes gripping the manicured grassy surface. Their golf shoes, discarded, lay at intervals around the green. The sexualizing of the female golfers had increased the profile of the sport. But it also created more pressure. These girls not only had to be great golfers, they had to be sexy and gorgeous and charming, too. Almost every one of them seemed to be managing that just fine.

"Barefoot putting! I like it," said Vanessa, stepping out of her gold flip-flops and trying a putting stroke on the bare grass.

"I'll try anything," Margo said, kicking off her sandals.

The conversation continued, but Beth heard only roaring in her ears. Two of the girls on the green had long dark hair. Her vision of the girls began to blur and, feeling nauseated again, she headed toward a stone bench under a nearby magnolia tree. The porous surface was slightly cooler than the air.

One girl was African American, with a compact, sinewy build, like a cheerleader. The other was short, with hair frizzier than the girl in the newspaper photo. Neither one was Sky.

Beth went over ways she might introduce herself. She could picture a teenager's wide-eyed, wary face. Maybe she would lose her nerve altogether.

Look how focused these girls are, Beth thought. Literally cocooned in concentration. Their putters clicked against the white dimpled balls like the measured ticking of a clock. Beth could almost feel the burgeoning of their potential, both as human beings and as young women, skimming like dolphins just below the liquid surface, ready to leap free.

These girls had to be tough, mentally. Golf took stamina. Like running a marathon, the person who took the lead out of the gate was not necessarily the one to win. Winning took staying power, concentration and control and iron will for eighteen holes.

Serious golf was deeply ethical. It was the only sport in the world in which a player was expected to call a penalty on him or herself. One world-class player had once failed to call a penalty on himself during a tournament and that one action had cast doubt on his reputation for many years. But could people ever really live up to this? People were so imperfect. Almost every time Beth played, someone cheated. Found a better lie. Dropped a ball in the woods. Counted wrong. Took a mulligan. Beth and her gals offered each other mulligans all the time, like gifts on bad days, fairytale second chances at life. But in competitive golf, there were no second chances.

On the other hand, paradoxically, on every hole, there was a fresh chance to make things right. And maybe today, in finding Sky, Beth would have a chance like that.

Margo sat next to her. "I got a pairing sheet. Sky teed off at seven thirty. She's probably already on the back nine, maybe on number ten."

Beth took the pairing sheet, ran her chewed fingernail down until she found the crisp black letters. Sky Sawyer. It was real. The dizziness passed and the pieces of the world settled back into place. Beth bit her lip and stood. "Let's go."

Great fear suddenly rose inside her. What if Sky rejected her?

"Are you okay?" Margo's weathered face floated close to hers. Vanessa was on the other side of the putting green, still watching the girls putt.

"Yeah." She and Margo headed down the cart path to rejoin Vanessa, and the three of them hurried down number ten's fairway. The girls were in twosomes today, and most had caddies—either fathers or brothers, it appeared. There was none of the joking or banter that Beth, Margo, and Vanessa enjoyed during their rounds. Instead, stony competitive silence. Game faces all around. Occasionally a girl exchanged a clipped word or two with her caddy. Fathers who weren't caddies watched by the greens. One or two of them looked to be clenching their teeth hard enough to crack diamonds. Most girls had no more than five or six spectators following them. Mothers, aunts, uncles, friends.

Beth's heart pounded against her chest wall. The idea that Julie might be here snaked its way into her consciousness now, like a faint pulse of electric current, and of course it had always been there, coiled in her mind.

"Hey, if we cut through these pine trees, I think we'll come out close to the number eleven tee," Margo said after briefly studying the course map.

In the blue-white sky, weak, hot breezes fluttered a few wispy clouds. The tree branches waved, making a sound like a mother shushing a baby. Beth and the others plunged into the cool dark shade of the pine grove between holes, the bed of copper needles spongy under their feet. Beth was enveloped in an eerie, dappled coolness, and goose bumps peppered her arms. The voices of her friends receded. The pump of blood in her extremities echoed the beating of her heart. Two female figures, still too far away to identify, stood on the tee on the other side of the woods. Beth walked more slowly, deliberately falling behind. She felt as if she were suspended in the slowing of time before the gunshot to begin a horse race. The arc of the sun and the flow of time seemed to stop.

Maybe this was not supposed to happen. This could change everything about Beth's life. About Sky's. She passed pine trunks lined like dominoes that, once they began to fall, perhaps could not be stopped.

She already wanted to love her so much.

Beth was still in the woods when she saw her. Leaning on her club, waiting to tee off, her silky dark hair a heavy mane on her neck. Beth wrapped her arm around the slim trunk of a dogwood.

She had a flash memory of Julie, at fifteen, leaning on a fence outside a horse ring.

Beth felt her face collapse. Vanessa was beside her. "Beth, is that her? Beth?" Vanessa's fingers grasped her arm like vines.

Sky looked coltish, with strong legs and triangular, boy-like shoulders, and long-fingered hands. A serene, focused expression filled her face, like the smooth marble of a Greek statue.

She was teeing off now. Two taps on the ground, stepping into it, leading with her chest, her swing too aggressive to be gorgeous, moving through the ball, almost like a baseball swing. But she finished with a smooth, textbook turn of the shoulders. Still so young. And so serious.

Julie hadn't played sports, though she was coordinated and loved to dance. She'd closed down the dance clubs, in fact. She prowled at night and slept like the dead during the day, hating the light almost like the vampires in those old black and white horror films.

Mostly, she left. Jumped in the car, careened out of the driveway. Like a moth in a jar, flinging herself at glass walls, leaving bits of herself clinging like pollen to everyone she met. Beth and Mark watched it happen, too helpless to do anything.

Margo was next to her now, gripping her elbow. "Beth, that's her, right? The one who just hit?"

Beth nodded, her eyes burning, trying to keep the girl from swimming out of focus.

"Oh, good grief, Beth." Vanessa noticed that Beth was crying, and Margo squeezed her shoulder. They huddled in the pine grove and waited for Beth to pull herself together.

"I'm okay, thank you, ladies." Beth wiped her cheeks, took a deep breath, and stepped out of the woods and into the rough beside the fairway. She jammed on her sunglasses to hide her reddened eyes, raked her bangs off her face. "Come on, let's go." Sky was talking to her caddy now, a pale balding man who looked like a walrus with wire rim glasses, as he slid the cover onto her driver and shouldered her bag. Golfer and caddy headed down the fairway.

"Her caddy," said Margo, as, in unspoken agreement, the four tramped down the edge of the fairway, following them. "That her dad?"

"I don't know," said Beth, clearing the vestiges of the crying jag from her throat. "That's not the boy Julie ran away with."

"Maybe the club assigned her that caddy," said Margo.

"You're not going to say anything to her yet, right?" said Vanessa.

"No, I'll wait," Beth said, and felt relief run through her like sparkling water. She had time. Time to watch, to get to know her a little. What if Sky didn't want to meet her? What if she had built up years of anger?

"There's hardly any other people," Margo said. "She'll probably keep wondering who the hell those three old ladies are who are following her."

"Don't call *me* old," said Vanessa.

Beth stopped beside the fairway and looked at her two friends. Margo, with her intense face and ponytail of gray hair, already sweat-soaked and awry. Vanessa, deer-like, her braids swinging. "Girls, I know I begged you to come. And it was so sweet of you to take care of me when I fell apart back there. But now I feel like we're a *posse*." Beth took a breath. "I just want to follow her by myself. Do y'all mind?"

Margo and Vanessa looked hurt, but agreed, and they set a time to meet for lunch at the clubhouse bistro. Suddenly, Beth found herself standing beside the manicured emerald fairway alone.

WHILE THEY'D BEEN talking, Sky had marched down the fairway and was now fifty yards ahead of Beth, preparing to hit her approach shot. Beth hurried to catch up. The pasty, rather unsteady caddy lowered Sky's bag to the ground beside her.

Sky's opponent was a powerful Black girl with hair like cropped velvet clinging to her perfectly-shaped skull and a narrow-eyed expression of determination. According to the scorekeeper's board, her name was Erika Sanford, and she was beating Sky by two strokes. That was okay; the way qualifying worked, you were just playing your own game against a score, and Sky could still qualify even if Erika beat her.

Beth watched Sky, studied her, memorized the way she pursed her lips when she putted, the way she cracked her knuckles when she was waiting and thought no one was watching. Beth was aware she was trying to drink in the girl's very essence. It reminded her of the time she and her friends had followed Tiger Woods at a tournament in Charlotte. Four hundred people crowded so suffocatingly close around a tee their sweaty elbows poked her and their hot breath permeated her skin. The car keys in the pocket of the man beside her practically left an open wound on her bare arm.

And everyone's eyes were trained on Tiger, as if he were a god. He'd stood motionless, staring straight ahead, as if none of them were there jockeying for a tiny piece of him, to breathe the same air, to step into his aura, to drink in what it was that made him so great. The crowd was so quiet, yet packed like chickens in a crate, a challenge even to expand your lungs to breathe. It had been only a few months after Tiger's father died and Beth had wondered what it would be like to have to grieve while still being on display like that every day.

Just like that, she studied Sky. It seemed nothing short of amazing that this girl could be her own flesh and blood, that, after all these years, she might have found a connection to Julie. Everything seemed heightened, sharp, vivid, like a camera rolling focus—the click of the club heads against the balls, the etched green leaves against the whitewash of the sky. Her stake in every passing second seemed more intense.

On the pond in front of the green, wind gusts drew sparkle patterns on the water surface like a child's glitter pen. Sky swung, totally ignoring the pond, putting her shot in good position ten feet below the hole. Beth climbed to the green and stood just back from the edge. Erika had hit her shot in the trap, and as the sun climbed and the heat began to radiate from the sand, the small gallery watched her descend to the bottom, her golf shoes sinking into the pinkish, shifting grains.

Beth took the opportunity to scan the other eight or so people following the twosome and decided that all of them were Erika's family and friends, with the exception of one tall teenaged boy with freckled milky skin and nearly white hair. There was no one who could possibly be Julie.

Erika, meanwhile, opened her clubface and blasted the ball from the trap, hitting it too hard and leaving herself a long downhill putt.

Sky's caddy seemed unhealthily pale and breathless. He looked as though it would be touch and go for him to walk the full eighteen. Beth stepped a bit closer to the edge of the green, close enough so that she might be able to overhear Sky's conversation with her caddy.

"Two inches left of the hole," he said.

Sky knelt and plumb-bobbed the shot. She did not respond.

He said something else that Beth couldn't hear.

"Dad, sh!"

So Sky was calling this man *Dad*. Beth caught her breath. Her mind raced ahead, tumbling and leaping over the possibilities. Where was Julie?

Sky holed the putt, then crossed to the edge of the green and handed the putter to her caddy. Erika two-putted, and the group took off for the next hole at a brisk walk. Beth fell in behind Sky and her caddy.

"See? Two inches," he said.

As Sky approached the tee, she pulled a black golf glove from her shorts pocket and popped the knuckles on each hand before she flexed her fingers inside, readying herself for her drive.

The heat was increasing so fast Beth could almost see steam rising from the grass. Sky and her caddy toiled toward the green.

And just as the caddy was about to crest the hill, he swayed, sank to his knees, and sat down. Beth was close enough to hear when the clanking crash of the clubs made Sky turn around.

"Dad! Are you okay?"

Beth watched Sky almost slide back down the hill, lean over him, put her palm on his cheek, and give him her hand.

Erika, her caddy, and the scorekeepers stopped, and a half dozen people gathered around the fallen caddy.

"Give me a minute," he said.

No one seemed to know what to do. The caddy tried to stand, moving his bulk slowly, but sat back down. Beth's stomach fell into nowhere. The man's face was the yellow of chicken skins. A marshal—a man wearing a polo shirt with the club insignia—drove up in a cart and jumped out.

After some discussion, it was agreed that in this heat he should not continue to carry Sky's bag. The marshal helped the caddy, supporting his elbow as if he were an elderly person, into the passenger seat of his cart.

"Are you going to continue to play with no caddy?" the marshal asked Sky.

"I never use a caddy anyway," Sky said. "Dad? Are you going to be okay?"

"I'm okay," said the man. He leaned back as if in slow motion and held a cold bottle of water to his mottled, flushed forehead. "Sorry I let you down, honey."

"Dad, go sit in the clubhouse, have a glass of ice water, and let the air conditioning cool you down."

"I could call on the walkie-talkie," said the marshal, "and see if I can get you a caddy from the clubhouse."

"I can carry my own bag," said Sky.

Beth's heart began to pound, and adrenaline buzzed in her brain, making her light-headed. Beth had caddied for Paul in a tournament once, when he was about twelve, when Mark had had to go to an optometrist's convention. Paul had been mortified. Of course she'd been much younger then. She hadn't carried her own bag in about ten years.

"I've got it." Someone shouldered past Beth and she turned around and the tall milk-skinned boy with the white straw hair looped the bag's sweat-soaked strap over his shoulder and gave a practiced shrug to settle it more securely in place. "Let's go."

Beth could see that Sky was the kind of girl who made a point of not showing her emotions, so she didn't smile at the boy or even nod, but she let her body incline just slightly toward his.

Sky glanced at the marshal. "Is it okay? I mean, rule-wise?"

"No rule against it," said the marshal. "So you're good?"

Sky nodded, and the marshal stomped his foot on the pedal of the cart and drove away with the man Sky had called Dad.

Beth climbed to the green and stood on the fringe. The boy set down the bag, and, after a brief search, pulled out Sky's putter and handed it to her. He had fringed, laughing green eyes, and a look of amused expectancy on his face.

Sky's ball was about six feet from the cup. Erika's was closer, which meant Sky putted first. Beth held her breath as Sky stepped up, executed a quick pendulum practice swing, and drilled the ball into the hole. Her confidence seemed to have soared.

When she handed her putter back to the boy, they had a brief exchange, sotto voce, both smiling, and then stood, leaning toward each other, almost but not quite touching, as Erika crossed to her ball.

Erika, clearly trying to play her own game, was unable to keep from glancing at Sky's new caddy as she addressed the putt. Erika's family gave audible groans when she missed her five-footer and made bogey. And suddenly Erika and Sky were tied.

Sky and the boy barely waited for the ball to drop before turning heel, almost as one, to press on. Beth watched Sky and the boy settle into a rhythmic, habitual lope to the next hole, like two rangy dogs that hunted together, side by side.

Beth followed. Once, Sky hit it into the woods and Beth was amazed at how level-headed she was in assessing her options, how patiently she swung the club, checking to see if she had a full swing, examining her angles through the trees. She didn't get flustered the way Beth always did, worrying that she might be holding people up. Beth felt proud, seeing how confident Sky seemed about her own time and place in the universe. The nearly-albino boy stood with his arm circling Sky's golf bag, and they barely spoke to each other at all. Beth found herself remembering when Julie used to sneak out to see Russell Ray, seeing them together, the way she circled her arms around his waist, the way he possessively laced her fingers through his, and knowing that it had happened, that they had been intimate. She had known Mark didn't know, or didn't want to know, and she hadn't told him.

Sky finished her round tied with Erika. Looking at the leader board posted by the eighteenth green, Beth was pleased to see Sky two strokes off the lead. She was almost sure to be one of the six who made the cut. With a start, Beth saw Margo and Vanessa at one of the café tables behind the putting green, waving to get her attention. She'd forgotten all about meeting them for lunch!

But this was her only chance to speak to Sky. They would understand. She waved, then hurried over to Sky and the boy. They both smiled back, blankly, politely.

"You played well out there," Beth said. "It was a pleasure to watch."

Sky squinted at her, kept smiling. "Thank you so much." Beth noticed that the bone structure of Sky's hand, as she passed her putter over to the caddy, was almost identical to her own, and her nails and cuticles were bitten and red in almost the exact same way. She felt a surge of emotion that nearly caught her off guard. "You played your own game. I really admired the way you've developed that at such a young age."

"Thanks. I appreciate it."

"Do you know if what you shot was good enough to make the cut?"

"Not yet. We have to wait for everyone to finish."

"And then, you'll go to the girls' junior in Charlotte?"

"I don't know. It costs a lot of money."

The boy turned away, busied himself cleaning Sky's clubs, but Beth thought he might be listening with half an ear.

"I wanted to introduce myself. I'm Beth Sawyer, and I live about a half hour southwest of here."

"Hey, we have the same last name." The girl smiled cautiously, shifting her weight from one leg to the other, clearly wondering what Beth's point might be. Sky was taller than Beth, and she had to look up to meet her deep-set, almond-shaped gray eyes.

"Your parents must be so proud of you. Are they here?"

Sky glanced at the clubhouse. "My dad is. My mom . . . I don't have a mom. But I need to check and see how my dad is doing."

Beth plunged on before she could stop herself. "Yes, of course. I hope your dad's okay. I have . . . had . . . a daughter named Julie. I heard she had a daughter named Sky, and her last name was Sawyer. Of course it was, cause my last name is Sawyer. I'm sorry, I'm rambling."

The girl had been staring at her feet and when Beth said this, her head snapped upward like a rifle stock snapping into place.

"I was wondering . . . if I might be related to you. If I might be your grandmother."

"My . . . grandmother?" Sky couldn't get the word out all the way and had to clear her throat and start over halfway through. Impossible to guess what was going on behind those determined gray eyes. But now, suddenly, she was cracking her knuckles. There was a beat and Sky said, "So you know where she is? Your daughter?"

"No," Beth answered, nearly blushing. "And I guess that means you don't know where she is either. What was your mother's first name? *Was* it Julie? Do you remember her?" Beth stopped herself, embarrassed. "I'm so sorry, I must be coming on a little strong."

"No, it's all right." Sky looked straight at her as she seemed to be weighing her words. "Julie, yeah, that was her name. I don't . . . I mean, I can't . . ." She glanced toward the clubhouse again. "I better go check on my dad." Sky crossed her arms over her chest, rubbed her palms over her upper arms as if she'd been struck with a chill, and took a step toward the clubhouse.

"Wait!" Beth reached in her back pocket for the envelope she'd prepared, each photo chosen with care. "These are copies of pictures we took of Julie when she was a teenager, in the year or so before she left. Maybe you could compare them to pictures you might have. I included some of her as a little girl because I thought maybe you'd be interested." The tears came again now, as hard as Beth tried to stop them. "And you don't have to look at the pictures now—maybe it would be easier later. But there's one in there of her when she was fifteen. Exactly your age, right?"

"These are for me?" Sky took the packet, taking another step away.

Beth glanced at the young caddy, still cleaning Sky's clubs. He cast a cursory look at the packet of photos. His eyes danced even when he wasn't smiling. Greenish-brown, like fringed windows of darkness in the opaque whiteness of his skin. "Yes, they're copies I made for you. Show them to your dad, if you'd like to. And here's my email address and phone number, if you want to get in touch."

"Did she . . . have a white bathing suit?" Sky's eyes glistened and she seemed to be holding her breath.

"A white . . . Yeah, there is even a picture of her in a white bathing suit in there."

"I should get my dad," she said, but Beth was almost sure she hesitated.

"I saw that your father wasn't feeling well earlier, and maybe this isn't a good time. Would you and your father and your friend like to have lunch?"

"What friend?"

Beth turned around. The boy with the straw hair had vanished into the blossoming heat. Sky's clubs were leaning on the club rack. "I'm sorry, I thought you knew the boy who stepped in to carry your bag."

Sky gazed at Beth for a second, blinked. "He plays on the golf team at my school." She gave a shrug.

Beth nodded. Julie used to do the same thing, keep her relationships secret. She believed it gave her more power over her own destiny. And maybe it did. The trait had made Beth furious with Julie. The more she tried to pull information out of her, the more stubbornly she'd kept it to herself.

Maybe she should walk away now. But at that moment the father shoved through the turn room door and shuffled toward them. Beth glanced over at Margo, sitting bolt upright at a café table, staring at her, evidently trying to figure out what was happening.

The sweat on the father's clothes had dried while he'd been in the air-conditioned clubhouse, leaving wandering white salt lines over his stomach like the edges of land masses on a map.

"Hi," she said, holding out her hand. His was cold and clammy. "I hope you're feeling better. I'm Beth Sawyer. I know this will probably sound crazy but . . . My daughter Julie disappeared fifteen years ago, and I was wondering if there's any possibility Sky might be her daughter. My granddaughter."

The father swayed slightly but did not respond. His large mustache made it hard to read the expression on his lips, but he narrowed his eyes. Sweat sheened the top of his bald head. He glanced at Sky, then pulled a wadded dollar bill from his pocket and said, "Honey, we're going to talk a second. Why don't you go get a Gatorade?" When he spoke, Beth recognized a Midwestern accent.

Sky stood for a full three or four seconds, no emotion showing on her face, then said, "Dad, I can stay." Beth saw Sky had put the pictures and contact information she'd given her in her back pocket. She didn't think the father had seen.

Beth rushed in. "Sky told me her mother's name was Julie. And there's the Sawyer last name."

"Sky, go get a Gatorade."

Sky's face went inscrutable, then she finally stepped away.

"There are probably fifty Sawyers in this area," said the man in an offhand, semifriendly way. "A Julie Sawyer in every town."

"I know, it's a long shot, it's just that she resembles my daughter so much. Do you know where Sky's mother is? Do you have any pictures of your wife?"

The father blinked and looked at the ground. "I have pictures. I don't know where she is. She disappeared when Sky was two. Sky doesn't remember her." Beth felt the blood drain from her face and her throat close.

"A lot of people look alike," he added. "I don't know," he suddenly said, becoming more breathless, running his hand over his bristled head. "It's probably not a good idea for Sky to be thinking about this. She shouldn't be thinking about anything except how she plays in the US junior. She needs to concentrate on her game." He turned and watched Sky standing in line to get a Gatorade, and Beth could see, from the way his eyes softened, how much he loved her. "You don't know how much she wants to find her mother. Maybe we shouldn't be getting her hopes up."

"She can't want to find Julie any more than I do," Beth heard herself say in a taut voice. "And if she's my granddaughter, then we should know each other."

"I need to think about this," he said. "Give me your number. You live nearby? I'll call you."

Beth's mouth fell open, and she took a step back, mentally scrambling for a reply. Of course, he felt ambushed. Maybe she should have done this some other way.

She decided not to tell him that she'd already given her number and the pictures to Sky. She nodded and pulled one of her business cards from her purse, circled the home number. "I hope you will call. Please call," she said. "At least let's investigate and find out for sure. What's your name, sir?"

She met his eyes beseechingly, but he didn't answer. Girls were finishing their rounds and heading for the clubhouse, and people flowed around Beth and Sky's father like waves around a stone. Finally, he took her card. Beth couldn't detain him any longer. "Please call." He turned and moved unsteadily through the crowd.

"Beth!"

Margo was waving at her from a café table.

"Well?" Margo demanded and Vanessa looked on wide-eyed as Beth sat down with them. "What's the scoop?"

"Sky says her mom's name was Julie. But her father . . . I think he feels ambushed or something. He didn't tell me his name and he didn't give me any way to contact them. I have to wait for them to contact me."

"Shit," said Margo.

"What do you think, Beth?" asked Vanessa.

"I know this sounds crazy, but her hands look like mine," Beth said. "And we both pick our cuticles in exactly the same way."

Something occurred to her.

"Maybe I should call Mark."

"Why? You don't know any more now than you knew before," said Margo. The lines around her mouth deepened and she exchanged a glance with Vanessa.

Beth let her eyes drift from Margo's face to some leftover potato chips on her paper plate. Suddenly she was ravenously hungry. "Are you going to eat those?"

Margo, without a word, shoved the plate closer.

CHAPTER TWELVE

Sky

"Why do we have to leave?" Sky tried not to raise her voice.

"I have to get back," her dad said. The rusty door of their red truck squealed as he threw it open.

"But I don't even know if I made the cut." Sky knew this was about that lady who'd approached her.

"You can find out later. Let's just go." Her dad's shirt was soaked with sweat again. A bead of sweat trembled from a hair at the end of his mustache and the skin underneath was a painful-looking red. Bits of grass still clung to his pants and the dome of his stomach where he'd fallen.

His voice rose and Sky's inner alarms went off.

"You've played lights out. Now, back to reality." Her dad spread his arms around, encompassing the club's manicured foliage and marble walkways. "Come on, honey. This isn't us. You know it, I know it. Time to go home."

What do you mean? Why isn't this me? Her heart began to thump. "I thought this was your dream, Dad. Our dream. Our way to get Mom back. Like the girl on *American Idol.*"

"We gotta go, Sky. I've got a job to start in the morning."

"Well, I left my clubs in the storage area." Sky had saved her money and haunted used club shops for every one. Mr. McLean, the cigar-chomping starter at Solomon Municipal, had found her driver on eBay and lent her the money for it. She'd only finished paying him back a month ago.

Her dad straightened and looked at her. "Go get your clubs." He pointed his big finger at her. It shook slightly. "Then come back here. Right back here, right away."

Sky whirled and ran through the parking lot to the lower level of the clubhouse where the clubs were stored. She swiped hot tears of fury from her cheeks. She was glad she hadn't shown her dad the pictures this woman had given her and glad she'd kept Silas a secret from him, too. She couldn't wait to look at the pictures by herself.

She jogged inside the club storage area and gave her claim ticket to a skinny boy in an Izod shirt. "I need my clubs back." She turned her face away quickly, and, as soon as he disappeared into the back of the locker room, she used the end of her T-shirt to wipe her face. She stepped behind a wall of lockers and punched in Silas's number.

"What's up?" he said.

"Do you think I made the cut?"

"You were only two strokes off the lead, so yeah, I think so."

"I do, too. But Dad won't let me stay to find out." She pulled her damp pony tail off her neck, used the end to wipe her cheek.

"Who was that lady?"

"She thinks she might be my grandmother."

"Don't you know your grandmother?"

"No."

"Weird. Well, do you think she might be?"

"I don't know." Sky thought she might have a panic attack. She stared at a table in the corner of the storage room for repairing and regripping clubs, trying to take calm, even breaths. She focused on the table. There was a vise for holding the shaft, tape, and solvent for regripping, a box full of utility knives, and boxes of rubbery grips in different sizes. Sky could smell the solvent, sharp and unpleasant, like lighter fluid. Somehow that smell kept her grounded. Three shaftless clubheads lay on the table, and it was spooky because they looked like people's heads without their bodies. She wiped her nose with the back of her hand and cleared her throat. "Where are you right now, anyway?"

"On my way home."

"Want to sneak out later tonight?"

Silence from Silas. Sky picked up one of the grips and bounced it on the table rhythmically, listening to her heart thud, waiting for Silas to answer.

"Okay," he finally said. "Meet me in the woods across the street from the trailer park. Twelve thirty?"

Sky quickly clicked her phone off when someone entered the club storage area. Sky turned and saw Katherine Anne Boyd with her spiked hair.

"Didn't know you were playing today," Katherine Anne said. Then, to the guy behind the counter. "The Calloway Fusions in the gray and white striped bag."

And Sky couldn't believe it. The attendant, who was supposed to be looking for Sky's clubs, immediately took Katherine Anne's claim tag and handed her the bag, which was leaning just to the side of the counter. "Here you are, Ms. Boyd."

Sky kept her game face. "How'd you hit it today?"

"Good. I was happy with my game." Katherine Anne tossed the attendant a five dollar bill and shouldered her clubs. "What about you, Cloud, find any water today?" She grinned.

"*Sky*. My name is Sky. And no, didn't find any water. But thanks for asking." This to Katherine Anne's back as she walked away. She hadn't even waited for Sky's response.

Sky slid the phone in her shorts pocket and stepped in front of the counter as the attendant finally returned with her clubs. He gave a cursory scrub with a dirty cloth to the head of her five iron as he set them in front of her. Katherine Anne had tossed him a five. Shit, she was supposed to tip him. She dug in her pocket. The boy gave her a withering look and turned away when she produced a quarter and a dime.

"Sorry," she called back over her shoulder on her way out. She aligned the shoulder strap in the customary spot over her right shoulder and felt the comforting weight of the clubs settle onto her back, the rhythmic clanking as she walked, trying to forget about what an arrogant jerk that Katherine Anne was.

She took her time returning to the parking lot. Her dad had always acted like he wanted to find her mom, but now when this lady stepped up and claimed to know something, he freaked. Was he hiding something else from her?

She'd been ashamed of him for a long time, and ashamed of being ashamed, but suddenly she was wondering whether she could trust him. That was a completely different thing. It made her feel dizzy.

Sky's dad sat in the front seat of the truck with his head resting on the steering wheel. Sky threw her clubs in the back and got in. She was silent as they drove west on I-40. She thought about all the other girls milling around at the club, waiting for everyone to finish so the top six could be named.

"Nobody else who had a chance to be in the top six would have left," she said.

"I can't help it, Sky. This is the way it's gotta be."

Katherine Anne would be first, she'd bet anything.

They drove directly into the setting sun, a blazing red-hot explosion on the horizon that seemed to singe the trees into black silhouettes. It was giving Sky a monster headache. Her dad lowered the visor and put on his sunglasses. Because of the glare through the window, her dad's face looked like it was on fire.

"Sky," he said. "We need to talk."

"What?" Her mouth felt dry. She remembered breaking the window to escape from the bathroom that time at golf camp, dropping on the dumpster. If she sneaked out her window tonight, she'd have to drop two stories. If her dad fell asleep, she could just walk out the back door.

"I want you to promise me you won't try to get back in touch with that woman who came to talk to us today."

"Why?"

"I just want you to let me handle it. There are too many crazy people in the world."

Sky recalled the woman's thin tanned face. Sky had been studying women that she thought might be her mom's age all the time, but she'd never paid attention to grandmother types. She'd never even thought about her mother having a mother. Never considered that she might have a grandmother.

Crazy or not, she was going to call her. That lady knew something Sky had wanted to know for a long time.

CHAPTER THIRTEEN

Beth

Driving home, Vanessa sat up front with Margo, who was telling some story about running a marathon near Stonehenge. Beth, sitting in the back by herself, zoned out of the conversation. She looked out the window and watched the shiny leaves in a grove of oaks tremble and shush in the breeze as they drove by.

"Beth, you know who you ought to call?" Margo pulled Beth back into the present. "Barry Redmond, that's who. He told Buddy's wife he had a great time with you."

Beth tried to focus on Margo's comment.

"I'm playing a golf match with him next week."

Beth's thoughts wound back to years ago, when Mark taught her to play golf. Other women she'd known had been persuaded by their husbands to try the game, but most, after a few feeble attempts, had ended up refusing to play with their husbands ever again. The husbands impatiently described to their wives what must be done in terms of grip, swing, course management, and most important, reading greens. Then the husbands sputtered and criticized, as their wives teed it up again and again.

"Couldn't you see that break? Are you blind?"

But Mark had cheered on Beth's every shot, decent or not. He had been the most patient of all teachers. His passion for the game had been so consuming, and his desire to share his passion with Beth had been too genuine for her to resist.

"Your swing is pure," he'd told her. Well, all this time Beth had been walking around thinking she was a perfectly ordinary person. But no. Her swing was pure. He'd made her think that she had something special, and his belief in her had inspired her to keep playing. When she'd made her first par, he'd galloped across the green yelling with joy. When she made her first birdie, she'd thrown down her club, run across the green, leaped, and wrapped her legs around his waist. When she beat Mark the first time, instead of getting angry, he'd appeared nearly overcome with pleasure. Even now, the fact that Beth still played golf had a great deal to do with maintaining a thread of connection with Mark.

And of all the people that she wanted to tell about finding Sky, she wanted to tell Mark the most. She didn't say it out loud, though, because she knew Margo would yell at her. Margo's opinions about Mark were pretty clear—the less contact the better. Every time Beth talked about him, about connecting with him, Margo encouraged her to move on. Plus, judging by their last encounter, she had to admit that Mark might not even want to hear about her encounter with Sky.

"So . . . playing next week with Barry Redmond will be pretty interesting, won't it?" Vanessa said. "Have you ever played golf with a man other than Mark?"

Beth watched the shadowed trees slide by on the highway. "No."

CHAPTER FOURTEEN

Sky

Sky thought her dad would never fall asleep in his chair that night. She cleaned up the dishes, then did a load of laundry. Then she went into her room and watched the girl from *American Idol* on YouTube again. When she cracked her door open and peeked out, he was still watching the news.

She wedged herself into her closet between her sweaters and dresses, many of them too small by now, and used the light on her phone to look through the photos the lady had given her for probably the tenth time. The girl in the white bathing suit. The girl riding the regal-looking chestnut horse. The girl skating on rollerblades with one leg in the air.

Finally, finally, she heard her dad's soft snoring, and, just to be sure, she peeked outside her door and saw his head slumped forward on his chest. Then she tiptoed back inside her closet and stood in between the clothes. With trembling hands, she pulled out the slip of paper that lady, Mrs. Sawyer, had given her and dialed the number scrawled upon it.

"Hello?"

"Hi. This is Sky."

The lady gasped. Then she started talking, kind of rattling on about how exciting it was that Sky had qualified, and how she wanted to come watch her play in the tournament.

"So, I did qualify?"

"Oh, yes, you did. I looked for you—I guess you'd left." Sky, so relieved to have it confirmed that she'd made it, half-listened to the lady's chatter, and with the hand that wasn't holding the phone, played with a smashed yellow ribbon on the front of a dress that she'd worn a long time ago. Sky listened to the high swoops of Mrs. Sawyer's voice and let her eyes wander around the inside of the closet, trying to think about times she'd last worn these dresses, wondering if she'd made a mistake with this call.

"Do you have any more pictures of her?" Sky asked, peering through the slit in the closet door, making sure her dad hadn't woken up and was checking on her in her room.

"Oh, yes, I do, and I'd love for you to see them," said Mrs. Sawyer. "I have albums and albums of pictures. I used to look at them all the time. Can we meet somewhere?"

"I work at the driving range at Solomon Municipal Wednesday through Sunday."

And so Mrs. Sawyer had said she would come and bring the pictures on Thursday.

A few hours later, when Sky tiptoed out the back door and closed it quietly behind her, she skimmed across the dewy grass and the soles of her feet seemed not to touch the ground.

As she approached the edge of the woods, she thought about that picture of her mother in the white bathing suit, the one that matched her dad's story. It was so strange and discomforting to think that someone could look so much like her—like a twin with the same dark hair and shape of face and almond eyes—but be just without a doubt a different person. She was prettier than Sky— beautiful, while she herself was just solid looking—but there was nothing peaceful or satisfied about that face. When Sky looked into Julie's face, she could see a teasing vibration of the air around her. Julie's eyes promised a connection with what was real and true and thrilling about life.

You'd want to be near her, you'd stay there and hang on to every word she spoke, even if she was in a terrible mood and insulted you all day.

You'd try to make her happy, even though there was a strange glinting off-centeredness in her eyes that implied you never could.

Sky had also studied the picture of her leading an enormous chestnut horse into a ring. Still small, maybe nine years old, she was leading an animal with a face the size of half of her body. Commanding this animal five times her size with the sheer force of her will. And the eyes of the horse seemed mesmerized by her.

When she arrived at the woods, a car blinked its headlights. She ran down the hill with her backpack swinging, hopped into the Jeep, and immediately saw the gleam in Silas's eyes. Maybe he liked it that sensible, solid Sky was acting a little crazy. And then they took off, spewing gravel behind the Jeep, driving past the dark woods, then the wooden trailer park sign and the back road to the interstate. The air seemed electric, as if tonight the stars weren't held in the sky but were zooming all over the place.

"So . . . no problems, then?" he said. His hair almost glowed in the dark.

"He fell asleep." She leaned her forehead against the window. "I'm so pissed at him. I mean, why couldn't he stay for thirty minutes so I could be there when they announced who'd made the cut." She paused. "Do you think my dad is weird?"

"I don't know. Kind of. He's different from my dad." The air conditioning wasn't working, so Silas rolled both windows down and the wind started roaring through the car.

"I looked at the pictures that lady gave me," Sky shouted.

He glanced away from the road at her, knitting his brows. He hadn't heard.

"Never mind," she said. They were driving past some dark fields and the smell of cow manure permeated the air. Silas put his hand on her knee and squeezed. "Where you want to go?"

She grinned. "Anywhere." Silas knew someone who had a party that night and so they went to his house. The garage had been turned into a party room with a big refrigerator and a foosball table and a few sagging brown and green chairs that smelled like stale beer and pot. The host was older and had graduated from their high school a few years before. Bottles of booze littered the bar, and a downstairs bedroom was being used as a make-out room. The other guests were mostly older and she didn't really know anyone. So after Silas had a beer or two, Sky told him she wanted to leave.

They went to the quarry again. Sky had never been there at night. She got goose bumps on her arms and could hear her teeth chattering even though it was the middle of summer. They sat on the damp rocks and looked at the moon on the water, a bright crescent, the water so still you thought you'd smash into a mirror if you jumped.

"A fingernail moon," said Sky. "That's what I always called those."

Silas got up to look for a few pieces of shale. He wound up and tossed one out into the lake. It smashed the surface into a million pieces of dark glass. When he released the rock, his weight shifted precariously.

"You're making me nervous. You could fall over the edge in a heartbeat. Why don't you sit back down?"

Silas threw another rock and smashed the surface again.

"That garage party . . . was that the same house where Maeve was last seen?" she asked.

"Yeah." Silas sat down again beside her.

Back in May after an end-of-school party, a girl named Maeve had run away and disappeared. After a three-week search, her parents had found her living in an apartment with a much older guy she'd met online. Everybody had been surprised that she'd been found and was all right. Somehow they'd all expected her to turn up dead. The guy was arrested.

"You know, my mom ran away," Sky said. "Only she hasn't ever been found. I mean, I don't even know if she's still alive."

Silas tossed another rock. "It would be unbelievable if she was, Sky. Unbelievable."

"But she might be."

Silas shrugged and threw another rock. "I wouldn't get my hopes up."

"I called the lady who approached me today, the one who says she might be my grandmother."

"Maybe that wasn't such a great idea. Maybe she's some kind of weirdo. My parents would freak out if I did something like that."

"Really? All I did was call her. She seemed nice."

"But are you meeting her somewhere?"

"At the practice range. Mr. McLean will be there. It'll be safe."

Silas ran his palm over the ground, looking for more rocks to throw. "It's just weird, Sky."

"So . . . you don't think I should go?"

"I think it's weird."

"Maybe you're right. I'll think about it." The water had settled again, but it was not as perfectly still as before. A slight tremble remained.

CHAPTER FIFTEEN

Beth

On the Tuesday morning after the tournament, the air was still relatively cool, and birds chirped with crazy frantic hope while lemony bands of sun filtered through the stand of pines in front of Mark's house. Beth slowed at the top of the driveway. He'd suggested she take him with her to pick up her car so he could pay for the repairs and then drive Courtney's car to his office. He stood waiting, gaunt and serious, his white lab coat over his arm. He pointedly glanced at his watch as she drove up, even though she'd agreed to pick him up at seven thirty and it was only seven thirty-one.

Beth was so excited to tell him about Sky's call. She'd scheduled the meeting with Sky for Thursday. It hadn't been a fully conscious decision to schedule it for Mark's day off, but she had to admit that it might have had something to do with it. She had a class later that morning and had tossed a change of clothes on the back seat because she was supposed to play golf with Barry Redmond in the afternoon.

Her old brown leather briefcase sat on the passenger seat, and she reached to move it to the back seat when Mark got in.

"I'll get it," he said, and his hand met hers briefly on the handle of the briefcase as he took it. His fingers felt surprisingly cold.

"Do you want to drive?"

"That's okay." He climbed in beside her and shut the door. She'd always loved the way he smelled, but today there was a faint sour whiff of decay, of age. He looked at his watch again. "It's definitely ready?" he said. "I can't wait around if it's not. I'm slammed today."

"They called last night; it's ready." She pulled out of the cul-de-sac and headed down the road toward town and the body shop. The morning traffic was backed up as usual, and the ten-minute ride would probably take thirty.

She looked at him. He'd slid over to the door and settled his elbow on the armrest, propped his forehead on his hand. He looked like he already had a headache. She realized she was just another obligation on a long, difficult to-do list.

Maybe it would be better to tell him about Sky another time.

No, she had to tell him now. She wouldn't get another chance without having to navigate Ronda.

"So . . . Saturday I watched Sky Sawyer play a qualifying event," she said.

"Really?" It seemed he suddenly stopped breathing. The traffic ground to a halt. They stopped behind a cement mixer, loud and grinding, its rotating belly dripping gray-white splats on the asphalt ahead.

Beth kept her eyes on the road. "I met her, Mark," she said, after a beat. "She's darling. Such a solid, sweet girl. And you should see her swing! I wish you could have been there. We talked after the round, and I gave her some pictures of Julie. And my contact information. Guess what?" Beth let the car slide forward, closer to the cement mixer, anticipating it soon might move.

Mark angled himself so that he could see her better, but still leaned away. His blue eyes seemed icier than usual. "What?"

"She called me, Mark. God, when I picked up the phone and heard her say, 'It's Sky,' my heart almost broke in two. She wants to see more pictures."

"This is crazy, Beth."

"She's very curious about Julie, wants to know more about her."

"Well, that's the sixty-four-thousand-dollar mystery, isn't it," Mark said, staring at the line of traffic ahead of them. "Everybody wants to know more about Julie."

"I'm going to Solomon Municipal on Thursday to show her some more pictures, and to chat with her. And I might try hiring another PI."

"Beth, you're chasing a ghost!" Mark sighed, then slapped his knee with impatience.

"I refuse to let you bring me down," she said. "I have been so happy the last few days, just thinking about this girl."

Mark stared at the line of cars ahead of them as if he'd like to blow them up. Suddenly he unleashed his seat belt. "I can't take this. Get out of the car. I'll drive."

Beth gaped at him, but he was already out of the car, crossing around the front, his thin face pointed, almost like a rodent's, with anger. Quickly, she undid her own seat belt as he flung open her door.

"Put it in park," he said.

Maybe he meant for her to slide over, but she was too old to climb over a gearshift, and so she got out of the car and their bodies came together just as someone beeped their horn because they were holding up traffic. He gripped her arms and literally picked her up and set her aside as he slid into the seat. She ran around the front of the car and ducked into the shotgun seat, slamming the door.

"Good grief, Mark."

Before she could put on her seat belt, he yanked the steering wheel to the right, and Beth's temple banged the window. The car groaned as he pulled onto the shoulder, skirting a full lane of traffic, and he drove with one wheel on the asphalt and the other four inches lower on the ground. Beth clicked her seat belt with emphasis and dignity and sat in silence, rubbing her temple while they bumped along, passing a half-mile backup of cars. One guy yelled "Asshole!" as they lurched by. Then, Mark cut through a service station, skidding past the gas tanks, barely missing an SUV, and zipped out the other side. He floored it once he got to the road, even though he had to turn in less than a block, then careened with squealing tires into one of the body shop's parking spots. Beth's head jerked forward when he slammed on the brakes.

"Whiplash. I'm suing you for whiplash, Mark Sawyer."

"Go ahead! You want a piece of me, go ahead, take it, everybody else has!"

"I was jok—"

"Beth, enough! I cannot think about this anymore. It makes my head explode. Leave me alone!" His face was red, his hands white-knuckled on the wheel.

Beth couldn't keep looking at him, so she looked at the floor. She didn't breathe. Couldn't.

Mark leaned back in the seat and closed his eyes. He looked exhausted. His hair had turned so gray. "I'm sorry."

Beth didn't answer. Instead, they both sat in silence. She could feel the charged atmosphere inside the car slowly release and soften. The seconds ticked by, and Beth could feel the anger turning to sadness, the way a candle melts to wax. She put her fingers very lightly on the back of Mark's wrist. After a moment, he turned his palm up and entwined her fingers with his.

She remembered a time only a year or so before Julie left, when she and Mark had rented a motorcycle to ride around the island, Beth holding tightly to Mark's waist, her chin nestled on his shoulder. They'd stopped at a café where they chatted with a man on the porch who claimed to have come to Grand Turk on vacation and simply never left.

Mark pulled himself away. "I need to go pay the bill and get to work."

"Okay. Thanks for doing this."

"Don't mention it," he said shortly, and climbed out of the car.

CHAPTER SIXTEEN

Beth

Beth choked down a dry peanut butter sandwich while driving to the golf course after her class. Something was going on with these pills. Or with her. Suddenly, after fifteen years of NPR, she'd lost interest and switched to some vintage rock station. So far today she'd filled her head with Van Halen, Springsteen, and Bob Seger singing about "Night Moves." Now she had Sting full blast, blaring African bongos and syncopated jazz trumpet and a deep driving backbeat. After that, she listened to Eminem, whom Margo couldn't believe she liked, but "One Shot" was awesome, and she sang to it at the top of her lungs. Paul had told her his club soccer team in college used to play it on the bus on the way to a game to get pumped up.

She was nervous about playing golf with Barry Redmond. But she hadn't missed the contrast between Mark's body language that morning and Barry's a few days ago. Mark had tried to get as far away from her as possible while trapped in the car together. During dinner, Barry had leaned toward her across the table, wanting to be closer. She should listen to Margo and Vanessa. She should give him a chance. She'd go to see Sky by herself. She wouldn't burden Mark with it anymore. She wouldn't burden him with anything. No, she'd move forward. And she'd have a darn good time.

She sat on the back bumper of her newly repaired Civic to put on her golf shoes and visor, and methodically took out three brand-new Titleists and her favorite-sized tees and dropped them into her pockets. She didn't bother with the ibuprofen for the back nine.

Heading for the clubhouse, she stuffed her glove into her back pocket and adjusted her visor against the sun. The heat shimmered in clouds off the cart path and the grasshoppers were clicking and flinging themselves like kamikazes through the high dry rough. It had been dry for several weeks, which was good for Beth's golf game because she could gain twenty extra yards of roll on a dry fairway.

Barry was waiting for her on the putting green, wearing wrinkled khaki shorts and a blue golf shirt the color of a Caribbean bay. The creases in the shirt were perpendicular, telling Beth he'd bought it new for today. He'd lined up three balls on the practice green, and Beth stopped to watch him before she walked over. He was small-boned and coordinated and seemed to take it for granted when he sank all three.

"Hi there!" Barry's face lit up when he saw her. Beth liked the crinkles around his eyes and a dimple on his left cheek that she hadn't noticed the other night. Sweat sparkled at his graying temples and the humidity coaxed his hair into curls. He was not wearing his glasses.

"We can tee off anytime," he said, crossing the green to put his putter back in his bag. "Almost nobody out on the course. I guess it's too hot today for most people. I've already checked in."

"You didn't pay for me, did you? I didn't want you to do that!"

"I did. I was the one who threw down this gauntlet, so I figured I better pony up and put my money where my mouth was."

"Well, thank you. Goodness, you've only been in the South for a few weeks and listen to you."

"Oh yeah," he said with a grin. "I definitely got me a dog in this race." He drawled out "dawg" just like the good old Southern boys in the clubhouse. His whole being seemed suffused with happiness, and Beth felt another flicker of hope and relief that she hadn't found another sad man. She could see him trying to pretend that his eyes weren't traveling over her body, but when he met hers traveling over his, he raised his eyebrows. "You look nice," he said, indicating her white shorts and pink tank.

"Oh, this old thing," she joked. "You, too."

"Ready to play?"

"I am."

He looked at her golf bag, examined her clubs. "These clubs have been around awhile."

"My ex-husband bought them for me, probably fifteen years ago. The only club I've bought myself is this one—the rescue." She showed him the hybrid rescue she'd found in the half-price bin last year.

"Ooh, nice," he said. Once she'd admired his clubs, which she knew he expected—a solid but not showy set—he added, "Well, do you want to practice before we tee off?"

"Practice doesn't seem to help me whatsoever." She felt a recklessness she hadn't experienced in a long time.

"Ha!" he said. "Me, either!" And that made him smile and brought a slight flush to his cheeks. "Well, then. Ride or walk?"

"Walk."

"Now, are you sure? This course doesn't circle back after nine—it's straight out and back, so you'll have to walk eighteen."

"I'm aware, it's no problem," she said. They went to the senior tees, which they agreed were a good compromise between the men's and the women's, and Barry put on his golf cap, pulled a tee from his pocket, and flipped it to see who hit first. When he won the toss, he pulled out his driver.

Beth was happy for him to hit first. She admired the smoothness of his swing, the way the muscles rippled in his back when he finished. He hit a solid, beautifully arced shot right down the middle.

Beth wasn't at all nervous, the way she thought she might be. She set up and thought about Sky's swing. And then, like Sky, she stepped into the ball, let her body move through the swing, and finished with a strong shoulder turn. She couldn't believe it when she knocked the cover off the ball. Man, she wished she could grab that girl and hug her to pieces.

She was matching Barry drive for drive, approach shot for approach shot, putt for putt. They could get to know each other later but right now they were just playing golf and she was firing at the pin, her clubs connecting with the most satisfying thwack. It was a magical round of golf, unlike any she'd ever played. She couldn't seem to do anything wrong. The result of copying Sky's swing was nothing less than thrilling. She was driving it in places she'd never driven it before, she was in a zone so pure that she was reminded of the Scottish legends where the old duffers holed their balls and then climbed an invisible stairway straight to heaven.

Barry was being gentlemanly and the slightest bit condescending at first, but then she saw him frown when she drilled a twenty-foot putt and tied him on the fifth hole in a row. "Even up," he said, glancing at her as he bent for his ball. "No blood."

Beth knew she was being obnoxious. She yelled, "Get up!" at her ball when she knew good and well it had already made the green. She yelled, "Get in the hole!" when it was foregone it was headed for the center of the cup, and she jumped up and down like a teenager when she made a birdie on the par three at number six. Just to fluster Barry, she commented to him how funny it was that so much golf talk was sexual. But who could blame her? She'd never played like this. Never. She hadn't been in a single trap, not in a single pond, not in the woods. Who ever heard of such a thing? She'd been on every green in regulation and only was over par because she'd missed a few putts.

And then Barry stopped being condescending and gentlemanly. She knew the moment when he turned on his A game. On number seven he stepped up, raised his arm to wipe sweat from his brow, gave her an almost angry look, and pounded a gigantic drive almost through the dogleg of a par five. She loved the fact that she'd goaded him into his A game. But then, he'd stopped smiling.

By number nine they were still tied up and the course was like a sauna. Beth's shirt was completely soaked, her silk underwear beneath her shorts wet and clinging. Her arms and legs were damp and shiny, and when she licked her lips, she tasted salt. Barry's new golf shirt had turned several shades darker and hung on his shoulders like a wet towel, and semicircular stains spread from his belt down both the front and back of his shorts. They both panted slightly when heading up the hill to the ninth tee.

"Okay, watch where you're standing, you never know where my ball is going," he said, but that wasn't true at all. She stepped behind him to watch his shot. Number nine was the longest par three on the course, about two hundred yards with a difficult green nestled behind two giant bottomless traps. Barry mishit his shot and landed in the right trap. It was the first bad tee shot he'd hit all day. Unlike Mark, who used to slam his club into the ground, once breaking the head off a club, he just shook his head and stepped back for Beth to hit.

Once more, she conjured Sky. She'd never hit this green before in her life, but she knew, even before she hit the ball, that she would today. She stepped into it, felt the corkscrew twist of her shoulders at just the right instant, and when she finished, Barry was behind her saying, "Oh my God, that is a gorgeous ball."

It landed airy as a bird on the center of the green and rolled pertly up to stop only about three feet left of the pin.

As they headed down the fairway, Barry was out of breath and he said, "I left the door wide open with that shot."

She did have quite an advantage at that point. Barry had a difficult up and down from a deep trap, and she had a three-foot birdie putt. The thought of purposely missing her putt wandered unbidden into her head and she swatted it away. "Nobody's ball is in the hole yet," she reminded him.

"This is true," he said, then looked at her. "This is such a fun round, Beth. My wife didn't—" he stopped. "Never mind. I was going to see if you wanted to go double or nothing for the back, but I don't know, you might have me on the run here."

"We're even up. There's no way you're on the run," Beth said. "I'll take it, though. What's the bet?" Her heart gave a pleasant thud, and she felt thoroughly present and alive.

"Dinner?"

"Okay, if I win, you make dinner for me," said Beth. "If you win, you get to make dinner for me."

"Hmm," said Barry, hitting a high note with his laugh that sounded very young. "Not a cook, huh?"

"I'm kidding. I'll make dinner for you. *If* you beat me."

When he climbed down into the trap, Barry almost disappeared; Beth could only see his eyes and nose and the brim of his hat over the edge. She warned herself not to gloat, but getting the ball over that cliff would be no mean feat. He centered himself, digging in the heel of his golf shoe, and blasted the ball; it spun lightly as a popped cork up and out of the trap and rolled to a stop a few inches outside Beth's ball.

"Whoa, nice out," Beth said.

"Thanks," he said, his eyes sparkling as he climbed out and methodically raked, all the while sizing up his putt. And then, brandishing his club like one of the three musketeers, he crossed the green and sank his putt.

"Great save."

Beth kneeled and took her time looking at the putt, although it looked damn straight to her. Then she stood, practiced once, and put the ball in motion, trying not to hit it by. It rolled right up to the lip and stopped.

"Damn! I am such an idiot!" And she hadn't done it on purpose, she'd really tried.

She tapped in her par.

"Nice par. No blood," Barry announced, bending to retrieve Beth's ball for her. "It's so hot out here there's no one else on the course," he commented, still trying to catch his breath. A droplet like a diamond trembled on the fuzz of Barry's forearm when he handed Beth her ball. "I haven't seen a single other person, have you?"

"I haven't." As they passed by the water fountain and small restroom building at the turn, Beth pulled out two paper cones and filled them with water. "Here," she said, handing him one of the cones. "It's really cold."

He pursed his lips to drink, and his eyelashes brushed his cheeks, and she saw the most fleeting look of sadness. His features were fine, with full lips and a sharply defined jaw, and she was close enough to see the webbing of lines around his eyes and mouth, close enough to smell his sweat, not acrid but sweet like grass and dirt and outdoors. "Mmm. It is cold," he agreed, and his lips, previously pale and dry, were wet and slick. It would have been easy for Beth to stand on tiptoe and kiss him. She drew in her breath and tried to step away but felt as though she was stretching some fine invisible fishing line that tangled her to him.

She turned back and touched his shirt over his rib. "Let me see where I hit you."

"Oh, it's nothing." He drank the water, then smoothed his hand over his shirt, as if to prove his ribs were solid and healed.

"Just let me see."

Barry hesitated. "It's kind of ugly." He pulled out his shirttail, modestly, in just one spot, and raised it up, showing her a yellowish-purple welt just above one rib. She reached out, grabbed the shirt herself, and pulled it back to get a better look. Before she knew what she was doing she had slid both hands under and stroked her palms over the fuzz of his chest hair, a half inch above the skin.

His eyes widened and, even in the heat, his shirt dimpled where his nipples were. And her own nipples tightened in response, sending twin shudders down to her pelvic bone.

And then he bent his head and touched her lips with his and the dried sweat on him was like fine sand, like the beach, and she loved the taste. He pulled her to him, backwards into the alcove with the water fountain.

"I guess . . ." he glanced back at the ninth green, stipples of red creeping up his neck. "I guess if someone comes, we can just let them play through."

This struck Beth as hilariously funny. Of course a man's first thought would be about someone playing through.

"We might violate the four-hour rule," she said, her lips brushing his ear, as they pressed up against the water fountain. She also meant to say, "There's nothing worse than slow play," but then he deepened his kiss and the words flew out of her head. Kissing salty, sticky, breathless, her clothes glued to her.

Tenderly, he blew on her temples, and it felt amazingly cool. For a moment, she had the most exquisite sense of well-being. Her body seemed to be floating in air.

"Let's quit. I don't have to play the back. We tied. No blood."

"Quit?" Then she cut her eyes over to the ninth tee and saw a tiny foursome of men approaching. "Oh, God, I know those guys, they call them the Slowsome Foursome. We can't let them get ahead of us." In her imagination, she suddenly had a vision so vivid of Mark walking up the path she nearly threw up. "I don't want to quit," she said, breathless, wrenching herself from the dreamlike place where they had been.

When they disengaged from each other it was like two dividing cells pulling apart, slow and reluctant, but necessary.

CHAPTER SEVENTEEN

Beth

B eth went straight home after the round. She stood at the
bathroom counter, glared at the dialpak of yellow pills, and
heaved them into the trash. Then she showered, climbed into
bed, pulled the sheet over her head, and slept. When she woke, it was
nearly nine in the evening. She made herself a bowl of cereal and ate
it without tasting, blindly watching TV, shuddering with pleasure as
she let herself recall the feeling of Barry Redmond's hands on her
skin. She wanted to call Paul but remembered that he played league
basketball on Tuesday nights. It was better to wait until their normal
Sunday night mother-son conversation, anyway. Her voice might
sound funny, and Paul would ask questions. Sons were like Puritans.

When she couldn't stand it anymore, she called Vanessa and
asked if she could come over. She felt she'd arrived somewhere safe
as she followed Vanessa's long narrow feet padding silently on the
terra-cotta tile past the stairs into her kitchen. Vanessa took out two

hand-blown glasses and poured them each a glass of golden wine, which conjured for Beth an image of a potion that turned mermaids into humans until sunset, or, as in Shakespeare's comedies, made people fall in love for a fortnight. Or, better yet, truth serum. Margo made Beth laugh but Vanessa always made her tell the truth.

They sat on the screened back porch, curled on honey wicker furniture, listening to a frog sing in the dark pond out back, like the plucking of a single low note on a cello.

"It's beautiful out here," Beth said. "Justin still at work?"

"It is. Yes, still at work." Vanessa was wearing the prettiest pajamas—silky pale green material that contrasted beautifully with her skin, with off-white lace tracing the deep V neck. "I got a new trainer today," she said. "I like him a lot. He told me he knew exactly what a woman my age can do." She winked.

Beth laughed.

"But that's not why you're here." Vanessa propped her elbow on the back of the wicker loveseat and leaned back, waiting.

"We . . . made out," Beth said.

"Well, finally. Good Lord, I'm glad."

"It was only our second date."

"You're fifty six years old. It's not like you have a lot of time, honey. How was it?"

Beth tapped her fingernail on the crystal of her wine glass, and it gave a faint clear ringing sound. She felt herself getting teary-eyed. "Tragicomic? We were both, I don't know, out of practice."

"Come on, honey, it's like riding a bicycle. You don't forget."

Beth remembered Barry's hands on her breasts and her stomach tilted. She took a sloppy gulp of wine. "More like a bicycle wreck." Beth rubbed her hands over her eyes, flashing back to the slide of sweaty flesh and the feel of his palm as he cupped the back of her neck.

Vanessa gave her throaty laugh. "When are you seeing him again?"

"I keep owing him dinner. First for hitting him with the golf ball, now because I lost our match by one stroke. I'll see if he calls to collect."

"He will." Vanessa leaned forward to pick up her wine, then curled her feet more tightly on the loveseat and changed the subject. "Does he have kids?"

"His son will be a freshman at Davidson. His daughter has one more year of high school, I think."

"The kids both okay?"

"I'm not sure. He showed me pictures on our first date and both of them looked so sad. You just wanted to give them a hug. Last semester the daughter was suspended from school for fighting."

"The daughter?"

Beth nodded, and they both went silent again, their thoughts suddenly elsewhere. Beth knew Vanessa too well not to know who she was thinking about.

"How's Michaela?"

"She's great, Beth. She got a big promotion at the lab."

"Such an achiever! I know you're proud. You know how sometimes you just feel a connection with a person? I guess it's chemistry. I always did with Michaela." Michaela had Vanessa's lean build and striking features. She was a beautiful girl. She had always been at the top of her class, in high school and later at Duke. She had a skewed, funky sense of humor and when she was a kid, she had deeply admired Julie, who was a year older. "Remember when Julie put the vintage posters of Kurt Cobain all over her room, and Michaela copied her?"

"Yeah." Vanessa nodded, hesitantly, as if she were trying to decide whether to say something more. "Being honest here—I trashed those long ago." She laughed.

Beth laughed, too. "Me, too. I ripped them off Julie's wall and tore them into a million pieces."

Yet Beth had always felt that Michaela's interest in Cobain had an air of the tongue-in-cheek; it was more a statement of how she felt about Julie, while Julie's adoration of him and his music had a ferocity that had scared Beth. Soon after Julie left, Beth spent many evenings listening to his music, trying to understand what it might have meant to Julie.

Sometimes when Vanessa and Beth talked, they agreed that sometimes things happen and it's nobody's fault. Other times Beth was sure that with Julie, Mark had been too uninvolved and she herself had just been too accepting. She had not demanded enough of Julie. Beth used to read the "sample scenarios" in books about parenting teens, and while they worked with Paul, they were no help at all with Julie.

A memory of Julie surfaced now. She'd been a dead-on mimic and she'd loved to make fun of Mark and Beth's musical tastes. Once when they picked her up from one of her waitress jobs, wearing her uniform of black pants and white apron, she'd sung a tuneless, screeching version of Dylan's "Gotta Serve Somebody," using her order pad as a prop.

Beth had laughed so hard she'd thought she'd never catch her breath.

"Oh," Beth said, finally getting to what she wanted to tell Vanessa. "Sky called me! I'm meeting her on Thursday. She wants to see pictures of Julie."

Vanessa smiled. "I want you two to get to know each other."

"I'm almost afraid to talk about it too much, like I'm going to jinx it. I'm so afraid I'll get there and she won't show up, or she'll be like a wild rabbit or one of those feral cats, and I'll get just so close to her and then she'll run away." Beth leaned forward with her elbows on her knees.

"This is not Julie, remember. This is possibly, but only possibly, her daughter. A different person," Vanessa reminded her.

Beth nodded, a charged silence ensued, and now Vanessa looked away, then down at her lap, and in the low light Beth saw the outline of the whitish curve of her neck, and the sharp line of her jaw.

"Vanessa, are you okay?"

Vanessa waved away her comment like a gnat, and picked up her wineglass and cigarette pack. "I'm fine. It's late."

"No, wait. There is something wrong. I want to know—why did you quit golf?"

"Time to go to bed."

"No, Vanessa, it feels like an existential thing to me, and that scares me. You're the epitome of a woman who's got it all. So why would you quit?"

"It no longer makes me feel good to play. I like to be good at things I spend my time doing."

"I don't want to make you play if you don't want to. It's just, I miss you. And, you know how some people suffer tragedies you can't imagine, and then they go bake a perfect birthday cake, or how the English say, yes, that was bloody awful, but oughtn't we to have a spot of tea? And then they polish the silver tea set or the cracked mugs and pour themselves a cup. I don't know, it helps me make sense of life. The rhythm of it helps me keep going from one day to the next."

"You are a more hopeful person than I am, Beth," Vanessa said.

"Why do you say that?"

"I've had . . . I don't know exactly how to put it. I feel like I'm standing at the edge of this terrible empty place. I know that sounds corny."

"Vanessa, what are you talking about?" Startled, Beth sat down next to Vanessa.

"Uh . . . Michaela said I was the source of her anxiety. Somehow, I was too controlling when raising her, her perfectionism being my fault. I don't know. I'm trying to understand but I don't. We had another of those horrible fights and now she won't return my phone calls."

"What?"

Vanessa shook her head, stared at the floor. "And I'm sorry to complain to you, since you've lost Julie for what seems like forever."

"Give it time. I know, as a mother, you'd do anything—"

"Yes, I would. There's just this moment, when I first wake up, when I'm standing on the edge, and I think, well, it's such an effort, I don't believe I have the energy today." Vanessa's gravel voice crawled to a halt. Beth took Vanessa in her arms and hugged her tightly. Her shoulder blades felt like a bird's, sharp, brittle, and thinly covered, and she held her even more fiercely, until she realized that Vanessa was not hugging her back, was just accepting this with a strange, passive limpness.

How strange and painful it is to have a daughter, Beth thought, as she let go of Vanessa. They are so much our flesh we can barely separate ourselves. When we look in their young faces, we see ourselves with fresh opportunities to get things right. But then they grow up and away and hate what they see of their mothers in themselves.

CHAPTER EIGHTEEN

Beth

"Mom?" Beth let herself into the house. Chi-Chi raced up to her, stood on his hind legs, his bulging eyes frantic, then raced back to the den, then back to the hall to make sure Beth was following, and led her to her mother, who was in her blue leather La-Z-Boy, leaning forward with her head in her hands.

"Mom, what happened?"

Her mom's shoulders were shaking and when she looked up at Beth, her entire face was wet with tears.

"Mom?" She knelt beside her, put her hand lightly on her arm, and she flinched. Her mom wore a threadbare nightgown and a robe that needed to be washed. Her normally clean and fluffy white curls were matted and greasy, and her cheeks were splotchy and chapped. Beth's throat grew instantly raw. "Mom, what's wrong?"

Her mother straightened and dabbed her eyes with a damp tissue she withdrew from one of the pockets of the robe.

Chi-Chi jumped on her mother's lap and tried to lick her cheeks.

"Oh, stop that, Chi-Chi," her mother said, attempting a smile. She let out a long sigh of anguish and exhaustion, sat back and cradled the dog. "I don't know what's wrong with me."

Beth sat on the arm of the chair and put her arm over her mother's shoulders. "Did something happen?"

"My friend Sally Griffith died yesterday."

"Oh, Mom, how awful! Why didn't you call me?"

Her mother shook her head. "Oh, I didn't want to bother you."

"You should have bothered me! You can always bother me."

"Beth, it was the most awful thing. We were taking a painting class together, and we were just laughing, and she told me that my peony looked like it was made of pink tissue paper and I agreed with her, and then she just fell out of her chair and just lay there, dead."

Beth drew her mother into a tight hug. "That must have been horrible."

"It was. The shadow of a cloud moved across the window of the studio, and we were all so shocked we just sat there and watched it crawl over Sally's body. The eeriest thing I've ever seen. Then, I jumped out of my chair and tried to give her CPR. Her lips were blue, she wasn't breathing. And Louise called 911."

"Right."

"We kept trying CPR until they got there—it seemed like an eternity, but Louise said it only took them eleven minutes."

"Oh, Mom. Poor Sally. And all of you, having to watch it happen like that." It occurred to Beth, with a slight amount of embarrassment, that while her mother had been giving CPR to Sally Griffith, she had been having another sort of mouth-to-mouth resuscitation with Barry Redmond. "Have they scheduled the funeral?"

"It's the day after tomorrow. If I can manage to go out in public. I can't seem to stop this crying."

"I'll go with you. Besides, Mom, it's a funeral. It's okay to cry."

Her mother dabbed at her welling eyes again. "And, I don't know why, but I keep seeing her falling over, again and again. Like an instant replay. You know, we've been taking art lessons together for ten years. It sounds strange, but we weren't that close. While I was giving her CPR it occurred to me that I had only hugged her a few times over all those years. And there was a second when her eyes just flew open"—her mother blinked her eyes wide in demonstration— "and she said, 'Gerald?' I took her hand and said, 'Sally, don't you do this.' Then she gave a little sigh and closed her eyes." Her mother's lips began to tremble. She covered her face again.

Beth rubbed her shoulders for a few minutes, trying to imagine how shocking the scene had been. Then her sadness transformed to curiosity. "Who was Gerald?"

"That's just it. I don't know. Her husband's name was Henry. And her son's name is Randy."

"That's kind of strange, isn't it? Gerald. It's an old-fashioned name."

"Goodness, do you think Sally had a secret life, Beth?"

"I think everyone has secrets."

Her mother looked at her, blinked, then looked out the window at the flamboyant sunflowers she grew every year on her back deck. "This crying jag started a few hours after it happened, and it only seems to stop when I sleep. I didn't cry this much when your father died. And my heart is racing, too, Beth. It's pounding so hard it feels like my ribs are going to cave in."

"Well, let's call the doctor first thing tomorrow morning. Have you eaten anything?"

"I had a little something."

Beth took that to mean no, so she fixed some instant coffee and made a chicken salad sandwich. She persuaded her mom to come to the table.

"You know," her mother said, taking an eager sip of the scalding coffee. "I think about dying all the time. I know I told you once that I was ready to go. But really, I'm not." She took a bite of the sandwich, and the color began to return to her face. "Sally would have been pleased with that last painting. It was her best."

Beth smiled.

"I have always been terrified of long, drawn-out illnesses, having to hang on in some hospital bed for months on end."

"Mom, why don't you come stay with me for a few weeks?"

"Absolutely not. I won't consider it. What would happen to Chi-Chi?" Carla Swenson tore off a piece of ham and held it above Chi-Chi's head until the dog rose up onto his hind legs and began what they called his "begging dance."

"You can bring him."

"No."

WHEN BETH CALLED her mother the next day, she didn't sound good.

"There's something wrong with me, Beth. I can't stop crying. If I hear children singing somewhere, I cry. If I see a bird fly across the yard, I cry. And forget sappy commercials that have puppies in them or young men coming home from the war."

"I thought you were going to the doctor."

"I did. He says I need some medication to calm me."

"Really."

"Can you believe that? I told him that was ridiculous, and I came home and mowed the lawn. But I could barely see to mow."

"Mom, if he says you need medication, maybe you do."

"Oh, Beth, it's such a slippery slope, I just hate to get started. I've always prided myself on my positive outlook."

"But, Mom, it's completely normal for people to take medication after a trauma."

"We'll see, Beth."

AT THE FUNERAL, Beth's mother looked lovely, her curly white hair washed and set, wearing a black silk pantsuit Beth found in her closet. But she cried the entire time, not bothering to try to muffle her sniffling or throat-clearing.

Beth sat with her in the pew and kept her supplied with tissues and listened to the tributes to Sally. The speeches by Sally's children and grandchildren were moving.

Her mind wandered back to Sally saying Gerald to her mother while lying on the floor of the art studio, and she scanned the people in the sanctuary to see if there might be someone who looked like they could be Gerald and have a secret relationship with Sally.

Then Beth's mind wandered to Barry Redmond, and she relived their sweaty kiss at the turn, sneaking a peek at his eyes, closed and lost in concentration, and remembering the feel of his sandpapery cheek against hers, the warm rush of his breath against her neck, his hands on her skin. It wasn't often, at this age, that you even touched an unfamiliar person, much less kissed someone. She ducked her head, embarrassed at the thought that she was sitting here in the Methodist Church pew thinking about kissing while Sally lay in her coffin at the front of the sanctuary and the minister droned about death. But then she got worried. It had been three days, and Barry hadn't called.

Life was short, as the coffin in front of her testified. Maybe she should call him.

She stood in the parking lot with her mother and her friends. At the cemetery she met Sally's husband, her children, and some of the grandchildren. She and her mother didn't speak of it, but as she was pulling out of the parking lot and her mother was continuing dabbing her eyes with a disintegrating tissue, her mother said, "I didn't meet anyone named Gerald, did you, Beth?"

And Beth touched her arm and said, "I thought about that, too. I asked her sister if she knew a Gerald, and she said yes, they had a younger brother who died of scarlet fever when he was three."

"That was Gerald? Her little brother?"

"Yes." She felt pleased to have been able to help her mother with this.

Her mother nodded, and fresh tears slid in a layer almost like Saran Wrap down her cheeks.

"Did you think any more about staying with me, Mom?"

"No." She shook her head vigorously.

But when Beth got home, as soon as she checked the phone messages (noting with disappointment that there was still no call from Barry), she went into Paul's old room and put sheets on the bed, vacuumed and dusted, and made room in the closet. She hung towels in the bathroom and opened fresh bars of soap. She emptied the drawers in Paul's room and packaged up a collection of his things to mail to him in California: old school notebooks, moldy photos from a hedonistic trip to Italy seeking his great-grandmother's hometown the summer after he graduated from college, his high school and college diplomas. Going through Paul's things must have created a tremor in the universe, because, as she was sifting through the carpet-like sports letters that he'd earned playing soccer and basketball, he called.

"Mom, you busy?"

"Never too busy to talk to you, sweetie." She explained why she was getting his room ready for his grandmother. "I have these sports letters here that I never bothered to sew onto your letter jacket. You were the only guy on the team who never had his letters sewn on."

"Bobby Pappas didn't either."

"Well, his mother had an excuse. She was a surgeon and she already sewed all day." Beth tested the nightlight, taking pleasure in the fact that it still worked—Paul had always been afraid of the dark. What a fearful, serious little boy Paul had been. Then, when he was in fourth grade, after the first time Julie ran away, he'd brought home a joke book from the school library. With intense solemnity, he'd said, "I'm going to be funny, Mom."

"It didn't matter to me, Mom. Honestly, I didn't care."

"That's sweet of you."

"So, you told Dad about that girl? He called me. He thinks you're on another one of your half-baked missions. I thought you were going to wait until you had definite proof."

Beth hesitated. Then, "I thought he needed to know."

"Have you seen a birth certificate? Have you compared DNA?"

"No."

"Well, then, you shouldn't have told him. I mean, Dad thinks in terms of facts. It's just . . . everybody has finite resources they would be willing to spend on a search."

"Finite resources? I'm talking about having a relationship, maybe forming a bond. I really don't think that the amount of love I have to give is finite."

"Mom. You know that's not what I mean. You're the one who opened this Pandora's Box and that's what's at the bottom of it and you know it."

"Paul!"

"I just think you're going to need some solid proof before you go any further with this."

Beth and Paul talked about a few other things, but their voices were still strained when they hung up. Was he right? She didn't want to think about it. Should she ask Sky for a birth certificate? A DNA test? It seemed awkward at the very least, horrible at its worst. God, she didn't even want to think about it.

All Beth wanted was to learn if Sky was indeed her granddaughter. She imagined herself going shopping with her, maybe having her come spend the night sometime. She pushed open the door to Julie's room. She could hang up a girls' golf calendar. She opened the window to let the stale air out, stripped the bed, and put the sheets in the washing machine. She'd seen a cute throw rug somewhere that would brighten up this room. Where was that? She could just picture Sky lying on this bed, reading a book, twirling a strand of her hair, a stuffed animal under her arm. If that could happen for just one night, Beth thought she might be happy.

CHAPTER NINETEEN

Sky

Two horrible things happened on Thursday. First, when Sky arrived on her bike at the course in early afternoon, Mr. McLean told her that Mulligan had died. The dog had grown so feeble he could barely hobble from his food dish to the oak tree by the putting green. When he wrenched himself to his feet, the bones of his hips stood out like the handles of a plow. His eyes ran. His gigantic head seemed too large for his shrunken body, and his yellow fur had turned grizzled and white around his muzzle and chest.

Mr. McLean put his arm around Sky, breathed cigar breath across her face, and squeezed her shoulder. "I'm sorry, kid. You know old Mulligan's been doing an imitation of being dead for a mighty long time. I guess he finally got it down."

Sky tried to keep her game face, but she couldn't. She threw her bag on the ground and broke into violent sobs that came from deep inside, sobs that seemed to wrench her whole body inside out. She wailed, covered her face with her hands and then got the hiccups. Mulligan had been moving pretty slowly when he followed Sky and Silas and Bart on that last round a few weeks ago, but she certainly hadn't considered that he was about to die.

That old dog had been her first friend on this golf course, the first living thing besides her dad that thought she was special. She would have never made it through that first week of golf camp if not for him. She thought about him eating the baloney out of her sandwich, how hard he had tried to avoid the mustard, and felt her face crumple up. It was so painful, like the rocks of Mount Rushmore cracking and crumbling.

"I took him to the vet's office and he's going to be cremated," Mr. McLean said. "If you and Silas and Bart want to go out on the course with me to spread his ashes, we could all say a few words."

Sky nodded.

The second bad thing that happened was that Jordan showed up at the range. She didn't ever come to Solomon Municipal; she played the country club course, and so when the fancy rims on the electric blue Honda Civic with the sunroof, which she'd gotten for her sixteenth birthday, crunched the gravel parking lot, Sky knew something was up. Sky thought she'd started to look different at the end of school. She had more of a sway when she walked. She blow dried her hair now, giving it a glossy look and an evanescent gel smell that it never had before. She wore lip gloss and black shadowy streaks above her eyes; her jeans and T-shirt showed off her lithe, almost breakable figure.

Sky felt big and clunky around Jordan, her face unadorned and her clothes ill-fitting. She had a film of dirt all over her and more dirt caked under her nails from driving the range tractor and scooping the balls into the giant ball washer.

"Hey, Sky," Jordan said. "I just wanted to talk to you about something."

They sat at the picnic table beside the putting green. Jordan crossed her legs—one thin thigh over the other, like a grown-up, not propping her foot on her knee the way she used to—took her car key and started carving lines into the gray cracked surface of the table.

"Don't tell me," Sky begged. "I don't want to know."

Jordan carved a deeper line. "You already know what I'm going to say."

They were both silent for a minute.

"You quit the team."

Jordan carved another line. She started to say something, and then only nodded.

Sky felt bereft, a feeling that had been as much of a surprise as Mulligan's death. She hadn't known until this moment how much she cared for Jordan. "Why?"

"It wasn't fun anymore. And, I started going out with this guy, Troy, and I couldn't ever see him because I always had a fucking golf lesson or practice. And the tournaments took all weekend. I kept wondering if he was two-timing me when I was playing in a tournament."

"God," said Sky. "You're such a good golfer! Who cares if he was two-timing you? If he doesn't support your golf, he's a loser!" She didn't even know who Troy was. She had no idea if he was a loser. She just said that.

"Sky, he's not a loser. And *I* care." Jordan dug the edge of the car key deeply into the picnic table, then cupped the keys in both hands as if to keep from doing more damage. "Come on, have a little respect for my decision. I was sick of my dad yelling at me, too, if you want to know the truth. It got so shitty, never being able to live up to what he wanted. Hell, I was sick of barfing in country club bathrooms, okay?" She smiled at Sky, a funny cross-eyed smile that asked for understanding.

"Well, I guess . . . if you really don't want to play anymore." Sky didn't know what to say. "You definitely don't? Because you're good, Jordan."

"I'd rather spend time with Troy. Besides, Troy makes fun of golf."

"Did he tell you to quit?"

Jordan's nostrils flared, and something glittered on the inside edge of her eye. "So what if he did? Maybe that means he cares about me, okay? I thought you were my friend, and now you're making me feel bad, too."

Sky spread her fingers out on the table, looking at how dirty they were, comparing them to Jordan's clean manicure, and she laid her forehead down in the small diamond-shaped empty place between them. In the background, the balls in the ball washer made that loud tumbling noise that sounded like a small earthquake nearby. She supposed she had known that first time she saw Jordan in the bathroom, barfing, and seen the way her dad had looked so mad, that Jordan would quit. Just standing next to her that day in the bathroom, Sky had been able to feel the weight of her misery. It had scared her so much, she hadn't even been willing to commiserate with her, give her a hug. "Sorry. I'm just in a bad mood because this old dog died. What the hell do I know. You should go have fun with Troy. So, are you and your dad okay?"

Jordan shrugged, then held up the car keys. "He gave me a car."

Sky spread her palms. "Well, there you go."

"Let's still try to do stuff together, okay?" Jordan stood and carefully dusted off the back of her jeans. "Just because I'm not on the team doesn't mean I never want to play golf again. Let's go play, just for fun sometime. That is, if you'll still play with me. I'll get worse and you'll keep getting better and then, I don't know . . ." Jordan shrugged and trailed off.

"Yeah, definitely. We'll play," Sky said. The ball washer ground to a halt, and she stood, too. "I better go."

"Okay."

She thought that she should hug Jordan now. So she leaned toward Jordan and then she saw Jordan angle her body slightly away at the last minute. Maybe she thought Sky was too dirty. Maybe she thought she was gay. So Sky just let her arms drop and kind of gave Jordan a playful pat on the side of the arm. "Okay, well, see you. Let's hang out."

Sky focused on counting out twenty-five balls to put in each of the wire buckets and didn't watch Jordan walk up the hill, with her new swaying walk, or the flash of bluish light in the sun as she left in her new car.

She climbed in the tractor and headed out to pick up the rest of the balls from the range. The trees cast inky silhouettes in front of a red sky. The tractor seat was surrounded by a wire cage to protect the driver from people's shots—everyone at the range always aimed right at her when she drove the thing; it was *so* predictable and juvenile. As she drove the back-and-forth pattern on the field, she thought about Jordan quitting. One of the best aspects of Jordan's game had been her putting. Sky thought about the fact that putting didn't require any of the qualities that were normally required for sports. Except maybe pool. A smaller person, even a weaker person, had just as much ability as a larger one to do well.

Putting was a gift, Mr. McLean had said. You had to see the line. You had to see the curve and undulation of the earth, read the grain of the grass. You could practice twenty-four seven, and you'd get better, but bottom line, you either had it or you didn't. And she thought she did. From the day she'd crawled out of the bathroom to get her golden boy for longest putt, she'd had it. And, as for quitting—if there was anything that Jordan's quitting did, it made Sky even more determined not to.

She was almost finished with the tractor, making the last looping turn when she saw Mrs. Sawyer standing by one of the tees on the range. Sky had purposely not thought about the fact that she was coming and, because of what Silas had said, had even toyed with the thought of leaving before she got here. But she waved and drove over, then parked and joined her. Mrs. Sawyer wore a pair of loose-fitting capris and a sleeveless tank top. She was thin and tan with a wrinkled, hopeful face and a long, slim neck. She looked almost pretty when she smiled. It looked like she might have forgotten to comb her grayish-brown hair. Sky bet anything she was one of those ladies who would go running around like a chicken with her head cut off thinking she'd lost her glasses and then reach up in her hair and say, "Oh! Goodness, they were sitting there on top of my head all along." Sky wanted to put her hands over Mrs. Sawyer's and say, "Chill."

Right away Mrs. Sawyer saw the jar that Mr. McLean had set out to collect donations to help pay for Sky to go to the girls' junior in Charlotte. She leaned down and Sky could see she was trying to count how much was in there. "So, how much have you raised?"

Sky squinted at the jar. "Forty dollars. My dad said he could pay a hundred."

"How much will it cost?"

"Mr. McLean said eight hundred to a thousand."

Mrs. Sawyer nodded in a thoughtful way, and Sky wished she wasn't thinking what she was thinking; which was, if she is really my grandmother, maybe she will help pay. Maybe everything about my life will change. But maybe if she does pay, she will want something from me in return, and what will that be? And if she does give me money, I'll have to lie to my dad about where it came from. And she felt her face get hot, thinking all of those things.

Mrs. Sawyer bought them both lemonades from the snack bar, and they sat inside in the air conditioning at a red Formica table. With very straight posture, Mrs. Sawyer set a stack of photo albums and two worn boxes of pictures on the table, and Sky could tell she had thought up a whole speech.

"First of all, I don't think it's such a good idea if you tell your dad that we met, just yet."

Sky nodded. "I didn't tell him."

"Is it okay if I ask a couple of things, Sky?"

Sky shrugged and bit at her cuticles. "Okay."

"When's your birthday?"

"June 20, 2005."

Mrs. Sawyer nodded and wrote it down on a notepad. "Do you know where you were born?"

"Chicago."

"What hospital? Do you remember?"

Sky didn't.

"What's your full name? Do you have a birth certificate?"

"I don't have a middle name. Just Sky Sawyer. And I don't know where my birth certificate is."

"Can you look around your house? Find out from your dad?"

"I guess."

"How long did you live in Chicago?"

"Until I went to school."

"Where did you live after Chicago?"

"Washington, DC, until four years ago, when we moved here."

"Do you remember anything about your mother? Did you bring the picture we talked about?"

Sky had put it in one of the compartments of her golf bag, inside an envelope, and now got it out. She laid it on the table. It was torn and darkened, slightly out of focus, the crown of her mother's head missing at the tear; and her bushy dark hair, like a screen, obscured the side of her face.

With a shaking hand, Mrs. Sawyer put on some reading glasses and picked up the photo. She stared at it for a long time. "You know, when it's been fifteen years since you've seen a person . . . and it's not such a good picture . . . I never imagined that I would ever look at a picture of my own daughter and not be sure if it was her. But I am not." She sighed deeply and put the picture down. She removed her reading glasses and dug at both eyes with reddened knuckles.

"Well," said Sky, trying to be helpful, "it is torn, and her hair is covering part of her face. And the room is dark."

"Yeah. Well, we could do DNA tests. I mean, I guess we'd eventually have to do that anyway."

Sky straightened. DNA tests? "Like CSI?" People sneaking around, yanking hairs from her head with tweezers, analyzing them. Analyzing her dead skin. Her sweat. The shock must have shown on her face because Mrs. Sawyer immediately waved her hands dismissively.

"Forget I said that." And then Mrs. Sawyer slid the first album over and opened it and started narrating, running her thin, nail-bitten fingers over the pictures as she discussed them. "This is when Julie had her first tumbling class. She wasn't really any good, but she loved the trampoline. She jumped higher than anyone in the class, of course. There she is at her first horse show. She got a blue ribbon, see? We leased a horse from the time she was ten until she turned fifteen—we couldn't afford to buy one. He was the most enormous horse you ever saw, a chestnut, and he followed Julie around like a great big dog. When that movie *The Horse Whisperer* came out it reminded me of her. She just had a gift with horses. Most animals, in fact."

Sky ducked her head. "I love animals, dogs especially. But my mom? I don't know. Dad said she left when I was a baby. I don't remember her."

Sky had to get up a couple of times to check out buckets of balls for customers, but otherwise it seemed as though the time went by in the flash of a second. "This is her grunge phase. She loved Kurt Cobain and Nirvana. She played his music morning, noon, and night. Did your father tell you that?"

Sky nodded, feeling a tingle of recognition. "I think my mother liked Nirvana, too."

"Do you like Nirvana?"

Sky shrugged. "Not really." Mrs. Sawyer seemed happy with that answer, as if liking Nirvana might be a dangerous thing. "I found this online video where Paul Anka, this really old singer, does a cover of "Smells Like Teen Spirit," and I thought that was pretty funny."

"Paul Anka covered a Kurt Cobain song?" Mrs. Sawyer seemed intrigued. "That's just plain hard to imagine."

"I know, right? Yeah. I can give you the website, if you want."

"Okay, I'd like to see it. Do you like Eminem?"

"Well, he's kind of old," Sky said, apologetically. "But I like that song 'One Shot.'"

"Oh, me, too!" Mrs. Sawyer grinned with such pleasure Sky started to like her. She touched Sky lightly on the arm. "I knew we'd have something in common."

Sky smiled. Mrs. Sawyer was trying *way* too hard, but she wanted to give her the benefit of the doubt. Maybe she was just nervous.

"Well, and golf," Mrs. Sawyer added. "I like golf."

"You play golf?"

Mrs. Sawyer nodded. "I'm a hacker. High eighties on a good day. But I love the game. Oh, and I should tell you—recently I tried copying your swing and played one of my best rounds ever."

Sky smiled. She hoped Mrs. Sawyer didn't ask her to play, and she must have read her mind, because she didn't. Instead, she resumed their journey through the albums.

Mrs. Sawyer nodded. "Anyway, the day Julie disappeared, we'd forbidden her to go to a concert in New York City and she went anyway," Mrs. Sawyer went on. "She went with a boy named Russell Ray. We'd forbidden her to see him."

"Why? Was he not a nice guy?" Sky wondered what kinds of guys her mother might have spent time with before her dad.

"Well, let's just say she missed a lot of curfews when she was with him."

"Do you have a picture?"

"I think so." Mrs. Sawyer produced a photo of her mother—or maybe her mother—with a boy with dark shiny hair, deep-set liquid brown eyes, and broad cheekbones. A dignified boy.

"And that night, her father said something I have always regretted. He said, 'If you go out that door, don't come back.'"

"Oh." Sky felt the blood drain from her face.

Mrs. Sawyer looked away, as if she was ashamed. "Yes. And I did not contradict him. I have thought back on that day so many times. I'm not proud of that. Now, I feel like we gave up, and we shouldn't have done that. You cannot ever give up on your child. Because she did exactly that—she just never came back." Mrs. Sawyer's voice got very wobbly and weak.

Sky yanked a napkin out of the aluminum napkin holder in the middle of the table and handed it to her. She had a lump in her throat herself.and was afraid to talk.

Gradually Sky got used to the timbre and cadence of Mrs. Sawyer's rather high voice, and she looked deeply into the pictures and lost herself in the details, in the way Julie's outlandish outfits combined different time periods and styles, in the coy, sexy wildness of her deep-set eyes in one photo, their smoldering, scary anger in another. And there was also something wounded about her, too, Sky thought. She had dark circles under her eyes, always, even as a little girl, as though she just didn't get enough sleep. No calm. Just mischief and excitement.

And Sky felt the beginning stirrings of jealousy and anger. These past few years she'd just been yearning and yearning to get her mother back and now for the very first time she could not stop thinking, *Why did you leave me? How could you? What was wrong with you? What was wrong with me, that you didn't want me?*

And then she heard herself say, "My dad and I have this thing where we talk about what might happen if I win a golf tournament. I got the idea from that girl on *American Idol*, who wrote a song for her mom, and then the mom came back." Sky immediately felt bad for telling Mrs. Sawyer this. She hardly knew her. The only other two people in the world who knew this were her dad and Silas.

Mrs. Sawyer looked at her strangely. "The thing that Julie was interested in most, I think, was freedom. From rules, from judgment, from the entanglements of any level of commitment. You know, honey, please believe me when I say that when she left, I'm sure it had everything to do with Julie and nothing to do with you. If indeed we're talking about the same person."

When Mrs. Sawyer said that, Sky felt such a terrible pain in her chest. Mrs. Sawyer tried to put her hand over Sky's. "You are such a special girl, I know your mother—possibly my Julie—would be so proud."

Sky moved her hand. She looked at the table and played with her straw, trying to keep her movements as slow and casual as possible. She thought she might burst into tears. Or maybe into flames.

Mrs. Sawyer jumped up, as if sensing some of her inner turmoil. "Well, maybe that's enough for today. You might be feeling overwhelmed. Would you like to come to my house sometime, Sky?" Mrs. Sawyer twisted her hands, hesitating. "I'd like to help pay for you to play in that tournament."

There it was. She'd offered. Sky felt relieved but kind of awful, too. "That's so nice of you," she said. "You don't have to offer."

"No, I really want to."

Sky didn't relinquish the stack of pictures. She rifled back through them until she found the picture of Julie and Russell Ray again. Something about his smile seemed familiar. A thick row of goosebumps traveled from Sky's shoulders up the back of her neck and into her scalp, like a column of red ants. Sky was so freaked that she started clearing away the lemonade and knocked over one of the cups, the liquid barely missing some of the photographs.

Mr. McLean came by and cleared his throat again and Mrs. Sawyer packed up her pictures and asked Sky if they could meet again.

"Maybe," Sky said and walked straight over to the tractor, climbed on. "Thanks." She drove out onto the field to pick up balls.

Why should she trust Mrs. Sawyer, anyway? Mr. McLean had gone upstairs to close out the register at the end of the day and Sky was alone when she drove the tractor back. As she dumped the last load of dirty balls into the ball cleaner, her brain went over and over everything Mrs. Sawyer had said. She was getting ready to go upstairs to talk to Mr. McLean about it when a thin gray-haired man came up, a leather golf bag with a nice set of Titleists over his shoulder, offering her a five-dollar bill.

"We're closing in fifteen minutes," she said.

"Can I hit just one bucket?" He was old but had the most arresting violet eyes.

"I really shouldn't let you. I've picked up the last load already."

"Come on. I've had a long week."

Sky raised her shoulders up to her earlobes and let them drop again. These old guys. Sometimes she felt sorry for them, really, she did. They wanted *so bad* to be good. And she couldn't believe the amount of money some of them spent on equipment, lessons, and golf camp. She was lucky that she had some talent. Some of these people, their swings were beyond hope. But they didn't give up. One time Mr. McLean showed her this article about the "World's Worst Most Avid Golfer." The guy was so bad that he *putted* down the cart path on number seventeen at Sawgrass because he couldn't hit it over the water. He took a 70 on that one hole. One hole! His score for the round was something like 915. When they interviewed him, he said, "It only takes one good shot to bring me back." There was something just unbelievably sad about that. But admirable, too.

Sky sighed and set a bucket on the wooden counter. "Well, Mr. McLean isn't going to like it, but okay."

The old man gave her the five-dollar bill, then added another five on top of it. "I really appreciate it. Thanks."

Sky started to tell him that tip was too much, but then figured she did need it for the tournament and stuck it in her pocket.

He took the bucket and his clubs out to the first tee position. He started out doing a couple of old man stretching exercises that made Sky want to laugh because she knew they didn't do any good. He got out his nine iron and hit a few and Sky winced; his swing desperately needed help. He even hit a shank.

He turned around and saw her watching. "What do you think I'm doing wrong?"

"Me?"

"Yeah. You a golfer?"

"Yeah."

"Can you tell what I'm doing?"

"I don't know," she hedged. "I'm not a teacher, I just play. Giving advice isn't always such a great idea."

"Well, I'm desperate. What am I doing wrong?"

"You really want to know what I think?"

"Yeah." He leaned on his club and gave her one of the most genuine smiles she'd ever seen. And the violet eyes. He seemed to be a very nice but tired man.

"I think you're standing too far away and swinging too fast. Slow it down. Give yourself time to connect."

"I'll try. Thanks." He took a few minutes with his stance this time, swung again and seemed to connect quite a bit better. Sky was kind of proud that she'd figured out his problem. But he hit it so much better that Sky got suspicious. Had he been hitting it badly on purpose at first? He hit the rest of the balls, and then came over to the counter, holding up the last one. "Hey, let me see you hit one."

"Why?"

"Show me what you were talking about with that swing tip, giving yourself time to connect."

Well, why not? Sky reached for her favorite stick—her six iron—and took the ball from him. She went out to the tee, tossed it on the ground, and knocked it ten yards past the hundred- and fifty-yard flag.

"Beauty," said the man. "Very nice. A swing for the golf gods."

"Shh!" she said, starting to laugh. "Don't say anything. If they hear you, it's all over."

"Oh, that's right."

"Never forget about the golf gods."

"I won't. Not ever again. You take care, young lady, all right?" He thanked her, and as she put away the last of the pencils and scorecards and closed the wooden shutters over the counter, she heard the crunch of his steps on the gravel in the parking lot, the slam of the trunk as he put his clubs in, and, after a slightly longer span of time than usual, the engine turning over.

She went upstairs to say good-bye to Mr. McLean. When she got up there, he looked at her with a broad grin, chomping on his cigar. "Guess what?" he said, holding up the collection jar. "We made eight hundred dollars for you to play the tournament."

CHAPTER TWENTY

Beth

The night of Beth's visit with Sky, the phone rang. She'd opened a bottle of wine and was in her pajamas, scrolling through information about making genetic matches, and didn't pick up. The visit with Sky had been both wonderful and stressful and had left her with more hope and questions than ever before.

The phone started ringing again. Again, she ignored it.

She kept going over the time she'd spent with Sky in her mind, as she continued to peruse the DNA websites. For only a couple of hundred dollars, she could find out all she needed to know right through the mail. It seemed obvious to Beth now that the only thing to do was get a DNA test. They couldn't speculate any longer. For a personal test with ninety-nine percent accuracy, the guardian's permission wasn't necessary, so she could handle it by only speaking with Sky, not her father. There was a problem, though. For a grandparents' DNA test, without a mother being present, it was impossible to prove a relationship without both DNA strands. So she'd have to get Mark and Sky to agree or get samples from them without their permission.

Do I really need to know this? Her head was pounding. *Maybe I should just leave this alone.*

She drank another sip of wine, knowing that would only make the headache worse. She didn't know the answers to any of those questions. What the hell, she'd decide all that later. She clicked to order, and she received an almost instantaneous email saying that she should receive her "Grandparents' DNA Test Kit" in three to five business days.

Mo, her fluffy black cat, meandered over her keyboard, pausing directly in front of Beth's computer screen, twitching his fluffy black tail over the bridge of her nose. He must have stepped on her "esc" key because the screen suddenly went black.

"Mo!" Beth gathered him onto her lap, where he began to purr and sharpen his claws on her stomach. His purr sounded like someone flipping through the pages of a thick book. She reopened her browser.

The phone rang again. Beth finally picked up. Her mother.

"Do you remember that joke Uncle Ronald used to tell," her mother said, "about coming home from school one day and the rest of the family had moved without leaving a forwarding address?"

"Yeah. I do remember that."

"I was just thinking about him."

"How are you feeling, Mom?"

"I'm not a bit better. There was just a Kodak commercial on TV with a son coming home from college and I've used practically an entire box of tissues."

"What about going to see a counselor of some sort?"

"Beth, you know good and well, this is probably some reaction to Sally dying in our art class, that's all."

"Any chance you'll change your mind about coming to stay with me?"

"I like my place," her mom said. "The only reason you want me to come there is to make your life easier."

Beth gasped at her accusation. She suddenly felt close to tears. "Mom, I'm asking you because I thought you'd want someone to take care of you, not to make things easier on myself."

"It would be quite a lot easier on you if I died, wouldn't it?"

"When you act like this, yes, it would!" Oh, she was furious at her. And herself. "Mom, how can you say that? I can't believe you said that." She'd begun to cry herself and, knowing it was very childish, hung up on her. Certainly her mom knew Beth didn't mean it, and she knew her mom hadn't meant what she said, either. But the words had been said, they were out in the universe, and there was no taking them back. And if her mom wouldn't come to her house, what could she do?

Would she be all right in her rancher? Was Beth to close up her house and go live with her? The very thought that her mother was sitting in a house by herself, crying in her nightgown with that little dog, upset her beyond belief.

And, ironically, she was sitting in her house, by herself, crying in her pajamas with her big pathetic cat. Maybe it was genetic.

The phone rang again, thank God, and she picked up without looking at her caller ID before the end of the first ring. "I'm so sorry," she said. "I promise I didn't mean it. You know I didn't."

"Gosh, I hoped you *did* mean it." It was Barry.

"Oh!" She could feel her entire face begin to flame. But, what was he talking about? The kiss on the golf course?

"The dinner?" he said.

"Oh, the dinner!"

"I won our bet. We tied the front nine, but I beat you by one stroke on the back, remember?"

"Oh, yes, how could I forget." Beth remembered very little about the back nine, but she did remember losing.

"You said you'd make dinner. I'm calling to collect my winnings."

Beth listened to the smooth buoyancy of his voice. She knew what Margo would say. *Go for it, girl.*

"I waited for you to call me," he added.

"I was waiting for *you* to call *me*," she said.

"You outwaited me. I'm calling in my bet."

"I'd love to," she said. "Saturday night, then?"

"That sounds great!" he said. "Tell me what to bring."

"Just yourself," she said with the typical Southern hospitality she so deplored in other women.

"I will," he said. And then she realized that he was giving his response a slightly different spin than your garden-variety hospitality and blushed again.

CHAPTER TWENTY-ONE

Sky

Sky turned on the hot water and poured the dishwashing liquid under the stream, threw away the empty macaroni and cheese box, then stacked the dishes in the sink as it filled up. Her heart was beating hard. She needed to hurry with the dishes. She didn't want her dad to drink his second beer before she tried to talk to him. The water was too hot, and she yanked her hands out. But no, she had to hurry and do this—so she plunged them in again.

She was suspended in a slow-motion bubble of disbelief, like swimming in a gel that dimmed light and sound, and the hot water felt good, actually, shocking her back to this room, this minute, this life.

When the dishes were dripping on the drainer, a few rainbow bubbles still slipping down the back of the thin white Corian plates, she wiped her red hands with the dishtowel and went in the TV room. He was in his maroon swivel chair with the duct tape covering the rips, still wearing the stained orange Steven's Roofing Moving Up in the World T-shirt he'd worn to work.

She thought maybe she should wait for an ad, but then, she just couldn't.

"Dad?"

He looked over at her and blinked. His eyes were bleary. Maybe it was already too late. Maybe she should wait for morning.

But he hit mute on the remote. The people on TV moved their mouths, slammed doors when they left offices, jumped into cars and sped away, but made no sound.

"What?"

She popped her knuckles, aware now that it was something she always did when she was nervous. "I've asked you a lot of times about yours and Mom's wedding, and you haven't ever really answered my questions. I told myself it was because it was too hard on you, thinking about how she died in that fire. But now that I know it was all a lie, that she isn't dead, that she just left us, I want to know why. I thought you wanted her to come back. But now I don't know what to believe. Everything you've told me is a lie."

Her dad blinked again and slid a little lower in the chair. There was a look on his face that reminded her of being in class when some kid made a smartass remark and the teacher nailed him right back.

"Did you talk to that lady?" His face looked like a weasel's.

"What if I did? I have a right to know about my mother!"

He pointed his big white finger at her, narrowing his eyes. "Who's been here with you, day after day, week after week, year after year? Not her! Me, I'm the one here!" He stood and threw the remote on the floor. The cover popped off and the battery skidded out.

Sky bit her lip, blinked back the tears, far, far back, until her eyeballs felt like the Sahara; at the same time, she shifted her weight to the balls of her feet in case she needed to lunge out of his way. "I deserve to know."

Her father was breathing heavily. She took one step away. She should have called Silas first. She should have set up a signal, blinking the kitchen lights or something. Why hadn't she done that?

Very slowly, her dad leaned over and picked up the remote. He walked a little farther to pick up the battery and, still breathing very hard, worked at putting it in with positive and negative in the right place.

By the time he got it right and put the cover on, he seemed calmer.

He sat back down in the swivel chair. With a shaking hand, he turned the TV sound back on and a siren started up. He didn't look at her. He looked at the TV.

Sky, her teeth chattering with adrenaline or fear, her stomach roiling, retreated to her bedroom. She grabbed her backpack and started stuffing it with things. She didn't even know what she put in. She put in some shirts, she took them out, put in something else, then took that out. She was so blinded she had no idea what she was doing.

The sound of the TV stopped again, and Sky turned around. Her dad was standing in the doorway of her room. He looked smaller now. "Sky, what are you doing?"

"I'm packing. If you won't answer my questions, I'm leaving." She held her hands behind her back so he wouldn't see them shaking.

"You can't leave. Where would you go?"

"Plenty of places!" She was screaming now and could feel the burn as tears slid down her cheeks.

"You're not leaving!"

"Then answer my questions!"

Her dad took a step inside her room. He stepped over a few of her clothes on the floor and slowly let himself down onto her unmade bed. They were both silent for what seemed like forever. Then he raised his eyebrows, opened his mouth, and plunged in like someone would dive into a wave. "I met your mom in this Chinese restaurant I used to go to outside Chicago after a day of roofing. She was a waitress there, and we'd get to talking. She told me her name was Libby Titus. Since then I found out Libby Titus was some songwriter in the seventies, but back then, what the hell did I know? One night after I'd fallen off a roof and messed up my back pretty bad, I went to the restaurant although I could hardly walk. She came to my place and brought me some food, then one thing led to another. Then one day she got fired for throwing a plate at a customer. A few weeks later she got kicked out of her apartment and moved in with me."

Sky sat down on the opposite side of the bed, facing away from him.

"She took care of herself. She was good at fixing things, taking TVs, cell phones, and car alarms apart and putting them back together. She could break into a car in about five seconds. And she was a pool shark. An amazing pool shark."

"Really?" Her mother used to break into cars? Sky felt a wave of shame. But pool. Seeing the line. Like putting. Sky liked that. She traced a pattern on her jeans.

"When you all moved into my apartment, you were only a few months old. She ended up staying until the day after your second birthday."

"Wait, what?"

The ceiling fan spun around and around but Sky had so much adrenaline racing through her body that she felt feverish. "What do you mean we moved into your apartment. I was already born when you met her?" Sky could not look at him. "You're not my dad?"

"I know, I should have told you, Sky, and I'm sorry." It was as though his words were coming from very far away. "I was working on it. I fell in love with her. With both of you, really. She was such an amazing woman. But on her bad days, watch out. She was always losing jobs, getting fired for mouthing off at people, throwing things.

She started working as a cocktail waitress at a place that closed really late. I started wondering if she was going somewhere else with someone else. Once, I was so jealous, I fell off a roof on purpose just so she would take care of me again. That first year I was the one who bought all your Christmas presents; I kept them in a big plastic Toys R Us bag in the cab of my truck. I spent so much more than I should have on you and Libby; it took me almost a whole year to pay it all off. And it was completely worth it. That was some Christmas all of us had together."

"What did you get me?" Sky knew her voice sounded small.

"That stuffed Elmo doll." Her dad pointed at the limp, threadbare Elmo lying on her bed. Elmo had slept on her pillow every day of her life since then. "One of those little See-n-Say things. I thought you were so smart, I wanted you to have every learning gadget there was. I remember spending over a hundred dollars. That was pretty stupid, huh."

Sky reached for Elmo and held him in her lap, using one of his matted, clubbed red hands to dab at her eyes. "Why was that stupid?"

"Well, because you oughtn't to spend money you don't have, that's why." He ran his palm over his head and took a deep breath. "Then Libby heard that your dad, a guy named Russell, might be around. She asked me if I'd watch you for the weekend while she went to try and get some child support from him. I didn't want her to, I told her the money didn't matter, but once she made her mind up, I couldn't ever stop her from doing nothing. So she went. And, well, that was that. She left your birth certificate in a plastic bag in the middle of the bed. That's how I found out her real name. I tried to track her down a few times on my own, but I didn't have much money, and I never went to the cops because I was afraid they'd take you away from me."

Sky finally looked over and tears were sliding down her dad's cheeks, sinking into his mustache. "So you didn't go look for her."

"I did, Sky. I asked around. I put ads in places. I didn't have much money. Somehow I think she went to Europe with him, and then they didn't ever come back. When a person who's an adult leaves and it seems like they just left on their own, the police don't really give a shit. And, like I said, I was afraid of losing you."

"I know," she said. Her throat went scratchy and taut.

"First, I went through all the steps for adoption, and I became your guardian. Then, later, I just . . . I can't explain what I did. Except out of love. My whole life, love has made me do stupid things."

Sky sat very still, softly rubbed her cheek with Elmo's matted hand. "You should have told me you weren't my dad."

He nodded. "I was going to. Then I put it off. Because of this, because of what's happening to us right now. You don't trust me now. I can see it." His eyes were glassy as he reached across the bed and gripped her shoulder. "Sky, maybe I'm not your real dad, but I love you like a real dad."

"I need time to think." He let go of her shoulder. It occurred to her that she was sitting here in her bedroom with a complete stranger, a person she didn't even know. She could feel her game face sliding into place. Otherwise her entire being would collapse into a million pieces.

"Don't do anything crazy, Sky. Let things sink in. If that lady is your grandmother and you want to get to know her, who am I to stand in your way? But you and me, we've been through a lot together. You know from all that I've done for you that there's love there. I feel like I've done okay by you. I've been a good father to you. I would do anything for you. You know that's the truth."

Sky wasn't going to cry. "Do you think my mother is ever coming back?"

He sighed. "She's been gone a long time, Sky." He turned to face her more directly. "On her up days, she didn't need me, she didn't want to hear nothing I had to say. On her down days, she needed me bad. She'd lie in bed and cry. I had to do everything. When she left you with me . . . I think it was because she trusted me to take good care of you. I never wanted to let her down. And I am your official guardian, Sky. I adopted you."

She sat there in silence, still facing away from him, until he left her room.

Sky knew he was telling the truth. In her heart she knew he cared just as much about her as he had yesterday. But what else had he lied about? She took out her cell phone and called Silas.

"What's up?"

"I need you to come get me," she said. She stuffed a few more things into her backpack. The last thing she added was the golden boy statue from the putting contest at Solomon Municipal. She'd won a few more trophies since then, and some of them were even girls swinging the club. But the golden boy was the only one she wanted to take with her.

CHAPTER TWENTY-TWO

Beth

B eth waited in a booth in Denny's with a cup of coffee. He'd said he'd be wearing a Florida Gators T-shirt. The PI she'd hired fifteen years ago had been a retired cop and looked like it. What kind of private investigator wore a Florida Gators T-shirt? Through the window, she watched cars pull in and out, and the Saturday morning stream of people enter and leave.

A battered white Mazda sedan with a coaster-sized Florida Gators logo swinging from the rearview mirror pulled in no more than five yards from Beth's window vantage point. This had to be him. With the painstaking care of someone with bad joints, a man with gray shoulder-length hair the texture of a Brillo pad and a face that was a ravaged twin for Bob Dylan unfolded himself from the driver's seat. A shapeless gray Florida Gators T-shirt hung over a pair of khaki shorts and amazingly spry-looking legs for a man of at least sixty. Before closing the car door, he took a small blue and yellow aerosol container from the front seat and sprayed it on the knobs of both elbows and knees, then rubbed it in. WD-40?

Then, as he was putting his wallet in his back pocket, he accidentally dropped a fistful of plastic IDs on the ground, like in a child's game of 52 Pickup.

When he bent to retrieve them, Beth glanced behind her at the door to the women's room. Did she have time to dash in there and hide? If this was Allen Cowan, maybe she needed to go back to the drawing board.

She turned back. As he was raking together the IDs, a little girl with gleaming corn rows squatted and collected the rest of the colorful plastic rectangles and put them in his hand. Smiling, he gave the top of her head the gentlest of pats.

Beth decided to stay.

She waved when he came through the door and he headed over with a rolling gait, still shuffling through the loose IDs. He slid into the booth and let the IDs clatter onto the linoleum surface of the table.

"Allen Cowan." He spoke with vestiges of a New York accent. His hand, when he gripped hers, was small, but feverishly hot, as if his wiry frame both required and produced a good deal more wattage than the average human body. He began organizing and stuffing his IDs back into his aging wallet. "Okay, I've got your basic visitor pass to the hospital, your basic photographer's license, a real estate license, a press pass, see?"

"That press pass is dated 2003." Beth scrutinized the photo on the press pass, of a dark-haired righteously idealistic Carl Bernstein look-alike.

"No one looks at the date."

"You're kidding."

"Nope. Award-winning investigative reporter for twenty-five years. And here's a military press pass, an appraiser's license. US Airways employee ID. Got the uniform, too. Also got a FedEx uniform and an FBI hat."

"Okay, so you're like the Frank Abagnale of the Charlotte metro area."

"I get information any way I can. I once called a guy while sitting in the lobby of the tax assessor's office. 'I'm calling from the tax assessor's office,' I said. 'I have these forms to be filled out.' Guy gave me all the info. Did I lie? Technically, no."

The waitress came by, and Cowan ordered a grand slam over easy, two Cokes and a glass of water, with a side of hash browns. Then he leaned across the table, his elbows sliding slightly on the linoleum. The faint oily smell of WD-40 rose up. "Okay, so let me lay my cards on the table."

Beth glanced at the colorful pile of ID cards already fanned on the table, then nodded.

Cowan pushed his flyaway gunmetal hair out of his eyes. "You're going to ask me how long it's going to take to find your daughter. I'm going to tell you I don't know. It could take two days, it could take two years. You're going to ask me how much it's going to cost. I'm going to tell you I don't know. I'll ask you for a retainer now and when that's gone, if I haven't found her, I'll ask you for more. I charge a hundred dollars an hour plus expenses. And this case won't be easy. She disappeared fifteen years ago. Cars have been junked and traded for parts. People have died, moved, changed their names. They've forgotten what they might have seen. People think being a PI is glamorous but a lot of what I do is mundane. Look for paper trails, records, jobs, arrests, hospital admissions, and so on. I got a hacker downtown I work with." He looked at the ceiling. "What else?" He sat back. "You lie to me, I keep your retainer and drop the case." He shrugged, spread his hands, and gave a sly smile.

"Okay," said Beth. Was she really going to hire this guy? Was she really going to try this again, after all these years? She'd gone to the bank yesterday and applied for a home equity line of credit on the house. They'd said they'd have her answer in twenty-four hours. She could get the call any minute.

Cowan's grand slam arrived, and he dug into the hash browns, cutting and eating efficiently, without taking time to turn the fork right side up. She liked the fact that he'd been an investigative reporter. She liked the fact that he had patted that little girl so gently on the head. She thought about all the reasons Mark would object to him. "Do you ever get emotionally involved with your cases?"

"Never," he said, shoveling hash browns into his mouth. "It drains you. It burns you out. Like this one case I've got right now. I just don't think the guy is guilty. I've visited him in jail six or seven times and I'm sure of it. You just can't get emotionally involved in things like that."

Beth smiled. "How do we get started?"

"You give me five thousand dollars. And a bunch of pictures of her. I'll interview you and your husband separately."

"Well, it's just me who wants to do this. We're divorced, and he doesn't want to get dragged into this again."

"I still need to interview him." Cowan sucked down half the tumbler of Coke.

"I'll give you his number. He might not talk to you."

"He'll talk to me," Cowan said.

"I have also found a girl I think is my granddaughter."

"What evidence do you have?"

Beth told him about the newspaper article, the photo, the name. "And we have the same hands." She smiled meekly, knowing that this would seem silly to him.

"You need a birth certificate."

"Okay, I'll ask. I have her cell phone number."

Cowan sopped up the last of the poached egg in his bread. "Did you do DNA tests?"

"I did order some tests online, but to be honest, I haven't even decided if I'll pursue it or not."

"You know the online kits are worth bupkus in court without a witness."

"I know. I'm not trying to get custody of her. I just want a relationship."

Cowan studied Beth. "I told you, if you lie, I keep your retainer and drop the case."

Beth nodded. "Sky lives with her father. I've given him my contact information but so far he hasn't gotten in touch with me."

"Okay," said Cowan, wiping the remnants of egg from his gray-stubbled chin. "Back to your daughter. Do you still have the reports from the guy from fifteen years ago?"

"Yes."

"Okay, I need those. And I need contact info for your ex-husband, the granddaughter, her father, and everything you know about the family of the boy she ran away with."

"Okay."

Beth straightened her knife and spoon and carefully arranged the fork in the center of her napkin. She'd ordered a bagel and hadn't touched it.

A FEW HOURS LATER, Beth raced into the club, straightening her top. She stopped in front of the white painted double doors of the board room. Closed tight. She looked at her watch. Hadn't Margo said three o'clock?

"Beth!" She turned and saw Margo striding down the thick-carpeted hall, fluffing her battleship gray ponytail. Margo's expression, meant to be a smile, was more of a grimace. Beth and Margo hadn't spoken but once since Sky's match, and that had been yesterday, when Margo called to remind Beth she'd promised to do this. Margo would certainly disapprove of the deal she'd just struck with Alan Cowan. She also seemed to disapprove of Beth telling Mark about Sky. But Sky could be his granddaughter, too, for goodness' sake. It was a possibility, anyway, wasn't it?

"Hey there! Ready to go in and do battle?" Beth said. "I read in a women's magazine that when you want to look threatening, you need to wear black or red." She indicated the red top she was wearing. "I did this for you, Margo. I look like shit in red."

"Here." Margo shoved a printout into her hands. "I made copies for all the board members. Whatever I say, back me up. Know what I'm saying?"

"I know what you're saying," Beth said, trying to focus on the first bold line of Margo's printout. "Ladies' Day: A Vital Tradition at Silver Lakes!"

"Anybody in there?"

Both of them put an ear to the door. "One droning voice," Beth said.

"What about cigar smoke?"

Both of them put their noses to the crack between the doors and sniffed. Somehow just being with Margo made Beth feel punchy and all the awkwardness between them drained away. She started laughing.

"Cubanos, ya think?" said Margo

"Hav-a-Tampa?" Beth countered.

"Smells like they're in there, all right."

"Should we be like Butch Cassidy and the Sundance Kid and just blast our way in? Thelma and Louise?"

"Shit, yeah." Margo did a move like she was pulling six-shooters from each hip.

"One," said Beth.

"Two."

"Three!" And, hardly believing that she was doing it, Beth kicked one door while Margo kicked the other, and, like in a saloon, the doors swung into the room in slow motion and Beth and Margo stood, their hands on their hips, facing the Silver Lakes golf committee.

Buddy Watkins, chair.

Cigar smoke billowed out like poison gas, burning Beth's eyes. Five heads turned as one. At the apex of the burn-marked cherry table, Buddy Watkins, his eyelids shiny and mottled like a turtle's, blinked as if in slow motion and adjusted his basketball-sized stomach.

"I believe we're on the agenda." Margo stuck out her lower lip and blew her bangs off her forehead.

"Yeah," said Beth. She wheezed and fanned smoke from her face.

A heavy silence followed. Beth assessed the players. Next to Buddy, Harold Boykin, secretary, a modern Ichabod Crane, scribbling what appeared to be prolific notes. His handicap was close to being a three-digit number, as Beth recalled. Then there was Charles, the perennially Izod-clad pro and golf shop manager. Margo had long ago dismissed him as a yes-man who blow dried his hair. Across the table, Raymond G. Harvisham Jr., a senior citizen who served as self-appointed monitor of the seventeenth green from a wooden swing on his back property line. He confiscated all balls hit onto his property and used a bull horn to accost players who failed to repair their ball marks.

Last but not least, Wild Wes Unger, financial wunderkind, who always played alone and never got out of his cart. In fact, he never even slowed the cart down. Wild Wes's golf game was more like polo, and he blasted, with a swashbuckling arrogance, shouting "Fore!" through anyone unlucky enough to be in his way. Numerous past complaints to the golf committee about his unsportsmanlike conduct had gone unanswered. *Duh,* Beth thought. *He was* on *the golf committee.*

"We're readin' last month's minutes," said Buddy. He loudly coughed up phlegm. "We'll hear your case if time allows. Take a seat."

Beth cut her eyes at Margo. No seats were left at the table. They sat gingerly on a couple of rusted folding chairs against the back wall.

Harold Boykin resumed his rapid, monotone reading of last month's minutes. "Efforts have been made to identify and eradicate poison ivy patches growing near playing areas. Louise Shackleford requested that stairs be installed at the ladies' tee on number four, as several elderly women have broken or sprained ankles attempting to reach the tee box. The committee unanimously voted *Nay* as the railing for the stairs could obstruct the view from the men's tee. Louise Shackleford also asked if it was normal for maintenance crews to follow groups as her granddaughter and her college girlfriends were followed for fourteen holes by a crew of seven workers who continued maintenance while the young ladies played. Wild Wes volunteered to follow up. Ranford, concerned with slow play, offered to investigate the cost of placing a clock on every tee box. Motion passed, five to zero, that visitors, in the interests of time, receive no more than three minutes to address this committee. Motion also passed, five to zero." Here, Harold took a breath, then said, in hyper speed, "*thatladiesdaybeeliminated*. Respectfully submitted, Harold Boykin." Harold looked up, cleared his throat, and pushed his glasses up on his nose.

"Motion to accept the minutes?" Buddy grunted.

"So moved, yo," said Wes.

"Second," said Raymond.

"Favor of accepting the minutes, say aye."

"Aye," they all said.

"Opposed?"

Silence.

"Minutes accepted. Now, old business. The poison ivy."

Beth shot Margo a look as Charles began a laborious account of every product that had been used on every hole. After that Buddy halted the proceedings for a moment while he lit a new cigar.

"I'm like J. P. Morgan," he said, grinning around the cigar. "My doctor restricts me to twenty cigars a day." He puffed until the end glowed. "Okay, go ahead. Any more old bidness, as they say, Mr. Boykin?"

The committee dragged through an hour and a half of issues at the speed of a snail until Beth was ready to punch somebody. Finally, after a ludicrous circular discussion about the costs of buying and installing clocks for every hole, Buddy wondered aloud if in the interests of time, Margo and Beth's appearance should be tabled until next month.

"Buddy Watkins!" Margo jumped to her feet. "If you don't recognize us I will make you regret it, sir!"

Buddy raised his eyebrows. "All right. Margo Fitzgerald and Beth Sawyer have requested to address the golf committee. And, according to the motion passed last month, you now have three minutes to state your case." Buddy set his watch alarm with his sausage-sized fingers. "Go." He glared, then blinked in slow motion.

"Three minutes?" Margo's voice trembled with fury.

"Well, two minutes and fifty-four seconds now," said Buddy, shrugging.

Margo's face was florid as she tossed her printouts like poison darts at the committee members. "Ever since Clarissa Hopewell took ownership of this club, there has been a Ladies' Day," she said. "Women should have one day when they have preferred tee times, since on Saturday and Sunday mornings we are not allowed to play at all. If the committee would like to allow women to play during those prime golf times, or would agree to change the ladies' tees to the forward tees, and restrict tee times based only on handicap, we would accept this as an alternative. My friend Vanessa, for example, has a lower handicap than Mr. Boykin. Why should he receive tee time preferences on Saturday mornings?"

"Right," said Beth, with conviction, ignoring the nasty look Boykin shot her way. So far all she'd said in support of Margo was *yeah* and now *right*, but she knew Margo appreciated her fellow outrage and moral support.

"Furthermore, the golf committee eliminated Ladies' Day without allowing the membership to vote on it, which I have shown here on my printout is a violation of the club's bylaws."

"Issues of this magnitude should be decided by the membership," Beth added. Quite forcefully, she thought.

With a flourish of his fat forefinger, Buddy punched the timer on his watch. "Time!" he said. "Thank you, girls, for your very interesting presentation. We'll get back to you." He grinned around his cigar at the committee. "Hear a motion to be adjourned?"

"I move we adjourn immediately," said Harold Boykin, still glaring sourly at Beth.

"Yo, second," said Wild Wes.

"Meeting adjourned." Buddy tapped the ash from his cigar and, with great fanfare, pushed back his chair.

"OH, GOD, THAT MAN makes my blood boil!" said Beth, as she and Margo stomped across the steaming late afternoon parking lot.

"His penis is probably one centimeter long," said Margo.

"I know, right?" said Beth.

Margo stopped and stared at Beth.

"And to be honest, I would have liked more support from you, Beth."

Heat rose to Beth's face. "What do you mean? I followed your lead, just like I said I would." She could feel anger pulse to the ends of her fingers almost immediately, as if it had been already there, waiting for the slightest provocation to be released.

"Well, it would have been nice not to have to do *all* of the talking."

"Margo, this was your deal. I told you I'd rather have needles stuck in my eyes than do this. But I did it anyway because you asked me to."

"We were going to write the sheet together." Margo stood outside her car and hit the clicker to unlock the doors. "But you didn't have time because you were so wrapped up in connecting with Sky. You know what I think about you running to Mark all the time. I saw you and Mark early in the morning driving down the shoulder of the road. A lot of other people saw you, too. Now, *I* know you wouldn't be sleeping with Mark, but these suburban bean brains will gossip about anything."

"What?" Beth caught her breath, remembering the moment in Mark's car and the slumbering feelings it had reawakened all too well. "Ronda hit my car and he lent me Courtney's car. We were on our way to pick up mine from the body shop."

Margo put her hand on her hip and glared at Beth, breathing heavily. "Of course *I* don't believe it. But I want you to think about what you're doing." Margo opened her car door. "Beth, we've been best friends for a lot of years. You can't lie to me. I know you too well." Margo got in her SUV, slammed the door, and put it in gear. "You have a perfectly lovely single man knocking on your door."

Beth scrambled out of the way so Margo wouldn't run her down.

CHAPTER TWENTY-THREE

Sky

"You can stay here a while, honey," Silas's mom said, pouring two glasses of milk, then sliding the gallon jug into the giant stainless-steel refrigerator. "Of course you can. But you have to follow our house rules, and I will have to call your father and make sure he gives permission and knows everything. Parents worry."

"He's not even my father." Sky took the milk Silas's mom handed her and sipped. Cold. Silky. It seemed better than the milk at home.

"Well, he's your stepfather, then. He raised you, and apparently he's your legal guardian, so he's your father in my book. And that's my rule. We don't have secrets around this household, and we're not going to start now." Silas's mother was taller than Sky, and heavyset with short, bleached hair, huge bosoms, a scary tan that couldn't be real, and steely humor in her hazel eyes. Silas looked a lot like her, only he was skinny. And of course he lacked the tan.

"Please. Give me a couple nights."

"Nope." Silas's mom shook her head, crossed her arms across her expansive stomach. She was ridiculous looking, really; she wore a matching shortie nightgown and robe in a pink hibiscus pattern and giant puffy pink flip-flop slippers. "You're gonna have to call him and tell him you're okay. Either you do it, while I stand right here and listen, or I do it. I know I seem like a big old grouch, but that's just the way it's going to be, honey."

Sky looked away, and then her eyes bounced over to Silas, who looked at her, wide-eyed. She popped each of her knuckles, then played with a ribbon wrapped around a basket on the marble kitchen countertop. "Okay, you call him. But please don't make me go home."

She walked outside to the deck and looked out at the dark water while Mrs. Wade punched in the number. She couldn't see the lake except for an occasional flash of light skipping over the surface, but she could feel it out there, she could hear the faint slapping of the waves against the rocks at the edge of Silas's yard, and hear the mysterious, heavy hum of it. She heard Mrs. Wade's cheery, reassuring voice talking to her dad on the phone, and goose bumps rose up her arms.

Silas came out on the porch and stood beside her. His hair looked ghostly in the dark, its tips gleaming from the lights inside the house.

"My parents made me and Bart wear life vests outside all the time when we were kids," he said. "It was like, put on your T-shirt, put on your life vest. We hated it, but those were the rules."

"Is your mother going to make me wear a life jacket if I go in the backyard?"

Silas laughed. "If you don't have your junior lifesaving card. She doesn't make exceptions."

"That would be okay with me," Sky said.

A FEW DAYS LATER, Sky and Silas sat in shorts and T-shirts on the butter-soft, brown leather couch in his basement game room, shoulder to shoulder, thigh to thigh, their bare feet propped on a quadrant of square leather ottomans. Outside, it was dark, and a few steps beyond the sliding glass doors the underwater pool lights cast a half-dozen eerie greenish-white cones under the liquid surface.

The TV down here was huge, with a big flat screen, and behind the leather couch stood a dark wood pool table and a marble-countered bar, its surface shot through with veins of what looked to Sky like real gold. Behind the bar was a climate-controlled wine cellar, with rows of dark heavy bottles lying on their sides.

A reality show was on, and all the people were ratting out each other, complaining about the way one guy was being a slob and a jerk.

"Nobody would really act like that," Sky said. "The only reason they put him on there is so they can have fights on the show. I'd kick him out in a heartbeat."

Silas scooped his bare foot under her ankle, so her leg was propped on top of his. "You are so right. The guy is a tool. A loser. A complete scumbag." His feet were wider than hers, much paler, but not that much longer. "You got big feet, Spiderwoman."

"Yep." Sky loved it at his house. She loved the guest room where she slept, with the yellow walls, a little blue antique desk, and the blue and yellow flowers on the bedspread—Silas's mom must love flowers, because they were everywhere. She loved getting up in the morning and going out on the back porch to see what the lake looked like. Every day it had a slightly different color, a different mood. Slate-gray and slightly sparkly and choppy some days. Brownish-green and smooth as a bottle on others. On some days the water shone turquoise, some days a deep opaque indigo, others it gleamed an earthy translucent army green.

She loved sitting at the counter while Silas's mother took orders for breakfast and fielded all the guys' insults, tossing them right back like ping-pong balls. There was always a vase of flowers on the edge of the counter, something clipped from the yard, huge floppy pink flowers or a bunch of yellow roses with wicked prickers that could jump out and rip your fingers if you tried touching them—which Sky had found out the hard way.

She loved climbing the stairs to the second floor, looking at all the family photos stair-stepped there. The parents' wedding photos, pictures of Silas and Bart when they were little kids, posing beside the Easter Bunny in cute little white shorts with bow ties, with their pudgy knees. Her favorite picture, though, wasn't even of Silas or Bart, it was of their mom.

She'd been the captain of the basketball team when she was in high school, and while now she was built like the Statue of Liberty with huge boobs, back then she'd been tall and willowy with a long blond ponytail. She'd posed in her uniform with the ball on her hip and her chin in the air. The expression on her face said, "Bring it on, baby." Sky just loved that picture and stopped to look at it every time she climbed the stairs.

She loved going over to the golf course with Silas and Bart—they both had jobs on the grounds crew this summer—and a couple of times, the three of them played in the late afternoons after work. She loved the way Silas's dad would stand out by the eighteenth green and wait for them to come in, sometimes joking proudly with the people they'd been paired with. "I sure hope this crew of mine didn't lighten your wallet too much." He made them all talk about current events at the dinner table, quizzing them on their opinions. Each of the boys had to be ready to discuss one article from the newspaper at dinner, and even though Mrs. Wade said Sky didn't have to do it, she started reading the newspaper just so she could be ready when Mr. Wade asked, sipping his customary tall amber glass of sweet tea,

"Okay, who read something interesting in the news today?" And if he didn't ask her, she felt disappointed.

"I read one," she'd said that night, ready to talk about a front-page article on the war in Ukraine. "Ask me."

She even loved the way Silas's mother was always coming down here to the basement while they watched TV at night, with an excuse like bringing them Cokes, getting a bottle of wine, checking the laundry, or examining the thermostat.

"You all doing all right? Is it cool enough down here?"

Sometimes she sent Bart down.

"Alert, Fartster, Spiderwoman, I'm coming down," Bart shouted now, slapping the wall as he loudly descended the stairs. He appeared, flip-flops first, then shapely blond-fuzzed brown calves, baggy khaki shorts, faded T-shirt, and finally his head, his buzzed strawberry-blond hair lightened on the ends from the summer sun. Bart had grown, and even though he was two years younger than Silas, he was heavier-set and more muscular, and was also able to get a tan, which remained beyond Silas's abilities. "Your dad called, Spiderwoman," he said now. "And Mom was on the phone with him for fifteen minutes, telling him everything you've been doing."

Sky let her mouth fall open. "She did?" Her face turned hot. Sometimes she thought of him alone in the apartment, and her heart squeezed.

"No such thing as privacy, in Mom's opinion, if you're under eighteen," said Silas. "She reads our email and logs our online footprints. She makes us let her follow us on Find My Friends. She'll make you, too."

"We're freaking prisoners." Bart threw himself on the couch beside Silas and joined in the general insult-fest against the guy on the reality show who was being rude to the other housemates. Sky's cell phone rang. If it was her dad, she wasn't going to answer, though she'd still like it if he called. But it wasn't him; the caller ID announced "E. Sawyer." Her heart sped up. She untangled her foot from Silas's, jumped off the couch, and sat outside beside the pool, dangling her feet in the lukewarm water. It made them look swollen and whitish green, like a dead body in a horror movie.

"Sky!" said Mrs. Sawyer. "It's so nice to be talking to you. How are you doing?"

"Good." Mrs. Sawyer probably had no clue where Sky was, though it was possible that her dad had called her, thinking she'd gone there.

"How are you getting along?" Mrs. Sawyer said.

"Fine."

"Your stepfather just called me," Mrs. Sawyer said. "He's worried about you. He told me you'd left his house and you're staying with a friend. He said he told you that he's not your real father and that you're upset."

"Yeah." So he had called her. He must have been desperate. She lifted one foot out of the water, watching the way it appeared to shrink and turn to firm, living flesh when it moved from the liquid environment to the air.

"I hope you won't do anything rash, Sky," said Mrs. Sawyer. "Don't run away, like my daughter. There are so many people who love you."

Sky was silent. How could Mrs. Sawyer love her? She'd spent one afternoon with her. "I'm not your daughter."

"True." After a nervous beat, Mrs. Sawyer chirped, "What's it like where you're staying?"

"I like it here. A lot."

"That's great."

Sky was silent, spreading the nail-bitten fingers of her free hand for self-examination. Long, knobby fingers, maybe from cracking her knuckles too much. Sores around the cuticles from tearing bits of skin away with the edge of her front tooth.

"Maybe you should call your stepfather. He raised you all these years, you should put his mind at ease."

"Mrs. Wade called him. He knows where I am."

"I know. But I bet it would mean a lot to him to hear your voice."

"You're not the boss of me." Sky had never said that in her life. She didn't know why it popped out. But where did Mrs. Sawyer get off telling her what to do? How could she be having an argument with a person she'd hardly met? She realized that Mrs. Wade had been telling her what to do for the past few days; she'd in fact been much worse than her dad or Mrs. Sawyer, but for some reason Sky didn't resent her.

"You're right. I apologize. I'm glad you like it at your friend's house."

"Yep."

"You know, I hired a private investigator to look for my daughter again. I told him about you, and he wants to talk with you, and with your stepfather, about what you two remember. If you are indeed my granddaughter, which we really need to establish."

"I don't remember anything."

"He used to be an investigative reporter, he's very smart. Who knows, maybe we'll find her this time."

So this was the pair of aces Mrs. Sawyer had been saving. "You hired a private investigator to find my mother?" This was something she didn't think her dad had ever done.

"I did. He said fifteen years is a long time, but there is always a chance the first investigator missed something. And he wants some pictures of you, also asked about a birth certificate. Do you by chance know where yours is?"

"No."

"Well, if you could find it, it would be really helpful. He said a DNA test would be a good idea, too, just to be sure."

Sky listened as a frog down by the waterline sang out in the dark. What did a DNA test involve? Was it a blood test? Things were happy and uncomplicated here. Silas and his family had absolutely no expectations of her. It was like floating on your back in a pool on a sunny day, letting the time slide by, the sun shining reddish and warm through your closed eyelids.

Her dad had always had expectations of her, as though she were some lucky talisman that would bring back her mother. And maybe he didn't really love her, maybe she was just like a bright fishing lure to dangle on the water's surface, to bring her mother back. And maybe she was just the same thing to Mrs. Sawyer, a lure that would bring back her daughter.

She couldn't stay here indefinitely. She had to either go back to live with her dad or come up with a birth certificate and take the DNA test. What if she took the DNA test, and it turned out she really was Mrs. Sawyer's granddaughter? But if she took it and she wasn't Mrs. Sawyer's granddaughter, then what? Mrs. Sawyer wouldn't give a flip about her, and she'd have nowhere to go. Maybe a foster home. Maybe she shouldn't agree to any DNA test.

Everything was a big scramble in her brain right now. She had a headache.

She thought about what her dad might be doing right now, knowing he'd be sitting in his same chair, watching TV, and taking his pain pills. She pictured him eating alone at their small linoleum table with the cracks on the edges. She pictured the dishes piled in the sink, the dirty laundry wadded in the basket beside their temperamental washer-dryer unit, Hungry Man TV dinners stacked in the freezer, the occasional roach racing along the corner of the kitchen floor. She thought about the hallway with the mashed-down carpet outside her room where she'd spent so many hours practicing her putting and her dad had told her stories about golf.

"I don't know," she said. "What do I need to do?"

"We need your birth certificate," said Mrs. Sawyer. "And Mr. Cowan needs some pictures of you. I could come by the golf course sometime this week, if it's okay, and take some. And I'd like to do a DNA test."

"A DNA test sounds creepy." Sky turned and looked inside at the brothers—her brothers, sort of—sprawled on the couch in the dim golden light, their eyes bright with reflections from the TV screen. Their faces looked kind of blank, then Bart thumped Silas's ear and Silas, with cat-like reflexes, got him in a headlock and wrestled him to the floor. Sky, watching, felt a glow of warmth spread through her. But then the boys' lazy tousling changed; Silas suddenly lunged at Bart like a dog going for the jugular and Bart writhed and punched and slapped back with doubled fury, and then suddenly Bart shoved Silas off him, yelling, and they separated, wedging themselves into opposite ends of the couch. Sky couldn't see Bart's face, but she could see Silas's, sweat and a little blood glistening on his lower lip and a muscle pulsing in his jaw.

"I have to go," Sky said. "I'll try to bring some pictures and the birth certificate on Thursday."

The next day, while her dad was at work, Sky had Silas go with her to the apartment, and she grabbed the cigar box filled with old pictures from her dad's closet. When they got back to Silas's house, she closed herself in the guest room and looked through them. Pictures of herself as a toddler with her mom and dad, with the Elmo doll, clean and puffy and new, pictures of her in a snowsuit in Chicago, pictures of her and her dad on the back porch here, her mom gone then. She put aside every picture that included her mother; there weren't many. She thought it was the person from the photos Mrs. Sawyer had shown her, but she wasn't one hundred percent sure. And then she found another photo that she put aside. It was of her mother and two older people—her parents, Sky guessed.

Sky was eighty percent sure the woman was a younger version of Mrs. Sawyer.

CHAPTER TWENTY-FOUR

Beth

Beth pulled into the gravel lot at Solomon Municipal Golf Course and cut the engine. When Sky had agreed to meet her, Beth had rescheduled a conference with a student—something she had only done once, one afternoon years ago when Paul was in a fender bender—and jumped in the car. And here she was.

She'd closed her eyes and given Allen Cowan the five thousand dollars. He'd told her his first step would be to do a little computer sleuthing. She crossed the parking lot, fishing in her purse for her cell phone and tapping the camera icon. She also gripped a bag with a sleeveless Nike golf shirt in a vivid shade of purple she thought would look nice with the tone of Sky's skin. Beth had seen it and thought of her, though it was fair to say that she thought of Sky a lot now.

There were heavy clouds today and a lot of shimmering, threatening light but no real rain yet. She ignored Margo's voice in the back of her mind. "Listen, girl, you're way over the line, here." She and Margo hadn't talked since their fight.

She knew what Vanessa would say, too. "Beth, honey, I want you to have a relationship. But you and I both know from experience how delicate these things can be. They can't be forced; they have to happen on their own." By the time she pulled open the battered door of the Solomon Municipal Pro Shop, she'd tuned them both out. She approached the old man behind the counter who was chewing the wet end of a cigar that had gone out but still stank. "Hi, I'm looking for Sky. I didn't see her down at the driving range."

The old man looked at her with narrowed rheumy blue eyes shadowed by craggy overhanging white eyebrows. "She's out on the course right now. Spreading ashes."

"Ashes?"

"Burying an old dog. Don't know when she'll be back." The old man returned to his work, moving his gnarled fingers through a pile of translucent credit card receipts.

Beth went outside into the accumulating gloom and descended the steps to the empty driving range area. She paced behind the putting green, wandered to the driving range booth, and then headed back to the parking lot. She sat in her car for a few minutes, turning on the engine for brief periods to keep it cool, trying to ignore her growing fears that Sky had changed her mind and wouldn't show up.

Julie had run away as far as the beach the first time when she was fourteen, and she'd ended up calling home after she ran out of money. Without waiting for Mark, Beth had gone and found her under the pier, sleeping in a wet sandy sleeping bag with Russell Ray. They'd sat up, and Julie had been wearing a bathing suit cover-up and her bathing suit bottoms had been wadded in the foot of the sleeping bag. Beth hadn't offered Russell a ride home, but then, she hadn't killed him either, so everything came out in the wash, as Mark used to say. She felt a little bad, knowing he probably had no choice but to hitchhike. And Julie, wet and sandy, charged with silent fury beside her in the van. She lit a cigarette without asking Beth and rolled down the window.

From then on, her family's life hung on the breadth of a hair. Every minute of every day, Beth was worried that a word or a gesture would send Julie away again. As if they lived on a landmine, Beth tried hard not to let things tip one way or another, tried hard to keep the peace, but Julie behaved like a feral cat trapped into a corner—she hissed, growled, and lashed out. Julie's belligerence drove Mark to the breaking point. He wanted to send her to a military-style boarding school where a colleague had sent his pyromaniac son. Beth feared that a school like that would be the end of their relationship to Julie, perhaps even the end of her family. She and Mark did nothing but argue. First only over that school, but soon they argued over everything else—Julie's curfew, dress code, smoking, grades. Whether she should be grounded or met with understanding. Whether they should—or could—trust her. His hair turned gray in a matter of months. And then they began to place blame, pointed fingers at each other, said things that could not be taken back, and what she had feared would happen, happened indeed. Julie walked out. For good.

And then, Mark did, too.

Her heart was pounding now. She got out of her car and looked out over the golf course—to her right, the flat straightaway of the opening par four, to her far left, the downward sloping dogleg right of the tenth hole. She felt a cold shock of relief when she saw three figures loping down the middle of the fairway with the sun setting behind them. Sky was in the middle; Beth had already internalized the boyish aggressiveness of her stride.

And though none of the three touched, they seemed to walk as if riding the same wave, their rhythm implying an invisible but potent bond. It was the same feeling Beth had gotten when Sky walked away with her caddy at the golf tournament, and she felt a stab of jealousy. She realized that one of the figures was in fact the boy who had stepped in to caddy for Sky that day. She headed over to meet them at the putting green.

Would she ever have a bond that strong with her granddaughter? As they approached, the boys saw Beth and briefly closed ranks, and then the two of them gave a noncommittal nod in her direction and sat at the picnic table beside the putting green. Sky handed a carved wooden box to the pale one with the earring, the one who had been her caddy. Beth wished Sky would introduce them, even if just to be polite in that Southern way of past generations.

"Hi, Sky." Beth took a breath and stepped forward. Sky's face was streaked, and her dark eyes were red-rimmed, hinting at hurt deeper than the death of a dog. Beth, wanting to take Sky in her arms and run her palm over her hair, took another step, but then stopped herself, realizing that Sky might not want to be touched.

"Mulligan died." Sky ran the edge of her knuckle under her nose and wiped it on her shorts. Her eyes glistened and she blinked. "We took his ashes out and threw them in the pond by number eight." She ran the pads of her third fingers under each eye. "That's where he used to try to catch fish." Her shoulders slumped, the curve of her long neck like a Madonna's.

"I'm so sorry." Oh, no, Beth was going to cry now, too, and she'd never even seen this dog. She thought, strangely, of Barry Redmond saying to her, "I've got me a dawg in this race," before they played golf. "Did he ever catch the fish?"

"No." Sky half-laughed, half-cried. "He'd wade in the water and try to snap at them when they swam by. He never even came close. But he still tried, every time we played that hole." She sniffled, looked over at the two boys, who were cleaning clubs at a picnic table within earshot. "Remember that, Silas? Bart? Remember how he used to try to bite the water?"

"Yeah," Silas said. Bart nodded, glancing at Beth with a stoic expression. Both boys were struggling to keep from crying and turned their heads away.

"I thought it was so sad that he kept on trying to do that. Why would he keep doing the same thing over and over even though he never caught anything?"

Beth hesitated. Was it a rhetorical question? Should she stop what she was doing this instant? Then she tried to silence the doubts. "My cat chases flies. He's never caught a single one," Beth said, then added, as Sky moved toward the boys, "Hi, I'm Beth Sawyer."

"I'm Silas, this is Bart."

They said hello, then Beth said, "That must have been sad, spreading Mulligan's ashes."

"They weren't really ashes. More like little gray BBs," Silas said.

Bart cleared his throat and looked at the ground.

Feeling a little self-conscious, Beth handed Sky the bag with the new golf shirt. She purposely hadn't wrapped it so it wouldn't seem like a big deal. It was just a little something, as her mother used to say. Sky seemed surprised and pleased. Beth took several close-ups of Sky sitting at the picnic table. Most girls Sky's age had posed for thousands of pictures and taken hundreds of selfies, but Sky fidgeted, anxious for it to be over. Thunder rumbled in the distance, and a looming dark cloud rolled in.

"Okay," Beth said. "One with your sidekicks."

Sky grinned and put an arm around each boy, both of whom sprouted instant red spots on their cheeks. Beth snapped more, then Sky pulled Bart's cap down over his face. By that time the thunder was close, filling the sky, and a big drop plopped on Beth's viewfinder.

"I guess that's it," Beth said as she closed the lens. She felt closer to Sky and to both boys. "Anybody need a ride? It's going to pour."

"No, thanks," Silas said. "We rode together."

"Thanks for the shirt, Mrs. Sawyer," Sky said

"Oh, were you able to get a copy of your birth certificate?" Beth asked Sky.

Sky's almond eyes widened, then she looked away. "Oh, I forgot." Then she retrieved an envelope she'd left on the bench just under the porch of the pro shop and handed it to Beth. "I did find some pictures, though. I made copies for you."

"Oh, thank you." Beth took the envelope, but before she could look at them, the rain let loose, pounding on the roof of the prof shop like steel drums, then sluicing down the gutters in torrents, splashing their calves with gravel grit.

"Whoa!" said Silas. "Deluge!"

Beth had only time for a quick wave good-bye before she raced to her car. She passed Sky's clubs, leaning under the eaves against the clubhouse where she'd left them after hitting the balls for the photos. Sky's black golf glove hung over the curved edge of the bag, limp, but several of the fingers still shaped as though Sky's hand were still bringing it alive. The palm of the glove was dark and wet—not with rainwater but with Sky's sweat. The sight stopped Beth, and she remembered what Paul had said. And also Cowan.

"You're the one who opened this Pandora's Box, and a DNA test is what's at the bottom and you know it."

She hesitated. Even if Sky tried to get her birth certificate, maybe her dad wouldn't give it to her. She'd said a DNA test was creepy. It was. And yet.

Without thinking any further, she grabbed the glove and shoved it in her pocket. Hopefully, she wouldn't need it.

A HALF HOUR LATER, Beth pulled into one of the employee parking spaces in the back of Mark's practice. She knew Mark would be almost finished for the day. He was a man of habit. His last office call was always at five fifteen, he finished at five thirty, organized the day's files and receipts, closed out the computer, and generally headed home right at six o'clock. He had two technicians, and usually by this late in the afternoon at least one, if not both of them, had gone home.

The back door wasn't locked. Beth let herself in, carrying the envelope that Sky had given her, tiptoeing down the narrow hall that Ronda had decorated with a green and gold marsh bird theme. When she and Mark had been married, she hadn't bothered to wallpaper his office. It was in ways like this Ronda took much better care of Mark than Beth had. In fact, in most ways, Ronda was a much better wife. But Beth didn't think Ronda loved Mark any more than she had. It was just, after Julie, Beth had lost her ability to show it.

Her shirt was damp under the arms and in the small of her back, partially because of the rain but also because of nerves. If Mark was in a good mood, he might agree to this. Then again, he could have had a bad day. She knew him well enough to tell just by the way he held his mouth.

She passed the exam room in the back and was passing the one up front when the door opened and Mark charged out, looking at his watch and scribbling on a file with focused intent. His face was stippled with a graying five-o'clock shadow and pale with fatigue.

"Oh!" They almost collided.

"Beth?"

She glanced at the receptionist's desk up front to see if Mark's technician was still there. "I need to talk to you."

A cloak of guarded wariness immediately transformed the focused concentration on his face. "I'm with a patient, and I have to check her out because Ellen went home early."

"I can wait," Beth said.

Mark raised his eyebrows but didn't answer, just nodded and proceeded to the reception desk to check out his patient. Beth sat in the waiting room and opened the envelope Sky had given her and took out four photos. The photos were a revelation. Julie, without a doubt, and Steven Novak and a young Sky. Julie and Steven Novak at a music festival. Julie and Sky playing in the snow. And, on the final photo, Julie with Beth and Mark standing in the driveway on her fifteenth birthday.

She had to close her eyes for a moment as with a trembling hand she wiped tears from her cheeks. Without a doubt, Paul had taken this one. After all these years, the fact that Julie had taken this single photo of her parents with her when she ran away nearly caused Beth's heart to crack into pieces.

Meanwhile, Mark printed the paperwork for his patient, a fair, middle-aged woman who seemed shaken by the rapid advance of her presbyopia.

"I mean, at first I couldn't see far away. Now I can't see up close, either. All I can see is what's in the middle."

"It's the natural progression of things," Mark said. "It happens to almost everyone, if it's any consolation." Beth was sure he'd said this ten thousand times, and she admired the sincere way he made it sound, each and every time.

The woman glanced at Beth and smiled hesitantly. "Do you have it, too?"

"Presbyopia is the least of *her* problems," Mark said drily, his eyes suddenly sparking with a touch of humor his patient missed. Beth didn't.

"Oh, my, isn't it a nuisance?" said the woman.

"It certainly is." Beth smiled. She honestly could barely speak. She couldn't wait to show the photos to Mark. As soon as the woman left, Beth crossed to the counter, and laid out the four photos for him.

"Beth, please, not with the old photos again."

"No, Mark. I got these from *Sky*." She held up the photo of the two of them with Julie. "*Sky* had this photo."

Mark took the photo and looked at it for a long moment, wordless. His eyes glistened. "I remember that day," he said, his voice suddenly hoarse.

Beth then pulled the baggie with the swabs from her pocket. "I swear to God, this will only take two seconds, please don't say no," she said, leaning over the counter and holding up the baggie.

"Are you going to hit me with a paternity case?" He looked up and, surprisingly, smiled.

"No, a grand-paternity case."

"I see. And what if I don't cooperate?" As he said this, the edges of his mouth hinted at turning up, and he didn't seem uncooperative at all.

Mark took the baggie from Beth, withdrew one of the swabs, and put it in his mouth, rubbing it hard against his inside cheek tissue six or seven times. He put the swab back in the baggie and handed it to her. "There you go."

It was over in seconds. She took the baggie, confused. She'd expected to have to fight him, perhaps even to be forced to pull a strand of his hair out by the roots. She'd even briefly fantasized seducing him, like Delilah, for a lock of his hair. "Why are you being so agreeable?"

"It's less work than fighting," he said. "At my age, I have to conserve my energy."

Beth laughed.

"Don't laugh. Last week Ronda signed us both up to do a biking tour of Spain and Portugal. I've been having recurring nightmares about joining the running of the bulls in Pamplona, only on a bike." He went to the front glass doors, locked them, and put the keys in the pocket of his white coat. "How did I get myself into this?"

Beth laughed again. She liked the way the gray hair on the back of Mark's neck lay over the white collar of his jacket. For twenty years, she and Mark could touch each other, could make love any time they wanted to. And, at the end, they hardly ever did. Their marriage had been something precious they'd worked so hard for, and then they'd let what had happened with Julie destroy it, like carefully constructing a home and then having a hurricane or tornado twist it to the ground in a matter of minutes.

Beth looked at the swab in the baggie and took a marker from her purse and printed "Mark Sawyer, grandfather." She felt let down. "I expected to have to fight with you. I chickened out with Sky," she said, stalling. "I ended up stealing her golf glove."

Mark stopped and stared at her. "You stole her golf glove?"

"Well, Paul said I needed to get solid proof, and he has a point."

"Yes, but not behind her back!" Mark raised both hands in the air in a gesture of exasperation. "Beth! As usual, you do whatever it takes."

"And why is that a crime?"

"Actually, I believe theft is a crime indeed."

"Why is it that you're always so willing to give up?" Beth felt herself flush. The path the conversation was taking was familiar, painful terrain.

Mark must have sensed it, too. He clamped his mouth shut, then stood and slid the wheeled office chair under the desk. "She's a good kid, Beth. I'm sure she's scared. I mean, this is a lot for her to take in. But stealing her golf glove—that's stepping over the line."

"Now you're making me feel bad."

"Good. How do you expect her to trust you when you do things like that? It's like when we drug-tested Julie—I think about that now and feel like such a heel."

Beth hung her head. But then, something he'd said set off her antenna. "How do you know she's a good kid?" Warmth inched up her chest like advancing flame on paper.

Mark pretended to scratch his head so he could shield his eyes from her shocked gaze. "I went to that driving range at Solomon

Municipal. Asked her for advice on my swing. I didn't tell her who I was."

Beth gasped. "You told me you didn't want to be dragged into this."

He shrugged apologetically. "I was curious."

"I can't believe it."

"It's uncanny how much she looks like Julie. I have to admit, it wasn't easy to finish hitting balls and just go home."

"You didn't say anything to her?"

Mark shook his head. "I wanted to think."

"But you wouldn't go with me."

"It's not a good idea for the two of us to do things together, Beth." He went back to the narrow hallway, turned off the light, and just stood there in the sudden darkness. The front room was still lit, casting Beth, who stood in the doorway, in indirect light. "I'll pay for half of the DNA test," he said, with his back to her. "But only if you get Sky's permission."

"I hired a private investigator. You yelled at me that day when we were picking up my car, but I did it anyway."

"I'll pay for half." He hadn't moved from the hallway. He just stood with his hand on the light switch, his head slightly bowed. Beth felt her heart fill, looking at his humble silhouette. She took a few steps closer and embraced him, sliding her hands under his white coat and around his waist. She nestled the side of her own wet face against his chest, where the pen in his breast pocket poked her cheek. She could hear the labored thumping of his heart.

CHAPTER TWENTY-FIVE

Sky

A foggy shape, like a country, had formed inside the back window of Silas's Jeep and Sky traced her initials there, SS. Sky Sawyer. Was that even her real name? Who knew. How much of what her dad had told her had been lies? Her thoughts wandered to the hallway in her dad's apartment where she practiced putting, then to the poster of Annika on her wall, wearing her 59 cap, like memories from another life. She ran a knuckle across each cheek, swiping away tears fast enough that she was pretty sure the boys hadn't seen.

Silas pulled the Jeep into the circular driveway in front of the rambling, sharp-angled, gray and white Nantucket-style house. "Mom's not home," he said, cutting the engine.

This hadn't happened since Sky had been staying there. She liked the way Mrs. Wade lurked. Always checking on things and telling everyone what to do. It made Sky feel safe in a way she'd never felt before. Sky had been thinking about asking Mrs. Wade's advice about all the confusing developments in her life. As she got out of the car, Sky gently punched Bart's arm, just kidding around, feeling embarrassed but also powerful when she saw goose bumps stipple his skin in response.

Then she went upstairs into the yellow and blue guest room she'd come to love and shut the door without talking any more to either of the boys. She reached under the bed and got out *Tuck Everlasting*, sliding out the burned and faded picture of her mom, the note she kept hidden there, and the collection of photos Mrs. Sawyer had given her as well as the ones she'd taken from the apartment. Then she crawled under the covers and spread the pictures over the comforter. She thought about her dad, by himself, limping around the perimeter of houses with his bad back, trying to talk to his crew in his terrible Spanish. She'd never been able to teach him; it was like he had a mental block with languages. She smiled against her will as his sadness crept across her skin like a mist.

A soft knock sounded on her door.

"Come in."

Shyly, Bart pushed the door open. "I was just wondering if you were okay. Since you were crying and everything."

"I'm okay." Sky pulled the comforter over the pictures, but he had already seen them.

Red streaks suffused his solid cheeks. "Sorry."

"It's okay." She raked the pictures into a stack, put them back inside the book, and patted the end of the bed. "You can sit down."

Bart came over and sat down somewhat stiffly, leaning over with his elbows on his knees. He grabbed a decorative yellow pillow, twirled it in the air a few times, and then held it like a football in his lap.

"Are you going to go live with Mrs. Sawyer?" he said.

"What?"

"I just wondered. I figured you couldn't stay here forever." He shrugged his lean, muscled shoulders. "It doesn't matter."

"It doesn't?"

He ran his palm over his shorn hair. "No, it does. My mom likes having another girl here." It was funny that he called his mom a girl. It was odd to Sky that Bart had grown so big and muscled but that his thoughts were still so like a little boy's. Bart was smart. He made straight As. But when the two of them were alone, he could barely put three words together.

"You really think she likes having me here?" Warmth expanded in Sky's chest, to think that might be the case.

"Sure." Bart glanced quickly at her and then away.

"I love your mom," she said. "I wish she were my mom." She glanced at the door. He'd left it open, which everyone had been careful to do since the day she moved in.

The next day a couple of guys came over and they all played football in the front yard. She was having fun—she was pretty fast and a better passer than she thought she'd be—but then she threw a pass to Bart, and out of nowhere, Silas threw Bart to the ground and started punching him, even though they were playing touch, not tackle. The front door slammed as Mr. Wade came running out the front door to break it up.

Later that afternoon, a sharp knock on Sky's door announced Mrs. Wade. Drying her hands with a dish towel, she came straight to the point. "Sky, honey, I hate it that I am having to say this, but I think it's time you either went home or found somewhere else to stay."

Sky thought her heart would break, but she slid her game face into place. She'd expected this might happen, just not so soon. "I can't go home, not yet." She showed Mrs. Wade the photo of her mother with her parents. "I'm pretty sure she's my grandmother. My mom had this picture of her and my grandfather. Do you think I can go stay with Mrs. Sawyer?"

CHAPTER TWENTY-SIX

Beth

Thirty minutes before Barry Redmond was due for dinner, Beth sealed Sky's glove, carefully labeled, and the two swabs—"Mark Sawyer, grandfather," and "Beth Sawyer, grandmother"—into an envelope with the application form and a check, including extra for overnight shipping. But what Mark had said made her hesitate. Was she really willing to stop at nothing? She straightened her shoulders. Yes, she was. Those photos Sky had made for her gave her confidence. She put the envelope in the mailbox. The instructions said she would have her results in three to five business days.

She then reached into the kitchen cabinet and shook one shapely yellow pill from the estrogen dialpak into her palm. She'd fished it from the trash the day after Barry had called and started taking the pills again.

She didn't examine her motives. She tossed the pill back in her throat and washed it down. She also took out one of the tear samples

Mark had given her, turned her face up, and let a drop fall into each eye.

The phone rang. Beth hoped it was Margo. She'd tried calling Margo several times since their fight. She'd left one of those "Are We Okay?" Shoebox cards in her mailbox, but Margo hadn't responded.

It wasn't Margo.

"Mom! I was worried when you didn't call back."

"Well, I was in such terrible shape, I didn't want to call you," her mother said.

"What do you mean?"

The doorbell rang. Beth squinted at her watch. Was Barry thirty minutes early for dinner?

"Well, I started feeling pretty good," her mom was saying, "and so I stopped taking those pills and now the shaking and crying have started up again."

"Mom! You can't go on and off. You have to keep taking them, didn't your doctor tell you that? Hold on a second." Now she raced through the kitchen, tossing tortilla chips onto the plate with the guacamole she'd made, and checking the progress of the crab casserole. Surface beginning to bubble. Good. Then she galloped through the great room, scooped a pile of newspapers, books, and unfolded clothes from the couch, tossed them onto the floor of her office, and shut the door. She opened the front door, the oven mitt on one hand and the phone in the other.

Barry smiled, and his face took on that angular look that Beth liked so much. He wore his usual creased khakis with a subdued short-sleeved Hawaiian print shirt in shades of green and ivory. He must have played golf earlier today; his face was shiny with sun, the end of his nose slightly burned, white comma squint marks framing the edges of his eyes. He cradled a brown-bagged bottle of wine, like an infant, in the crook of his arm. He looked squeaky clean. And he smelled good.

"Sorry," she mouthed at Barry. With the mitt, she pointed at the phone. "My mother."

"I don't like taking pills," her mother complained into her ear. "It makes me feel weak."

"You agreed you'd take them, Mom," thinking about her own on-again off-again relationship with estrogen.

"I'm early," said Barry uncertainly. He had started to come in but stepped back "Should I drive around the block a few times?"

"No." Beth waved him in with the mitt, like a parking lot attendant. "Mom, I have a dinner guest. Can I call you back later? Or, I tell you what, I'll come over tomorrow, okay? And I want to talk seriously about you coming to stay here for a little while."

"Absolutely not, Beth!" With that, Carla Swenson hung up on her. Beth stood holding the phone, staring at Barry.

"She just hung up on me."

"Call her back."

"Maybe I should." She shook the mitt off, started to punch in the numbers, then hesitated. "You know what, I'll do it later." She turned off the phone.

"Sure?" Barry looked uncomfortable.

"I'm sure."

A flash memory of Barry's lips on her neck in the alcove by the water fountain ambushed her and her cheeks heated up. Tonight, would they continue what they'd started? She turned away. "Come on back." She led him to the great room in the back of the house.

She started to ask if he'd played golf today but realized she didn't want to talk about golf in the least and tightened her lips before she let the words slip out. She led him to the counter separating the living area from her small kitchen.

He offered the wine.

"You have a nice place," he said politely, leaning on the counter, looking around.

"Thanks," she said simply, scoring a circle of foil from the top of the wine bottle's neck. "I'm not really interested in decorating, and once I've got somewhere to sit, art on the walls, and light for reading, I'm pretty much good to go." She had a sudden ominous foreboding that the entire evening was going to be a catastrophe. The feeling of doom felt as sharp as the looming shadow of an ax.

Maybe they should just have sex now. Having sex would make them both ravenous and Beth's uninspired meals were best consumed that way. Wait—no, it would be better to eat first. He'd be anticipating sex and wouldn't notice what he put in his mouth.

"Need some help with that corkscrew?" Barry asked.

Beth looked down. She'd ground the cork to pebbles.

"Oh, God, yes, you do this." She slid the bottle toward him and crossed to her glass front cabinet in the dining area to get down two glasses.

THE CASSEROLE HAD BEEN excellent and the salad, while not exotic, had been crisp and fresh. She'd used two divine tomatoes from the farmers' market, and Barry had rummaged in the pantry and found a can of sliced olives and tossed those on top. She liked the way he naturally pitched in and helped without a fuss.

During dinner, conversation came easy, but she had great trouble concentrating.

"My favorite writer?" she asked, trying to answer his question. "Oh, the woman with the quirky characters. The bizarre family dynamics. They alphabetize their pantry. What's her name?"

"I have no idea." Barry smiled and stared at her. Was it fondly?

"Oh, I can't believe I forgot her name. I've read everything she's ever written. You know, they all live in those big old houses in Baltimore."

"Not a clue. Sorry."

"Well, I'll think of it. What about you?"

"I like that guy who wrote about the storm. All his stuff, true adventures. Everyone dies. You know who I'm talking about. His name is on the tip of my tongue. He wrote about that kid in Alaska, too."

"I do know!" Beth held up her finger. "It starts with an *M*."

"An *M*? No, that doesn't feel right. Oh, I'll think of it. I guess we're having senior moments. Pass the . . . what do you call it?"

"Wine?" Beth started laughing.

"Yes." Barry poured himself more wine and then held up his finger as Beth had. "The finger must be the sign that the memory is working. I'm trying it. I'm going to see if it works."

His nose was slightly red, and Beth wanted to kiss the end of it.

BARRY CLOSED THE DISHWASHER. "All done."

"Thanks for helping." Beth picked up the wine bottle, which had a few inches left in the bottom. "Half a glass more?"

"Okay. It's done wonders for my memory so far."

Beth put on the Alison Krauss playlist she'd made after hearing her at Margo's, and they sat on the edges of Beth's worn leather loveseat. Beth curled her feet under her, turning to face Barry. Alison Krauss's voice wove around them, silky and pure.

Her forebodings had been foolish. There was something elemental, stripped-down, about Barry. Beth had considered his cut-to-the-chase style at their first dinner as awkward, but now she thought it was one of his most endearing qualities.

"You're good in the kitchen," Beth said.

"I am," Barry said.

"And modest, too."

"If you've got it, flaunt it," he said. "Actually, I've done all the cooking at my house for the past four years." He took a beat, as they both considered why, then plunged on. "Once I get a place down here, I'll have you over for international night."

"International night?"

"Tacos, hot wings, and pork satay."

"Wow. A taste explosion."

Mark had always been a man of few words. Barry was more forthcoming, more honest and unself-conscious about what he said. Beth liked that.

"Tell me more about your kids," she said.

"Well, Aaron is like me, and Claire is . . . more like her mother. She is thoughtful, sensible, mature, like her mom. Because of Amy's illness, she seemed like an adult by the time she was twelve. Except for one incident of fighting, which I think may have been in defense of her brother, she has been as solid as a rock. I, on the other hand, was a late bloomer." He grinned and put his palm over his forehead. "Late frontal lobe development, I guess. Was really saved in high school by the nuns at the Catholic school in my neighborhood in Silver Spring. They took our car keys and let us play basketball and drink beer in the gym every Friday night. Then I flunked out of college my first year. I had to go live at home and put myself through community college before I transferred to Maryland." He shrugged. "Aaron . . . well . . . the vice-principal's number is on my speed dial. He's a camp counselor up in the mountains this summer, and I think it's going to be a great experience for him. Being responsible. I hope the temper and the wildness are just a stage."

Beth nodded and sipped her wine. "You sound pretty under-standing."

"I don't know." He ducked his head.

"I'm so sorry," Beth said. "It must be tough raising kids alone. And for them to grow up without a mom."

"We've all got to live through something, right? I hope they'll be okay. I can't say for sure that they will, though." He finished his wine and set the tall-stemmed glass on the coffee table a bit too hard. "I had started to think of Amy's treatments as a way of life, like AIDS maintenance. The treatments, then three nightmare days, then she'd slowly get better. I was thinking, 'Okay, we can do this; they say you somehow do what's asked of you, and we will.' We tried to take each day as it came. But it was a long haul, and after a while . . ." He stopped talking for a moment, blinked. He leaned closer to her, confiding. "You know, I feel guilty. There are periods during those last few months that I can't remember. It's always been survival instinct for me, forgetting the worst things. And I owe Amy more than that. I shouldn't forget." His eyes were wide and reddened around the edges. He looked down at his hands.

"Everyone has their own way of dealing with things, Barry. What you've lived through . . . you should not be feeling guilty." She so wanted to comfort him, to take away his pain if she could. She put her hand over his.

He was silent. Beth held her breath. The thread of Alison Krauss's hopeful soaring violin wrapped around Beth.

"Want to dance?" Barry said.

She blinked. "Okay."

Barry led her around the coffee table onto the small rug in her living room. They didn't really dance. They swayed, and it seemed to be exactly what they both wanted. Barry put his arms around her lightly, as if she were porcelain—and he surely already knew she wasn't—and she felt the pressing weight of his loneliness.

When he pulled her closer, she put her cheek against the soft silk of his shirt. The music and the smell of him. The thud of his heart, only thin fabric and a few layers of skin and bone away from her ear. A new song came on and Barry knew some of the words. He sang them as they swayed.

It was impossible to resist doing a little two-step to the sly syncopation of the song and suddenly the rug seemed too small for their feet. Both being out of practice, they stepped on each other's toes and bumped each other's knees and elbows. Barry laughed self-consciously. A few minutes later, Beth ran her finger down the bone of his forearm to the inside of his wrist, and then he led Beth by the hand upstairs.

BETH WOKE HOURS later to find her room in blue-black darkness, rain pummeling the roof and the smell of storm ions filling the air. Barry curled beside her, his arm and one leg across her body as snug as seat belts, snoring softly, his nose buried in her hair. She ran the backs of her knuckles over the soft salt and pepper hairs of his chest.

Her mind reeled back over their slow-motion lovemaking, how she had first held his face in her hands and kissed each of his closed eyelids and then he'd done the same for her. How it was like wading slowly into the ocean, the exquisite pain and pleasure of making it last as long as possible. And then when he finally rolled on top of her, the fine immersing sensation of their skin touching.

Moments later, when they were lying spent with the sweat pleasantly cooling, he started laughing, that high, boyish laugh she'd loved when they played golf. He rolled off her onto his back.

She'd started laughing herself. "What's so funny?"

"Jon Krakauer!" he said.

"That's it!"

BARRY STAYED FOR BREAKFAST, and even made avocado toast, which further endeared him to Beth.

His kiss when he left was soft and lingering.

"See you soon," he said.

"I hope so," she answered.

Afterward, she called Vanessa, both to share her good news and to see how she was doing.

"Have you heard from Michaela?"

"I did!" Vanessa sounded better than the last time she and Beth had talked.

"Did she call you? Oh, I'm so glad!"

"She did, in a manner of speaking. She came to say good-bye before leaving for her new position in DC. She's moving up there early to get settled. She spent the night in her old room, which was such a boon."

"Is she still with you?" Beth could feel the slightest twinge of jealousy and swatted it away.

"No, she woke up the next afternoon and was in the foulest mood ever, cussing a blue streak and blaming me for all her anxiety again. So I said all right and she left."

"Oh, Vanessa."

"I'm upset she left." Vanessa laughed. "And Beth, you're going to think this is sick. I loved every minute. No matter how contentious her stay was, I had her all to myself and she needed me. Now how is that for a desperate mother-daughter relationship?"

Beth and Vanessa both laughed until they were breathless. "I've got to say, Vanessa, you do sound pretty good."

"Honey, all I know is, anytime she wants to come back, the door is open."

After running some errands, Beth went to see her mom. She'd stop asking her to stay with her. She'd respect her wishes; she'd try to reopen lines of communication. Her mother hadn't gone to her art classes or really continued any of her normal activities since Sally Griffith's death.

When she arrived midafternoon, her mother was in her back-yard rigging up some kind of watering system for her sunflowers. She barely acknowledged Beth. She wore baggy denim pedal pushers, a gigantic floppy sun bonnet, and dilapidated topsiders, all of which were stained faint orange from the North Carolina clay.

Beth sat on the steps of the small deck behind her mom's condo, watching as she laid out lines of flat green hose along the base of the plants. Chi-Chi, still inside, barked ferociously through the condo's glass sliding door.

"Didn't it rain here?" she asked.

"No, Beth, it did not."

"Wow. It poured at my house last night."

Her mother stood, pinched a brilliant blossom from the vine, and handed it to her. "Put that over there in that basket by the sliding door."

Beth went to the sliding door and Chi-Chi lunged, baring his teeth, unleashing a snarling barrage of barking. "Nice to see you, too, Chi-Chi." Beth returned to the steps, sat down, and took a deep breath. "We keep hanging up on each other, Mom. I know I did it first. Maybe we should try to stay on the line and say what we have to say."

"Go over there and slowly reel out the hose as I position it," her mother instructed her. Beth sighed and stood by the hose cart, turning the handle as her mom fed the hose down one line of plants, circled around, and fed it down another. Her hands shook, but she moved with intense urgency, occasionally barking orders at Beth, who'd stopped trying to talk to her. She'd have to wait until the project was finished. At last, the hose was arranged around all four towering rows of sunflowers.

"Let's test it," her mom said. She spun the faucet, and water oozed from a dotted line of holes down the middle of the hose and soaked the broken clay, turning it a wild salmon red. Her mother adjusted her floppy hat, surveying her work, then turned off the water and carefully turned the dial on an old broken timer she'd fitted together with several thick rubber bands. Then, without further communication, she went inside, provoking Chi-Chi to perform an ecstatic leaping dance. Beth started to follow her, but, expecting her to come back out, remained seated outside on the steps.

A few minutes later, the glass door behind her squealed open and Chi-Chi, on his leash, shot out like dervish, her mother close behind. She struggled with two bulging suitcases. Clamped under one arm was Chi-Chi's dog bed, nested golden hairs swirling from it like slivers of glass in the afternoon sun.

Beth jumped to her feet. "Mom?"

"Let's bring some sunflowers with us," she said, handing Beth four or five clipped stems wrapped in damp paper towels.

CHAPTER TWENTY-SEVEN

Sky

S ky made Silas play eight ball on her last night, and first they said best two games out of three. When she won, they changed to best of five, and then to rotation. Then, even though she was beating him, and he usually wanted to keep playing until he won, he slid her cue into the rack and pulled her by the hand over to the couch. Confused, she freed her hand, and stood behind the couch.

"I need to pack."

"It's our last night; just watch this show with me." It was another one of those survival shows they liked to make fun of.

And so she sat. He moved closer as people on TV squabbled under palm trees. After a minute, casually, he moved one hand so that their pinky fingers lay next to each other, barely touching. Sky glanced down, her heart beginning to pound. Gradually, he slid his hand over hers, but he stared directly at the TV, rather than at her.

"What are you doing?"

"Holding your hand, Spiderwoman. Is that okay?"

"I'm confused. You and me, we're friends, right? Golf buddies. Living here, I've practically thought of you as a brother."

He whipped his face toward her. "I don't want you to think about me as a brother." With a deep breath, he leaned over and touched his lips gently to hers. "Not like a brother."

His lips were soft. A not unpleasant warmth bloomed in the pit of her stomach.

"Wait a minute." Sky pulled her hand free and stood up, straightening her shirt, pushing her hair out of her face. "I don't know, Silas. I just . . . I just need to pack."

"Fine. Go ahead and pack. But you can't deny that we're more than friends, Spiderwoman." Now he wouldn't look at her at all.

"Silas, don't be like that. Everything is so messed up. I like things between us the way they are, at least for now. At least until I can figure out where I'm going to live and whether I'm going to be able to compete at golf."

He didn't answer. Just stared at the TV.

"Are you still going to caddy for me?"

No answer.

"Silas?"

No answer.

"Oh my God, be that way! I'll find someone else." She could feel tears throbbing in her eyes, about to spill out, and at that very moment Mrs. Wade came down to check on them and Sky grabbed the banister and ran past her upstairs.

BACK IN HER ROOM, Sky folded her jeans, running her fingers over the edges of the new, freshly ironed hems Mrs. Wade had sewn for her.

She admired the neat, tight stitches Mrs. Wade had used to mend a hole in one of the pockets of her golf shorts. Sky didn't even know how to thread a needle. Once she had turned out the light she couldn't sleep. For hours she lay in the twin guest bed, thinking back over the time she'd spent here. It gave her a sore throat. The full moon shone into her room, painting everything bluish, and her lips still tingled slightly from Silas's kiss. Embarrassment and gloom had settled over her like a shroud.

In the morning, as she descended the stairs with her bags—Mrs. Wade yelled at Silas to go help her but he didn't—she saw her own reflected profile leap from the glass of one family photo to another, saw her face linger over Mrs. Wade's senior year basketball photo as she stopped to study it a last time, and then, at the bottom, she saw herself glide off the edge of the wall into the nothingness of the doorway to the formal living room.

In the driveway, squinting in the morning sun, Mr. Wade gave her a small salute good-bye. Silas had sneaked out last night to meet his friends after she went upstairs. His face was pasty and puffy today; he was probably hungover. She didn't feel like hugging him, and apparently he didn't either. He mumbled something and kicked a pinecone across the yard and went inside. Bart wasn't even there.

Mrs. Wade didn't seem to notice anything out of the ordinary— but maybe she did and just didn't say it—and talked like a game show host the entire time they were driving. She said because Sky was a female athlete, she was reminded of her senior year as basketball team captain.

"Listen, Sky," she said. "That was one of the best years of my young life. God bless it, I was hot, I was the captain, and our team won the state championship. Honey, it doesn't get much better than that."

"Right," said Sky.

Mrs. Wade pulled onto the highway. Sky couldn't believe how fast she drove. She drove inches behind other people's bumpers and then whipped out around and by them, like she was using them on the basketball court.

"There have been times in my life when things have not been so great," Mrs. Wade was saying. "And what do I look to? I look to that senior year of high school. I remember those games we won in overtime by one point because we just had too much heart to give up. And losing—when you get whomped the first half, and you walk back out on the court for the second half, girl, that takes guts! You've got to reach down deep!"

"Right."

"And that kind of effort stays with you your whole life, Sky. It does. It helps you get through difficult jobs, it helps you get through marriage, childbirth, family illnesses, I'm serious. You're facing something really tough, and you remember what you accomplished back then, and you say to yourself, 'I can do this.' You know you've got what it takes."

"Yes, ma'am." Sky had never said "ma'am" before she lived at the Wades' house, but Mrs. Wade made the boys say it and she'd gotten in the habit of it.

"When you play in the tournament, think about that. What I mean to say is, when you're good at something, you always have that core of yourself to fall back on. Will you promise me never to forget that?"

Sky looked at Mrs. Wade's full, cheery face and felt a yearning she could not put into words. She looked away, at the rows of gray-trunked oaks flashing by on the side of the highway. After a long silence, she finally said, "I wish I could keep living with you."

Mrs. Wade nodded her head, taking it in stride. "I wish you could, too. But, honey, I have to think of my sons. This is going to be Silas's senior year and sometimes, honest to God, sometimes I think that boy is one stick shy of a bundle, do you know what I mean? He's such a good kid but half the time he's on the edge of total catastrophe. He's so emotional. I have got to hold his feet to the fire."

Sky nodded.

"And Bart, he needs to find himself, he's got to get out of the shadow of his brother. I want you to come over whenever you can, and we'll always love you, honey. And I know Silas still wants to caddy for you in the tournament."

"Uh-huh." Sky was not so sure that after last night he'd still caddy for her, and she wasn't sure if it was a good idea.

Mrs. Wade never even glanced at her GPS system. She was not a person who seemed to have any doubt whatsoever where she was going. She turned into a neighborhood with a crumbling brick wall with kind of scuffed white letters that said Silver Lakes Country Club. A sign beside it said Memberships Available, only somebody had changed the *p* to a *t*.

"Someone ought to fix that," said Mrs. Wade. "In fact, I might stop by the clubhouse and complain on the way out." Mrs. Wade changed the subject almost immediately. "Did I mention to you that Mrs. Sawyer taught two of my friends' daughters during their freshman year in college?"

"No."

"Yes, they both said that, as a teacher, she was very fair and kind. And Mrs. Sawyer's ex-husband is my eye doctor. I'd never let you stay there if I didn't know of her through friends. And your dad confided to me that he remembers that photo of his wife standing with her parents, and he agrees that Mrs. Sawyer likely is your mother's mother."

"He does?"

"He does. Otherwise he'd never let you go for this visit."

The picture she'd showed Mrs. Wade told the story they all wanted to hear. Mrs. Sawyer was her mother's mother. And her mother's father was the man who tried to get golf tips from Sky at the range.

"I didn't even know you told him." Why was everyone talking to each other without even asking her?

"I had to get his permission, Sky. He's your adoptive father. Have you decided what you'll call her? You can't call her Mrs. Sawyer."

"I was just going to see what happened."

"Well, honey, I always like to have a game plan. What about 'Gran'? It's short and sweet, not too sappy."

It rhymed with bran. Sky didn't like it. "Let me think about it."

Now they wound through the neighborhood, passing stone houses and brick houses and stucco houses and Sky was getting the feeling that they were going to get there any minute and her heart started to beat faster.

"So, when will you know for sure? Did you do a test or something?"

Sky looked at Mrs. Wade, then down at her lap. "I'm not sure." She was starting to cry. She'd kept her game face about Bart not being there to say good-bye and Silas being such a jerk this morning for almost the whole ride here.

"Hey! Hey, honey, it's okay." Mrs. Wade pulled into a driveway and leaned over, seat belt and all, and smothered Sky in her big arms. Her breasts were huge and soft as pillows.

When Sky opened her eyes, she looked over Mrs. Wade's shoulder and saw an old lady in a floppy hat riding a lawn mower. Mrs. Sawyer stood on the front porch, one thin hand shielding her eyes from the sun. Mrs. Wade took one of Sky's bags, Sky took the other, and Mrs. Sawyer hurried down the sidewalk to meet them. She hugged her so tightly Sky thought one of her ribs might be broken and tested by taking a couple of deep breaths afterward. At the very least, all the air had been squeezed out of her lungs. Mrs. Sawyer squinted briefly at Sky's face but didn't comment, just teased Sky's hair out of her eyes with her cool fingers, and then turned to Mrs. Wade.

"I'm Beth Sawyer. Thanks so much for dropping off Sky."

"Hello, I'm Denise Wade, such a pleasure to meet you. Your ex-husband is my eye doctor." Mrs. Wade threw the duffel bag over her shoulder and gave Mrs. Sawyer a power handshake. They were shouting because of the lawn mower.

"Oh, yes."

"And you've had the children of two of my friends in your composition class. Not that I checked up on you, of course!" Mrs. Wade chuckled.

"Oh, I'm glad you did." Mrs. Sawyer laughed, but it seemed awkward. "We're so excited we can't stand it. Come in, come on in!" She waved them up the steps. "Mom, come meet Sky!" she shouted at the lady on the mower, who waved and smiled but kept riding in the same line. "Oh, well, you can meet her in a few minutes. She gets tunnel vision about yard work."

They went inside. A dog resembling a piranha on spindly legs raced up to Sky, barking. When she reached to pet him, he lunged, and she barely missed the razor edge of one of his teeth.

Mrs. Sawyer grabbed the dog by the collar and herded him in the bathroom. Sky could feel her game face crumbling. The roar of the lawn mower and the stupid dog were just too much.

She thought about her dad in his taped-up La-Z-Boy, trying to change his position so his back wouldn't hurt, and thought that maybe she should have gone back there.

He needed her. But when she thought about him, she still felt that pressure in her head as if it were going to explode, and she knew she was still too mad.

Mrs. Sawyer's house was smaller than the Wades', but it was cozy, and the colors were pretty—earth tones and greens and yellows. Light-colored furniture. No curtains on the windows, so lots of honey-colored light. Closed glass French doors leading to a dining room that had been made into an office. It was homey and welcoming. Papers and books lay around, and she picked up the swirling aromas of lemon furniture polish and Windex. Mrs. Sawyer had cleaned the house before she came.

SKY THOUGHT SHE MIGHT hyperventilate when Mrs. Wade put her hand on the doorknob to leave but she gave her a hug, thanking her for letting her stay there.

"Oh, honey, it was our pleasure. And we'll see you in a few weeks for the tournament, okay? We'll be your gallery, honey, we'll be with you every hole."

Sky followed her like a puppy on a leash as Mrs. Sawyer walked Mrs. Wade to the car. Mrs. Wade climbed into her van and leaned out the window to grasp Sky's hand. She squeezed hard. "Now, where is Sky going to practice, Beth?"

Beth. Mrs. Sawyer's first name was Beth.

"She can practice here at Silver Lakes. I've already talked to the pro," Mrs. Sawyer said. "She can use the driving range whenever she wants, and she can play the course using my membership."

"Do they have a female golf pro at your club?"

"No."

"Too bad. That would be ideal for her, I think."

"Well, I'll look around," Mrs. Sawyer said, looking at Sky, nodding, patting her back very lightly. "That's a good suggestion."

"I need a new golf glove," Sky said. "I lost mine. It was almost brand new. I hardly ever lose things."

"We'll take care of that tomorrow," said Mrs. Sawyer quickly. "Don't you worry about it, sweetie."

And then Mrs. Wade, the queen of basketball and unsolicited advice, was gone.

"THIS IS JULIE'S ROOM." Mrs. Sawyer spoke loudly because the lawn mower, now in the backyard, still roared. "I kept it the way she had it for a long time, but then I took all the posters down—just left a few pictures—and made it a guest room. But I want you to think of it as your room while you're here."

Mrs. Sawyer stood outside the room so Sky could go in first. She'd already put both of Sky's bags on top of the peach and yellow quilt that covered the bed. The dresser was of light-colored wood, and Sky liked it. A blue vase with some small pink roses adorned the dresser. She liked those, too. On one wall hung a painting of a big chestnut barrel-chested horse with a blaze on his face running on a track. She leaned close and read "Man o' War" on the caption. Two prints of Black Beauty hung side by side on another wall. There was a desk and a laptop computer folded on the desk. She'd never had a desk or a laptop. She liked everything.

"The laptop is from Mr. Sawyer, my ex-husband. Your grand-father, maybe," said Mrs. Sawyer.

"Oh, wow." Sky opened the laptop and touched the pads of her fingers to the keyboard, very lightly. "I can't believe it. Silas and Bart were letting me borrow one of theirs."

"Your grandfather and his fiancée want to take you to dinner later this week."

"Okay." There were woods outside the windows, and in the yard were some trees with frail white flowers. A breeze stirred the flowers and some petals floated to the ground like snow. Sky felt something soft trail across her face, and she wiped it away.

"If you want to put something up on the wall, like a poster of Annika, Juli Inkster, or Lydia Ko, go ahead. Whoever you want."

"That's really nice, thanks. Let me think about it."

"Use the closet, the dresser. All the drawers are empty. There are towels for you in the bathroom. I got shampoo and conditioner, but if it's not the kind you like, we can get a different kind. I know Julie was particular about her shampoo. Uh . . . I'm keeping the door to my bedroom closed because my cat has to stay in there while Chi-Chi's here. And the other bedroom is my son Paul's room. That's where my mother is staying. Take some time to unpack, and then come on downstairs. We'll visit and you can meet my mother and have dinner. How's that?"

"Sounds good." Outside there was a huge cracking sound and the lawn mower abruptly stopped.

"Uh-oh," said Mrs. Sawyer, listening.

"That doesn't sound good."

"I know."

Mrs. Sawyer came and gave her another slow-motion hug, whispering, "Welcome."

SKY WAS NERVOUS about just sitting around talking to Mrs. Sawyer, so she took her time unpacking and arranging her stuff in the bathroom. She took her golden boy statue from her backpack and put it on the dresser, running her finger, as always, over that place on the top of his head where it looked like his brains had leaked out.

She went to the built-in bookshelf and ran her fingers over the thick, bent spines of a bunch of horse books by Walter Farley. She pulled one off the shelf and opened it, as if somehow miraculously her mother might materialize from between the pages. She held the fold of the book to her nose and closed her eyes and breathed in. A dusty, bakery smell. She slid the book back into its spot on the shelf. But maybe she'd try and read it.

She'd never been a good reader. Her freshman English teacher had written on her report card, "Sky reads slowly and gets distracted easily. We would like permission to send her to guidance for some tests." Her dad had never signed the permission slip, and Sky hadn't wanted to go, either, because taking the tests would have meant missing golf practice. And she'd been embarrassed about what the tests would show about what might or might not be going on behind her game face. A stack of brand-new golf magazines—*Women's Golf*, and a few others—lay on top of the dresser. Also a new book with a pristine cover, *Seabiscuit*. Sky flipped through the first chapters. It was nice of Mrs. Sawyer to get these for her.

Sky lay on the bed, looked at the ceiling. Maybe her mom had done this exact same thing. Maybe she'd hated this room. Had she liked the picture of Man o' War and the two of Black Beauty? Sky slid off the bed and examined those two more closely.

In the first, Black Beauty stood under a tree, gleaming ebony, her neck arched, her tail in motion. In the second, she pulled an old wagon, and her coat was dull, her hipbones stuck out like Mulligan's, and her head, confined by a bridle, blinders, and reins, hung nearly to the ground.

Mrs. Sawyer was banging pans and dishes around downstairs, and she must have let the dog out of the bathroom. Sky heard the little galloping of his feet as he ran upstairs. Sky turned away from the picture, bracing herself for an onslaught of loud barking. Just inside the doorway of her room, Chi-Chi sat down, giving her the hairy eyeball.

"Why are you going around barking at people, anyway?"

The dog cocked his head and trotted out of the room.

"Good," Sky said. "Don't come back."

But a few minutes later the dog did come back with a chewed-up cat face squeaky toy and dropped it in the doorway. Sky was putting her shirts in one of the drawers of the dresser and ignored him. But then he carried the toy a few feet farther and dropped it again.

"What?" Sky stared down at the toy. Now the dog dropped it right beside her foot. Sky kicked the toy, connected pretty well, and it flew through the doorway of her room and halfway down the hall.

The dog tore after it, grabbed it and growled, shaking it feverishly, and then came running back to drop it at Sky's feet again.

He sat on his skinny haunches and looked up at her with liquid brown eyes.

"So now you're trying to make friends." Mulligan's big old yellow head rose up in Sky's mind, his rheumy brown eyes, his stinky coat and angular hip bones. She kicked the toy again.

Soon she was sitting at one end of the hall tossing the toy down to the end for Chi-Chi to chase. He was pretty smart.

She decided to make it more of a game, so when Chi-Chi ran down the hall she'd hide, ducking into the bathroom or squeezing behind her bed, or stuffing herself across the hall into a closet. Then she'd listen for the thunder of Chi-Chi racing around the house looking for her.

It sounded like a whole herd of horses—the galloping—and then, when he found her, he'd wiggle all over and touch his cold nose to her leg as if to say, "Found you!" She loved listening to the sounds of him looking for her, how anxious he seemed, how he never gave up until he could touch his wet nose to her leg. He always found her by smell. Standing in the closet, she heard him snuffling and whining outside the closed door, and she took pity on him and let him find her.

"What's going on up there?" came an old-woman voice from downstairs. "It sounds like someone called in the cavalry."

At the sound of the woman's voice, Chi-Chi raced downstairs, and Sky stood on the landing so she could see the old woman.

"I think Sky's playing with your dog, Mom," came Mrs. Sawyer's voice. "That's pretty nice of her considering he scared her to death barking at her when she arrived."

"He did? Goodness gracious."

She took off the floppy hat and her curly hair stood out like a bunch of cotton balls. Her tennis shoes dropped chewed clumps of grass onto the front hall rug. Chi-Chi ran along, trying to jump on her. "Beth, your grass was so long I think it's jammed the blade unit. I have no idea what we're going to do. And did you know you had pine seedlings sprouting in your yard?"

"I'm sorry, Mom," came Mrs. Sawyer's voice from the kitchen. Sky didn't think she sounded all that sorry.

A pan crashed. Sky got the feeling Mrs. Sawyer didn't cook that much.

"Not to mention those killer weeds wound around the shrubbery. And the crabgrass is having a field day. You should be ashamed of yourself, letting things get to this state of affairs. We have higher standards than this, Beth, and you know it."

"I'll come out and weed after dinner," Mrs. Sawyer said.

"I'll help," said Sky.

The old woman looked up at her for the first time. "Well, goodness gracious, hello there, young lady."

A HALF HOUR LATER they were all sitting at the table, eating a chicken dish that Mrs. Sawyer had made. It tasted kind of dry. Mrs. Wade was a much better cook. But there was plenty of bread, and so Sky had three rolls. And she liked the rice.

Mrs. Sawyer was running back and forth, fluttering over everything. The old woman had taken a shower and now wore large flat circular earrings that looked like sunflowers, a pair of khakis, and a yellow cotton shirt.

She sipped a giant glass of red wine.

"My mother used to teach high school history," Mrs. Sawyer was saying. "While she's here, I'm sure she could help you with school, once it starts, if you need it."

"Oh," Sky said. School seemed a long time away.

The old woman sipped her wine and didn't speak for a minute. Then, she said, "Oh, I'm sure you won't need my help."

"I need all the help I can get," Sky said, thinking that she'd never even tried to take an advanced class since there was no one she could ask.

"Are you being sincere?" The old woman glanced over, her eyes narrowed, sunflower earrings swinging.

"Sure." Sky gathered her hair in a ponytail, then let it fall onto her shoulders a couple of times, a nervous habit she had when she thought she might have to ask a favor of someone.

Sky ate some rice. It was plain, no sauce or stuff in it, just the way she liked it. Mrs. Sawyer had finally sat down and was drinking wine, too. Sky could always get more information out of her dad after a beer. "Hey, I like that picture of Man o' War in my room. And were those books my mom's?"

"Yes, Sky, they are," Mrs. Sawyer said. "She loved the story of Black Beauty. When she was ten or twelve, she'd sit up there and read it and cry, cry, cry."

"Julie was what in the South we used to call a wild child," said the old woman.

"Mom," said Mrs. Sawyer with a warning tone in her voice.

"Well, she was," said the old woman.

Sky liked the sound of *wild child*. She liked the rhyming. And it was so far from what she was.

"She was a free spirit," said Mrs. Sawyer. ·

"She lacked boundaries," said the old woman.

"Mom, stop it. Julie is her *mother*."

This talk had taken a wrong turn and could turn into a nasty fight any minute. So, Sky excused herself and went upstairs, closed the door to her room, lay on the bed, and began trying to read *Black Beauty*. But Chi-Chi came in with a squeaky toy. She put the book down and played with him.

CHAPTER TWENTY-EIGHT

Beth

Beth could not believe that the first thing out of Mark's mouth was, "So, Sky, do you remember me?" How could he put the girl on the spot like that? The ego of that man!

They were standing on Beth's front porch. He was taking Sky to an early dinner and to the Fourth of July fireworks at the club. But first, Ronda had wanted Sky to come by the house and see the room they'd prepared for her, in case she ever wanted to come and stay the weekend.

"I do remember you!" Sky's cheeks turned pink. "Your swing really stank at first. But it improved so fast that I suspected you had been faking to get me to give you a golf tip. And I did, and then you gave *me* a tip."

"I *was* faking," Mark said. "Or at least, that's my story and I'm sticking to it." He smiled. Beth hadn't seen him smile with that much animation in years. "Beth, have you seen this girl swing the club?"

"Yes, in fact, I have, Mark."

"What I would have given for one of our kids to have a swing like that. Absolutely a thing of beauty. As I told her, a swing for the golf gods."

Sky seemed to glow. And Beth, watching the two of them, felt that dry spot rise in her throat and had to blink and look away. It had taken Sky about thirty seconds to fall for Mark. The three of them standing together here on her front porch seemed almost too good to be true.

Mark escorted Sky through the front yard, his hand lightly touching the spot between her boyish shoulder blades, and opened the car door for her. Beth remembered, in contrast, the way he'd strong-armed Beth out of the way that morning in the middle of the highway when they were picking up her repaired car. "Tell your mother I sent my regards," he told Beth.

"I will."

Sky tossed back her mane of chestnut hair as she got into the car. She was enjoying Mark's courtly manners.

"Bye, Sky, have fun!" Beth waved as Mark backed out of the driveway. "See you later tonight!" She hoped she didn't sound paranoid. But Paul had driven off with his father one weekend and then made the decision to live with him, so he'd basically never come back. It could happen with Sky, too. He did live in a nicer house. He had a lot more to offer. Private school. Golf lessons.

But, of course, there was also Steven Novak, Sky's stepfather. She needed to prepare herself that Sky might not be with her for long.

Beth stood on the front porch until the car disappeared. Last night at dusk, Sky had carried Mo, Beth's cat, out into the front yard. Beth had watched from the upstairs window as Sky had sat down, cross-legged, as the breeze ruffled the grass, and let him walk away. Mo traversed the yard, nosing at the blades of grass, then he lay down and turned his black face up to the last rays of the sun, closing his eyes. Sky lay on her back and watched him, her hands behind her head. After a few moments Mo had stood and returned to Sky, waving his tail like a flag, preening his whiskers on her arm. Beth had watched breathlessly as he curled in the basket formed by her crossed legs. It seemed everyone was welcoming Sky, and Beth hoped she felt at home.

Everything felt surreal. She had received the DNA results the day before, and opened the envelope with trembling hands. The printout showed results greater than ninety-nine percent that Sky was their granddaughter.

Beth was in a euphoric mood, not just because of that, but also because Barry Redmond had invited her to dinner and to watch the fireworks tonight. She was dying to call Paul. She wanted to fill him in on Sky, but also just wanted to hear his voice. She glanced at her watch. Two o'clock California time. When she'd spoken to Paul the week before, he said he and Andrea were going boating with friends on the Fourth. If they were already out on the water, they probably couldn't get a cell signal, and even if they could, the wind would scream across the phone, and he wouldn't be able to hear a thing she said.

But, when she went inside and tried calling anyway, surprisingly, he answered. "Hey, Ma. We're still at the dock, waiting on some folks. We're going to head out and float around and have dinner and then watch the fireworks from the water. Happy Fourth."

"Oh, that sounds so great," she said.

"Looks like it will be gorgeous, but windy. Wish you could be here with us."

"Me, too." Beth heard the wind and the seagulls in the background. "Sky just went to dinner with your father."

"Really? Now, you don't know for sure yet if she's really Julie's daughter, right?"

"No, I do."

"You did a test?"

"I did. I got the results yesterday. Positive. The results were greater than ninety-nine percent. She's our granddaughter."

"Oh my gosh! That is incredible. How's Dad taking it?"

"He's thrilled to death; I think it might have something to do with her being a scratch golfer. He gave her a laptop."

"No way! He never gave me a laptop."

"Yes, he did."

"Yeah, but it was a cheap piece of junk. Did he give her a Mac or a PC?"

"A Mac."

"See? She is making out better. Damn. Dad likes her more. I'm calling a lawyer."

Beth laughed. "Paul!"

"Just because I sucked at golf? Is that it? If I had known when I was twelve that golf was the only path to my dad's heart, how much easier my life would have been!"

"Very funny. Ronda fixed a room for her."

"Does it have a hot tub? A new set of Callaways? Is Ronda giving her a diamond tiara? Fucking A, Ma, I want a court-ordered DNA test for myself today!"

Beth laughed, then said, "I am a little afraid she'll go there and never come back here."

Paul was silent for several seconds. "Because I did?"

"I don't know. Yes, I guess so."

"Hey, I shouldn't have done that. Keep in mind, I was fourteen with an emotional IQ of five. I was an idiot. Maybe I just wanted jet skis."

Beth laughed again. No one in the world was able to make her laugh like Paul. The very serious child who had one day, not long after his sister ran away the first time, announced he was going to be funny.

"Andrea says send a picture?"

"Yeah, sure. I took some the other day. She's adorable, Paul."

"Does she look like Julie?"

"Yes, very much."

"Is her personality like Julie?"

"No, at least, not that I can see so far."

"Well." Paul was silent for another second or two. "I've been thinking about Julie a lot lately. I hadn't thought about her in such a long time, Ma. You know, when Julie was happy, she was *really* happy. It was contagious. Remember that time we went to dinner for my eleventh birthday, and she started that conga line, and she took it all the way out to the parking lot and down to the corner? And the people in the restaurant, the wait staff, people off the street—everyone—joined in?"

"Yeah." That conga line. First Julie, then Paul, then Mark, then Beth. Beth knew that all she wanted was to have back that sense of belonging, of togetherness, of family.

"That was the best birthday I ever had," Paul said.

A gust of wind swirled through the phone, and Beth could almost smell the salt in the air. She was reminded of going on the whale watch last year and being chilled to the bone all day in spite of the sparkling sun, thinking of the cold, dark water nearly two miles deep beneath the small bobbing boat.

Neither Beth nor Paul said anything more about Julie. The dark times went unmentioned but understood, like the strange blind creatures floating in the black midwaters of Monterey Bay. Paul made more jokes about how scratch-golfing granddaughters really didn't have to earn their keep, and a minute or two later, they hung up. Beth felt buoyed, as always, after talking with him.

She knew Paul wasn't really bitter about the attention Mark and Ronda were giving Sky. And neither was she, although she was a teeny bit jealous.

The night before, after playing golf with the pro, Sky had had a headache from the sun, and Beth went in her room to rub her head before bed. She'd done the same thing for Julie, who'd suffered from headaches, too. Beth had developed a method of putting pressure with her fingertips and moving them in tiny circles on the temples, then moving slowly, keeping the circles small, around her scalp. Every now and then Julie would say, "That feels so good, Mom," and Beth would try to send love flowing through the tips of her fingers, all the love that somehow got tangled and twisted in her actions and words, willing it to leap from her fingertips and soak into her daughter's brain.

And so last night, when Sky said that very same thing, "That feels so good, Mrs. Sawyer," Beth had nearly cried with joy. "It means a lot to me, all that you've done. I like this room so much. And trying to find me a coach."

"Well, I haven't found one yet, Sky, so don't count your chickens." Beth wanted this moment to keep spinning out forever, to turn out differently this time, for all the love from her fingertips to burrow in this time and take root.

"But you don't even really know me. And you've done all this anyway. It just makes me feel good. Thanks."

Beth had kept making tiny circles, feeling the skin of Sky's scalp slide beneath her fingertips, feeling beneath her fingers the curved and vulnerable shape of Sky's skull.

Now Beth went into the kitchen and pulled the DNA envelope from the back of the drawer. When she'd fallen in love with Mark, she hadn't held back at all, she'd given her marriage everything she could give.

But after Julie, and the divorce, she'd held back, afraid to love anyone else completely for fear of being hurt. With a child you didn't have to hold back. She read over the positive result page once more. Ninety-nine percent.

Beth could love Sky regardless of whether Sky loved her or not. The way she'd loved Paul and the way she'd tried to love Julie. She shoved the DNA test results back in the drawer. The next question was whether to tell Sky or not, since she'd never asked her permission.

BARRY WORE A MELON-COLORED golf shirt that night, and Beth loved the way his freshly washed hair curled slightly at his temples. He was gallant and gentlemanly when he met her mother.

"I hear you're still mowing lawns at your age. You are an amazing role model, Mrs. Swenson."

"Flattery will get you everywhere, young man."

"I hoped it would."

When Beth climbed in his Prius, he turned to her and said, "Where should we go? Every restaurant is mobbed tonight."

"That's true." Beth was a bit disappointed he hadn't made reservations and wondered what he was getting at.

As he backed out of the driveway, he added, "Plus, if we want to be together, we can't come back here because of your mom."

"And we can't go back to your sister's place with the whole family there. It's like being back in high school."

"I'm telling you right now, I'm too old for the back seat. There's not enough pain reliever in the world. My knees can't take it."

As Barry drove toward the lake, Beth looked at his profile, feeling reckless.

"What about room service?"

He raised his eyebrows and grinned. "I didn't think you were that kind of girl."

"I'm not. But there is a small dive hotel right on the lake where you can see the fireworks."

THEY ORDERED SOME SORT of sausage half-smokes smothered in cheese and onions, with tiny paper American flags stuck in the buns, and wolfed them down ravenously while sitting at the rickety café table in their room overlooking the water. Beth hadn't eaten anything that unhealthy in a decade.

Beth, feeling ebullient, even drank a beer, which she didn't usually even like, as she filled Barry in on all the developments with Sky.

"That is an incredible turn of events," Barry said. "You must be over the moon." They ended up missing the start of the fireworks, as they were making some of their own. Dozing afterward, floating in a delicious state of semiconsciousness, running her fingers over the soft hair of his forearm, Beth heard a sound other than the fireworks. A guitar riff from Led Zeppelin, "Stairway to Heaven," over and over. She let her eyes wander to the clock. Just ten.

She pushed herself up onto one elbow, touched his shoulder. "Barry, your cell phone."

He rolled away from her, groaning, fumbling for the phone on the night table. He ran his hands over his eyes. "Aaron?" He sat up, and she lay watching the naked but suddenly protective curve of his back. "Okay, so what happened?" He listened, then sighed, running his palm over his head. "Oh Aaron, what were you thinking? You can't just . . . Never mind, do I have to come get you right now? Let me talk to her."

Beth sat up, pulling the sheets around her.

"I understand that was the agreement, Mrs. Treadwell, but I'm two hours away, I can leave first thing in the morning and still be there by eight." He listened, and the muscles in his shoulders slumped wearily. He leaned and picked up his pants. "Okay, fine. Tell Aaron to get his stuff ready. I'll be there at . . . let's see, about midnight." He spat the last few words and threw the phone on the bed.

Beth didn't ask anything, just waited.

He stood and pulled on his khakis. "He was in one of the girls' cabins. They had a bunch of beer, pot, prescription pills—I don't know, it sounds like they were playing strip poker." He buckled his belt. "Parents had to sign an agreement that if kids broke the rules, they weren't allowed to spend another night at the camp." He shrugged his shirt over his shoulders, hurriedly buttoned it. "So, I've got to go get him."

Beth remembered playing strip poker in high school once. Didn't everybody, at one point or another, give strip poker a try? She didn't say it. Instead, she pulled on her capris and top and plugged in the miniature Keurig on the dresser. "I'll make you some coffee for the road."

Barry slid his phone into his pocket. He hadn't looked at Beth once. "That would be good. Thanks."

LYING IN BED IN HER own room after Barry had dropped her off and she'd waved good-bye from the driveway, the memory of waving good-bye to Julie one morning forced itself upon her. That morning, Beth had raced out to the driveway in her robe, small pebbles bruising the bottoms of her bare feet.

"Julie, wait."

Julie had glared at Beth with narrowed eyes, her dark hair uncombed, eyeliner in black kohl around them, her hand on the door handle.

"You forgot your lunch."

"I don't want it. I'll eat in the cafeteria." Beth wanted to remind her that she had to serve detention during lunch that day for one infringement or another, but Julie's voice was so harsh she didn't want to seem confrontational.

"I'm sorry I lost my temper," Beth said instead. "I'm sorry." The night before Julie had told Beth to go fuck herself. Beth's vision had narrowed to a tunnel, whorled to a circular pinpoint around Julie's face, a red aura closing in.

Her rage became like a separate thing, like a red beast clawing to get out of her.

"Don't speak to me that way!" she'd screamed. Then she'd slapped her.

That next morning, Julie's face was inscrutable behind sunglasses. Beth reached up and just with her fingertips teased back Julie's dark unruly bangs. Julie flinched at her touch, grasped Beth's wrist, and flung back her hand. "Leave me alone."

And then she'd gotten in the car, careened out of the driveway, and never came back.

Beth could not call up this memory without a debilitating sense of guilt that felt as though the skin was peeling from the back of her scalp.

Her cell phone startled her. "Hi, Beth, it's Barry."

Her heart lifted only for a moment because she could sense a difference in his voice with only those few words. "Hi, is everything okay?"

"Yeah."

"Oh, good. I appreciate you calling. I'm worried about you driving so late, especially in the mountains."

"Yeah, I'm sure it'll be fine. Listen, I just wanted to thank you for everything. I've been doing some thinking, and Aaron and I are heading back to Maryland first thing tomorrow. He's not ready to make any kind of move, and I now realize I was asking a lot of him. Why would a guy want to move his senior year of high school? He has all his friends, the whole structure of his life there."

"I understand," Beth said. Of course, that was true. A dull ache started in her throat. "He's been through a lot. You, too."

"He's really not—" She could hear the hesitation as he chose his words. She thought of the strong muscles of his back.

"Beth," he said, in a quiet voice. "It's just too soon for him. Everything. Do you know what I mean?"

Beth closed her eyes. She licked her lips, which felt old and dry. "Yes."

"I just want you to know, that was the most unforgettable round of golf of my life." He laughed, but when she didn't, he stopped. Then drew a breath. "And the dinner at your house . . . I can't tell you how nice it was, having a meal, dancing with you, and then last night . . ."

"I'm glad you had a good time," she said, in a very formal voice.

"Okay, then," he said. He cleared his throat. "I wish I could have stayed."

"Me, too."

"Thank you again."

"You're welcome."

"Can I call you next time I get down South again?"

Her throat suddenly seemed constricted, and she couldn't speak.

"Beth, I wish I—"

"Sure," she interrupted. And with a "safe travels," she hung up.

Lying on her bed, motionless, she willed herself not to cry.

CHAPTER TWENTY-NINE

Sky

Sky ran up the steps to Mrs. Sawyer's house. Her shiny new key glinted under the porch light as she let herself in. It was about eleven o'clock and loud pops and whistles from random fireworks still erupted in the night sky.

The front hall light was on, but no one was downstairs. The old woman and Mrs. Sawyer must have already gone to bed.

Mr. Sawyer was so sweet! It seemed weird to think of an old guy as sweet, but he was. He had the kindest blue eyes. And he'd been so impressed with her golf abilities. He had invited her to play with him the next day. She didn't think he'd been planning to until she'd told him about her 76 from the men's tees the other day. She was a little nervous. She knew she could hold her own, but still.

Ronda, his fiancée, had fixed up a room for Sky at their house with everything pink and frilly in it and must have said ten times that they'd love to have her "any old time, sweetie-pie." Sky could tell that Mr. Sawyer *did* want her to come and stay there. And he said he'd pay for any golf equipment she needed, any coaches, just to ask him, not to hesitate. She started to say that Mrs. Sawyer was finding her a coach but suddenly she had a funny feeling about telling him and stopped. And he'd given her that laptop. She'd never had one of those before, either.

Sky went into the kitchen and took the ice cream from the freezer. She'd commented that she liked Moose Tracks, and Mrs. Sawyer went out and bought two gallons of it right away.

She had a funny feeling about everything, like Mrs. Sawyer and Mr. Sawyer were trying not to show it but they were competing to see which one of them she'd love the most.

She couldn't find the ice cream scoop and was searching through different kitchen drawers. In one of them she found a big green envelope. It had a helix on the outside and a DNA testing center return address. Her heart thudded. She stared at it a minute. It wasn't sealed. She reached inside and pulled out a baggie containing her golf glove—her golf glove!—with her name printed on it. And a letter saying that the results were ninety-nine percent conclusive, that the two samples provided were indeed the grandparents of the third sample.

Mrs. Sawyer had stolen her golf glove and tested her DNA without telling her about it.

She felt the heat of an angry flush creep up her neck and over her cheeks, and blood began to pound in her temples. Sky couldn't believe it.

She suddenly felt slightly dizzy. She stuffed the golf glove into her back pocket, shoved the DNA envelope back in the drawer and stormed up the stairs.

Approaching Mrs. Sawyer's bedroom, she saw the door was cracked and the light still on. She tried to sneak by, but Mrs. Sawyer came to the door in a blue short-sleeved robe and smiled. She wore glasses at night, which made her look older. Her eyes looked watery and weak.

"Hi, honey, did you have fun?"

"Yeah. The fireworks were good." Sky put on her game face, tried to say the same things she would have said if she hadn't found the envelope. She needed time to think. "We sat on the lawn by the clubhouse and Mr. Sawyer introduced me to about a million people. I think my hand is bruised from shaking so many people's hands. And he invited me to play golf with him tomorrow." She couldn't really meet Mrs. Sawyer's eyes, she felt so mad.

Someone set off a Roman candle just down the street and it exploded with a crack. Chi-Chi, inside Mrs. Sawyer's mother's room, whined and scratched at the door.

"Oh, that dog, he's terrified of the fireworks, he's been a basket case all night. Anyway, Mr. Sawyer invited you to play with him?" Mrs. Sawyer opened the door to let Chi-Chi join them and followed Sky into her bedroom, her hands nervously entwined. "That's nice."

Sky sat on the bed and petted Chi-Chi when he jumped up. He was shaking and crawled under the covers, reminding Sky of the opening picture in that book her third-grade teacher had in the classroom library, *The Little Prince,* of the lump under the covers which could be either an elephant or a man's hat.

Mrs. Sawyer waved her hand. "You should be very proud of yourself."

Sky shrugged. "Why?"

"What? Oh yes, you're right, of course." She seemed so distracted, as if she were as scared of the fireworks as that little dog.

"You'll have fun with your grandfather. Just go out there and play your game."

"Right." That was what Mr. McLean always said. *Go out there and play your own game.*

Sky remained on the bed, petting the quilt over the shaking lump that was Chi-Chi. But her heart started to pound. Sky looked into Mrs. Sawyer's weak and watery eyes and wanted to scream at her. Tell her how she hated that she pretended to be so nice when all this time she was really just making sure she was not a fraud.

"Well, good night, sweetie. I'm glad you had a good—"

Someone set off a string of firecrackers that sounded like a machine gun. Chi-Chi yelped and leaped from the bed and raced down the stairs, his tail between his legs.

A series of loud clicks downstairs meant the cat door had opened and closed.

From the corner of her eye, illuminated by the front porch light, Sky saw Chi-Chi's dark form race across the front yard, headed for the street.

"Chi-Chi ran out the cat door," she said.

"I didn't think he could fit!" said Mrs. Sawyer. "Oh my God." She clutched her blue robe close around her neck and turned for the door.

"I'm still dressed," said Sky, sliding her phone into her pocket. "I think I can get him to come." Moving without hurry, she headed downstairs, her heart pounding like a drum signal, stipples of goose bumps washing over her in an electric current. She felt the same warning buzz she'd felt that night at her dad's just before she left.

She opened the front door and stepped onto the porch, allowing the silky evening air to embrace her briefly. Mrs. Sawyer was running down the hall after her, yelling "Sky!" but Sky just kept walking, not looking back. She broke into a steady run after a while, pounding down the residential roads. She had stopped calling for Chi-Chi. She hoped he would find his way home.

She thought about Indigenous scouts back in the frontier days, and with them as her inspiration, she figured she could probably run at this pace all night. She had her cell phone in her pocket. She ran to the edge of the neighborhood, watching the bright fireworks like sudden bursts of cartoon tears in the sky.

She'd wanted so badly to get away from that thin dark hall with the mashed-down carpet where she'd practiced putting with her dad. But now, letting the ball roll so straight and true down that hall seemed simple and appealing. Solomon Municipal was her home course, it was where she had learned the game and where she felt confident and where Mr. McLean could talk her through her swing.

She missed her dad's golf stories, listening to the soothing drone of the golf announcers on the TV in the background. They always made everything about life sound so calm and reasonable, as if nothing was ever a crisis, nothing beyond saving. She wanted to go to Solomon Municipal and pick up the balls and put them through the ball washer and count them out, clean and gleaming, to put in the buckets. She wanted to go out on the course and play her game.

She passed the brick entranceway and jogged out onto the main highway, a cold sweat breaking out everywhere, and she thought she might throw up, just like Jordan on the day of that first tournament at Royal Run Golf Club. God, her dad had been right. They didn't belong there, they didn't belong in places like that. It wasn't them. But she would beat them all anyway.

She took her cell phone from her pocket and punched in the number. "Dad?" she said when he answered. A gigantic red, white, and blue chrysanthemum bloomed swiftly, with electric crackling in the sky above her head.

"Can you come get me?"

CHAPTER THIRTY

Beth

I n her robe and pajamas, Beth ran out the front door, turning on the porch light, which carved a semicircular pool of brightness out of the dark yard. She raced up the driveway.

"Sky! Sky!"

No answer. Beth's heart was pounding all out of proportion. Sky was simply chasing a little dog who probably would not run far. But Beth had been taken back in time all over again to the day Julie left, and a debilitating panic swept over her. People in her life left on innocent errands, never to come back.

When she got to the street, she had no idea which way to turn. She stopped and listened, hoping she might still be able to hear the pounding of Sky's feet or Chi-Chi's barks.

Nothing.

She ran across the street into a small park at the edge of the neighborhood, racing around the wooded paths, alternately calling for Sky and Chi-Chi. She tripped on a root and fell headlong to her elbows and knees. Tears from the impact started to her eyes.

As she pulled herself to her feet, feeling warm blood from her fall trickle down her shin beneath her pajama shorts, she saw a flashlight bobbing up her driveway and her mother's querulous voice calling, "Chi-Chi, come here boy!" Her mother's white nightgown glowed under the streetlight.

She limped back across the street. "Mom, you shouldn't be out here wandering around, I just tripped and fell, and you could, too."

"Well, I had the good sense to grab a flashlight, Beth, what's the matter with you? And where's Sky?"

"She ran after Chi-Chi." Not wanting to worry her mother, she added, "She'll probably catch him and be back any minute. Let's you and I go back inside. There's no use in us being out here in the dark." Yet she had a terrible feeling.

She took her mother by the elbow, guided her down the driveway, and helped her up the porch steps. A firecracker went off, making them both jump. Back in the kitchen, Beth saw a lake of melted ice cream on the counter, and the cabinet drawer standing ajar, where her mother had retrieved the flashlight, with the DNA test envelope nestled among the contents. Somehow, its position looked slightly different to Beth from when she'd hidden it yesterday.

With trembling fingers and a horrible premonition, she opened it.

The golf glove was gone.

And that's when Beth knew that Sky was, too.

CHAPTER THIRTY-ONE

Beth

Beth was in the same Denny's but at a different table this time. She sipped coffee as she waited for Alan Cowan, for something to do more than anything, though it had no taste.

Beth had never been depressed before. Even when Julie ran away, she'd avoided depression by channeling her grief into the manic search to find her. When her father died, she'd thrown herself into efforts to help her mother cope. But after Sky left, and Barry's call, she'd spent two weeks lying on the couch, unable to eat or sleep, unable to function on even the most basic level, unable to summon the energy to care about anything. If her mom hadn't been staying with her, she might have starved to death.

Beth remembered reading that the writer Dorothy Parker, at the end of her life, hadn't had the will to walk her dog. She made herself walk Chi-Chi, who had been found hiding behind a gardenia bush by a kind neighbor who called Beth's mother's number from

Chi-Chi's collar tag the morning after the fireworks. Sky wrote Beth a very sweet letter, saying how much she appreciated all that Beth had done for her. She said she'd loved staying in her mother's room. She said that she'd initially been furious about the golf glove and the DNA test, but as time went by, she guessed she had more understanding for what Beth had done.

Now, she wrote, she wanted to live with her dad but hoped to still have Beth in her life. Beth and Sky had smoothed things over, but all had not gone as well with Mark, who called Beth and told her he was not coming to Sky's tournament. "Look at all we offered her. And she turned us down."

"Oh, Mark, your pride is just hurt," she said. "You stuck your neck out for her—which was the right thing for you to do, by the way, since she is your granddaughter—and she was confused and didn't respond the way you wanted. That girl is wild about you, even if she did go back to Steven Novak. In her mind, he's her dad. We just need to take it slowly."

"What do you know?" Mark shouted. "None of this would have happened if it weren't for your insistence on doing a DNA test behind her back. Beth, you are a relentless woman. Relentless!"

"And what does it take to get you to take one tiny step out of your comfort zone?" A dozen years after their divorce, and they were still yelling at each other.

Beth had stood in her naked kitchen and her limbs felt like dead weights, too heavy to move, the gravity so strong her knees nearly buckled.

Now, waiting for Alan Cowan, Beth wrapped her hands around her coffee cup and took another sip. Six or seven robust Canadian geese landed in a field across from Denny's and waddled in a line, threading their bills through the grass. Two or three seagulls wheeled around above Denny's roof. The gulls, ocean bound, had found the lake, given up their quest, and stayed. People joked about these birds abandoning their supposedly hardwired migratory instincts. But their feathers gleamed with health, and they seemed content.

Beth didn't have a view of the front parking lot and couldn't see the battered Mazda pull in, so when Allen Cowan collapsed into the booth across from her, she jumped, clapping her hand to her chest in shock.

"Scare you?" He gave an uncharacteristic grin.

"Yes!"

"Good. Keeps you on your toes." He pushed a disheveled scrubbing pad of hair back from his face, revealing the weathered visage that instantly conjured a life suggested by the song "A Hard Rain's A-Gonna Fall." His calculating eyes swept the restaurant. Beth detected the smell of WD-40 again. "I need a Coke."

"I'm sorry, let me order your Coke." Beth thought to signal the waiter but lost her will before she did it. When she moved, it felt as though her limbs were struggling through a thick gel.

But the efficient young man stepped up to the table as if reading their minds. He poured more coffee into Beth's ceramic mug and stared wordlessly at his green-lined order pad with his pen propped at the top. Cowan ordered the Coke, the grand slam with the poached egg and the extra order of hash browns on the side. With nothing more than a tightening of his lips, the waiter pocketed the pen and pad and left the table.

While the waiter was gone, Beth searched in her purse for the stiff envelope she'd just picked up at the bank, found it, and pushed it across the table in Cowan's direction. "I hope this covers what I owe you. I want to thank you, Mr. Cowan, for all you've done. I did a DNA test, and Sky is my granddaughter for sure. But she went back to her stepfather. At the moment, I am not interested in moving forward. I'm a bit exhausted. And I wouldn't know where to go from here anyway." Beth was aware she was rambling and felt grateful when the waiter returned and placed a Coke and a straw in front of Cowan.

Cowan ignored Beth's envelope stuffed with his pay and instead tore the paper from his straw and sucked down the Coke like a wet vac. "Okay, I'm going to tell you that I've found Julie and you're going to ask me how I did it and I'm going to tell you that I can't tell you."

"What?" Cold waves of liquid shock shot through her.

"I won't be needing any more of your money." He slid the envelope back across the table in her direction. He gave a New Yorker's mock modest shrug. "I found her."

Beth's consciousness seemed to separate from her body and float to a spot on the ceiling above her, and then hung there, a loud roaring in her ears like ocean waves making it almost impossible to hear Cowan's next words.

"She's living outside Charlottesville, Virginia, on a small farm. About ten years ago she changed her social security number—which people do all the time, only nobody knows it."

Now Beth's hands and knees were shaking.

"And you're going to ask me how I know it's her, but I won't be able to tell you. You just have to take my word for it." Cowan reached onto the seat next to him and laid a medium-thick yellow manila envelope on the table. "She's married to a veterinarian named William Van Dantzig. On the property she keeps a refuge for exotic cats that have been abused. She goes by the name of Libby."

Beth reached for the envelope. The tips of her nail-bitten fingers lay where the edge of the envelope met the linoleum of the table, but she wasn't able to make them move any farther.

Cowan used his stubby but agile fingers to rip open the envelope and pour a stack of shiny four-by-six photographs in front of her like a jeweler pouring diamonds from a pouch. On top was a photo of a dark-haired woman with a lined but beautiful, almost mask-like face and sunken, bruised eyes. She was bottle-feeding a cougar cub. Fifteen years telescoped into the time it took a drop of rain to slide down a windowpane. An anguished sound that Beth could not control escaped her lips. Cowan was still talking but she could hardly hear him. It was just so much to take in. She thought she should go to the restroom and try and pull herself together. But she just sat there, the pads of her fingers on the edges of the photos, her eyes barely able to see them as tears were rolling down her face.

At that moment, the waiter brought Cowan's grand slam and hesitated about putting it on the table. Finally able to act, Beth raked the photos into her lap. As the waiter placed the plate in front of Cowan, the yolk of his poached egg broke and spread across the plate.

"Does she have children? I mean other than Sky?"

"Not unless you count the tiger cubs." Cowan began to eat, and Beth fell into the pictures. She kept swiping at her eyes so she could see the photos clearly. One showed Julie with her husband. He looked much older, maybe in his midforties, and Julie's face, as she looked at him, seemed suffused with love, fragile as a flower.

"The things that I've thought all these years. I imagined her in halfway houses, living under bridges, homeless. I had horrible nightmares about following some attendant into the morgue and having them open a drawer. Or someone handing me a watch or a ring or a necklace and saying, 'Can you identify these?' I can't tell you all that I've imagined."

Cowan wiped his mouth. "Some of that did happen. Your daughter was homeless in Amsterdam and did pretty much hit rock bottom. Sky's father ended up not being part of their lives. After coming back to the states and leaving her daughter with Steven Novak, she managed to turn it all around, found a new identity, and met this guy. And just about eight years ago she opened the wildlife refuge."

"You had a conversation with her?"

"No. It's my policy to leave actual contact up to my client. All the information you need in the event you wish to contact her is in the envelope I gave you." He sucked air from the bottom of the empty glass, making a loud burbling sound. His face twisted and he gave his New Yorker's shrug.

Beth nodded. Charlottesville was five hours away. She needed time to think. Would Julie see her? And what about Sky? Of course Sky would want to know this.

Beth realized Cowan had said something to her and she had no idea what it was. She rubbed her burning eyes and looked at him.

"The rest is up to you," he said.

On the way out of Denny's, Beth thanked Cowan, holding the precious envelope over her heart and shaking his feverish hand. She hesitated, and then on impulse hugged him, her nose buried in the dense forest of his gray hair. His bent knobby body burned like a furnace. "I'll be forever grateful to you."

"Glad I could help." Cowan stepped away. Hugging was not his style.

"Mr. Cowan, if you like golf, or even if you don't, come watch my granddaughter play in the Girls' Junior Championship at Carvelotte Country Club next weekend."

Cowan thanked her but politely declined as the day he went to a golf tournament would be a cold day in hell.

After he drove away, Beth sat in her car and examined the pictures, one by one, for close to an hour, crying on and off, unable to believe time and space had been bridged and she was looking at her daughter's face.

Then she drove to Margo's house. They still hadn't spoken, but she was the first person Beth wanted to see. Margo came to the door with a sponge in her hand. A pungent odor of bleach wafted out the door, along with Melissa Etheridge at brain-scrambling volume.

"I hired a private investigator and he found her, Margo."

Margo's weathered face fell apart and she dragged Beth inside and wrapped her in a bear hug.

FIFTEEN MINUTES LATER, Beth was still crying, and Margo finally went to the kitchen and got her a roll of paper towels. "Here, you're going to ruin my couch."

Beth took the roll, starting to laugh, then ripped one off. "So pathetic." She mopped her face with it. "Listen, Margo, you were right. I owe you an apology. I didn't think I wanted Mark back, but what you said hit a raw nerve, and I finally realized why. Finding Sky made me yearn for my old life. I just wanted to go back to when we were all happy."

Margo nodded.

"My old life with Mark, with Julie and Paul safe at home with us. I wanted that back. And none of that was fair to Sky, poor girl. No wonder she ran away."

Tears ran down Margo's cheeks and she grabbed the paper towel roll. "Just say it, girl. Life's a bitch." She wiped her cheeks. "So, when are you going to go see Julie?"

"I think I'm going to write her a letter."

And Beth did. When she arrived home, she sat down at the desk in Julie's bedroom and wrote a letter from her heart, telling her how much she loved and missed her, how she knew she had somehow failed her. She explained how she'd come to know and love Sky, Julie's daughter, and what a remarkable young woman she was. She enclosed an article from the local newspaper, describing the upcoming tournament. She told Julie that one of Sky's dreams was that one day her mother would come back to watch her play golf.

Although she was afraid that Sky would feel betrayed yet again, she didn't want to get her hopes up and decided to wait until after the tournament to tell Sky anything.

Then she took the letter to the mailbox, blinking in the sunlight that seemed to sear her eyes, and raised the red metal flag.

CHAPTER THIRTY-TWO

Beth

Carvelotte Country Club looked to Beth more like a sprawling brick fortress than a golf club. The four-foot-high brick walls that lined the entrance drive reminded her of a drawbridge over a moat.

"Jesus H. Christ," said Margo from the back seat as Beth turned into the drive. "Forget your game faces, girls, we shoulda brung our coats of mail."

"Beth, there's the parking lot, turn left," said her mother from the passenger seat. "There's a spot! Hurry and—oops, darn it, that other guy got it."

"We'll find another one, Mom."

Beth was doing much better, and so was her mom, and they'd agreed she'd go home next week.

"There!" said her mom, jabbing the air, her sunflower earrings swinging. "Hard right, around the corner! Beat that SUV!"

"Good eye, Mom." Sweat had popped out on Beth's temples by the time she got into the spot.

Vanessa tied her braids back into a ponytail when she got out of the car, and Margo made everyone put on SPF 50 sunscreen. Around the back of the clubhouse, they found the same scene as at the qualifying round in Winston-Salem, only with more people and the tension ratcheted up several notches.

Beth grabbed a preprinted program whose cover featured a silhouette of a girl with a ponytail at the top of her swing, and scanned the names, quickly finding Sky's. She had ended up fifth in the state this year and was paired with the girl who had come in first. A girl named Katherine Anne Boyd. They would tee off in just a few minutes.

Beth and the others hurried to the first tee. Beth had called Sky the night before to congratulate her on making the cut and to wish her luck, and they'd had a good conversation.

Now Beth, her mother, and her golf pals found Sky waiting for her partner to hit. Beth was reminded of the day she'd first seen Sky—only a few months ago—on the course in Winston-Salem.

The other girl—tall and lanky with dark spiked hair and narrow eyes—pulverized her drive, hitting it nearly two hundred and eighty yards down the middle of the fairway.

Come on, Sky.

The Wade boy—Beth was pretty sure his name was Silas—the near-albino with the earring, pulled Sky's driver from her bag and handed it to her. Sky adjusted her visor and pulled on her new glove.

Beth turned and saw Mark walking through the woods toward the tee with Ronda on his arm. Oh, God, she couldn't believe it, Ronda was wearing high heels, and they were sinking into the grass. But Beth watched the way Ronda clung to Mark's elbow, the courtly way he supported her, and something hard and painful racked into focus. Ronda was nearly turning her ankle with every step, but she was waving her thin, gym-toned arms, embroidering the air with her beautifully manicured fingers, telling Mark some story. She looked utterly ridiculous and out of place, yet he threw back his head and laughed. Then he affectionately took her hand in his and put his index finger to his lips, as if to say, "Shh! We don't talk while people are addressing the ball."

Beth blinked. She saw so clearly now how much Mark loved Ronda.

Someone on the other side of the tee box was waving at her and smiling. It was Denise Wade with her husband and their other son. And she saw Steven Novak, too, standing with them. He must have lost fifteen pounds. It seemed right that Sky should be drawing all of them together. And fitting that Sky should for the first time have a gallery to cheer her on.

Sky stepped onto the tee. She didn't seem intimidated by the other girl's monstrous drive at all. Beth loved watching the perfect spiral of her boyish shoulders as she executed a practice swing, like a time-lapsed photo of the uncoiling of a rose. And as Sky finished, she saw that tough, expressionless game face, and her eyes stung just knowing the volcano of emotions Sky was doubtless holding inside.

And then there was a hush, and Sky blasted her drive every bit as far as the other girl. In fact, it rolled two feet past.

CHAPTER THIRTY-THREE

Sky

At the beginning of their round, Katherine Anne had called her *Cloud* again. Sky wanted to smash her face with her four iron. "It's Sky," she'd said between gritted teeth. "*Sky.*"

But she wasn't calling her Cloud now. Sky was playing lights out. On the next to the last hole it was an even match so far, and she'd made Katherine Anne scramble more than once. She strode from the sixteenth green up to the seventeenth tee. Silas carried her clubs, flipping through his yardage book, talking as they walked. The seventeenth hole was a short par three with water in front of the green.

One hundred twenty yards to cover the water, one hundred thirty-eight to the pin.

A week ago, Silas had texted her.

Spiderwoman. Still need a caddy?

Affirmative. C U there, she had replied.

She could feel herself in the zone, like nothing could touch her. Her limbs cut through the heavy August air as if she were sliding without gravity or friction through pure light. Everyone else was sweating, but Sky barely noticed the heat. Out of the corner of her eye, the ghostly fox loped beside her. She didn't let herself look directly at him; it would be like looking at an eclipse. She thought about hearing Annika say once in an interview, "I can hear the heavy breathing coming up behind me and it makes me push myself to be the best."

"One-thirty-eight from here to the pin, Spiderwoman. Nine iron. Nice and easy."

Silas gave her the iron and he seemed a little breathless and she knew he wouldn't jinx anything and say it out loud, but she knew he thought she could beat Katherine Anne. But she shouldn't let herself get tricked; success always lay in playing your own game against the course, not against another person. She took her warm-up swing. She liked this match play format. If you totally fucked up the hole, who cared? It only counted as minus one. It was a fresh start on the next hole.

She'd never had a gallery before, and it was pretty damn cool. Her dad, who had told every heroic golf story he knew on the way over to pump her up, always looked at her and nodded, no matter what, as if everything she did was right and perfect. He'd told her on the way to the first tee that she had an advantage, having learned to hit the ball from bald fairways and clumps of crabgrass, having learned to scoop it out of sand traps that were either full of water or hard as cement, how to steer her putts over lumpy greens that didn't roll true. She had the advantage over a country club girl like Katherine Anne, who was only used to playing pristine courses in perfect condition, he'd said. She believed him.

Then there was Bart, who always found the spot beside the green that was closest to wherever Sky was, his blond buzz cut kind of like a halo, shoulders hunched, and his hands jammed into the pockets of his cargo pants. Mr. and Mrs. Wade were right behind him. And then there were her grandparents. It was still a little weird to think of them like that. Grandma Beth? Maybe someday she'd be able to call her that. And the two fun women Mrs. Sawyer played golf with. And Mr. Sawyer's wife.

Twice he had to tell her to stop talking on the tee.

"Spiderwoman, she's on the green with a twenty-footer. Put your shot inside hers," Silas said.

"No problem." Sky visualized the shot landing about three feet in front of the cup and rolling right in. She took a smooth practice swing, lined up again, and hit the ball.

Silas watched it rise. "You're going to like it," he said, and when it landed about three feet below the hole, he looked at her and grinned. "Fuckin' A!"

Katherine Anne and her caddy had barely waited for Sky to complete her swing before they were off. Katherine Anne's jaw was set hard.

"She can make that putt, Silas. She drills twenty-footers like gimmes."

"Well, you can make yours, too, so no worries." He slid the iron back into the bag and shouldered it. They walked together past the water hazard to the green.

"Hey, I can go to school on you, Katie," Sky said pleasantly as she stepped onto the large, squarish green. "I appreciate that very much."

As Sky predicted, Katherine Anne made the twenty-footer. But as Sky stood over her three-footer, she wasn't nervous at all. The line was crystal clear, emblazoned on her brain, and she drilled it.

No blood. And she met Silas's eyes. All square. On to number eighteen.

A long par five.

She and Katherine Anne both hit long straight drives and strong second shots. Then Katherine Anne's approach shot leaked right and landed in the greenside bunker. Whoa.

"The door creaketh open, Spiderwoman. Hit your best shot," Silas said.

She had about a hundred and twenty yards. When Silas pulled out her pitching wedge, it made a metallic shearing sound like a sword. As she was lining up, she saw Mrs. Sawyer standing under a big oak tree to the left of the green, about thirty yards away. She stopped and squinted hard. Mrs. Sawyer was talking to a thin dark-haired woman who looked incredibly familiar.

"Spiderwoman," Silas said. "Get your head back in the game."

Sky nodded and addressed the ball again. She had her chance now. Katherine Anne had left the door wide open. She blinked and looked down. Those pictures.

That dark-haired woman.

"Spiderwoman!" Silas said again. "What are you doing?"

"I don't know," she said. She rubbed her fingers over her eyes. She looked again. Mrs. Sawyer and the woman were both watching her.

"Okay, I'm trying to figure out what you're doing here," Silas said. He grabbed Sky's wrist gently and put his face up next to hers. The sun was behind him, and his face was dark, but a streak of sunlight threaded through his earring. "Come on, Spiderwoman, you're playing lights out, you can't quit on me now."

Sky stepped away from the ball. She closed her eyes and took a breath. She could feel the adrenaline racing now, and that was dangerous because it would make her hands and knees shake or cause her to fly the green. She wouldn't be able to putt for shit either.

Excuses, excuses. If she didn't win, no one would care *why* she hadn't. She looked up at the spot on the green where she wanted her ball to go.

And then she took her shot.

It landed past the cup, then curled its way back, inch by inch, and dropped in.

"Oh my God!" Silas started leaping up and down. He grabbed his cap from his head and threw it in the air. He grabbed Sky in a bear hug. "You holed it! The match is over! You won, Spiderwoman! You won!"

Silas hugged her so hard she felt like her teeth might fall out, and her gallery, her family, up around the green, was jumping up and down and from back here they looked like marionettes or jumping beans. Sky wandered up the fairway, feeling dazed, an electric crackling in her brain, while Silas galloped past her yelling, her bag on his back perpendicular like the wings of a plane. She searched under the tree for the dark-haired woman.

Where had she gone?

Katherine Anne was on the green, waiting to shake her hand. "Nice shot. Good luck in your matches this afternoon and tomorrow." It was true, there were matches yet to play. But for more reasons than one, this was the match Sky wanted to remember forever.

"Thanks," Sky said, trying to break the bones of Katherine Anne's fingers before Katherine Anne broke hers. "Good round." Katherine Anne turned and stalked toward the clubhouse without waiting for her caddy to retrieve her ball from the trap.

And then Sky walked off the green and her dad hugged her, laughing while tears ran down his sun-weathered cheeks, and then kissed the top of her head. Bart grabbed her and picked her up and twirled around with her. Mr. Sawyer was ebullient, saying over and over, "Did you see that shot? Did you see it?" And his wife kept saying, "This is so *exciting*, I think I'll be forced to have some kind of reception." And Mrs. Wade hugged her and said, "Girl, does it get any better than this? Does it?"

And Sky laughed and said, "I don't think so."

Her great-grandma and Mrs. Sawyer's golf girls were hugging her, too. A man in a navy-blue sport coat came up to her. "Nice round, Miss Sawyer. One of the hardest things about my job is waiting to approach athletes until rules allow. Maybe I'll see you in a few years."

Sky was confused and her dad took over for her. He shook the man's hand and started to talk.

Then Mrs. Sawyer, a big smile on her face, was giving her one of those hugs that made you feel cared for and cherished and safe. After a long while, she broke the embrace and looked up. Mrs. Sawyer's eyes were red and swollen and Sky grabbed her hand. She skipped over everything else. "Who was that dark-haired woman?"

"That's your mother, Sky. That's Julie. Want to talk to her?"

And then Sky realized the woman was standing just a few feet away.

So many times Sky had imagined what this moment might be like. She'd dreamed there might be a dawning of love on her mother's face, and that she would rush forward and gather her into her arms, but of course that didn't happen. The woman stood quite still, looking at Sky from a distance. Mrs. Sawyer gently grabbed Sky's hand and pulled her closer.

And then standing in front of her, Sky found the right words. "You came."

CHAPTER THIRTY-FOUR

Beth

Margo, Beth, and Vanessa stood on the first tee at Silver Lakes. The wind gusted, and from the oak tree beside them, a few hand-shaped red leaves swirled to the ground.

Beth was feeling good today. Since finding Julie, she found she had more patience with her students and could help them more. She tried not to have too much hope for the future, but to just be pleased about the way things were now. And she was thrilled that Vanessa was playing with them again. Neither she nor Margo had asked too many questions.

That was an after-the-round conversation.

"You're up," Margo said. "Hit a good one."

"Smash it, girl," said Vanessa.

"Love to." Nowadays, instead of visualizing Annika or Lorena Ochoa, Beth visualized Sky. Beth knocked a solid drive down the middle. Nowhere near the woods.

"Nice," Vanessa said. Her swing was as effortless as usual, and she outdrove Beth by twenty yards.

"Very nice," Margo said. She stuck her tee in the ground, waggled, then outdrove both of them.

"Damn," Beth said. "You are a beast, woman."

The three of them sauntered side by side down the fairway, their clubs clanking behind them on pull carts. "So, you heard anything from Sky?" Margo asked.

"Yep. She wants to play with us next week."

"Get out! Sky Boom-Boom Sawyer playing with a bunch of old biddies like us?"

"Sorry, Margo, I do not answer to biddy," said Vanessa, using air quotes.

"Well, she's got a day off school. She got her learner's permit, and Mark and I helped Steven get her a car, and she said she wants to try driving it over here. I can't wait to play with her."

"Are you kidding? Me, neither."

"Ditto."

Beth knew Margo and Vanessa wouldn't bring up Julie. Not during a round of golf. Their old rule about avoiding devastating subjects held. In a week or so, Beth was taking Sky up to Charlottesville to visit the compound where Julie kept the dozen wild cats she'd rescued. She could still feel visceral regret at what might have been, but there was a sense of freedom in letting go of the anguish and the blame, in starting anew.

"So," said Vanessa. "We still have Ladies' Day."

Beth's clubs rattled as she pulled her cart over a small dry gulley. "I guess Buddy did one nice thing."

"Probably his wife made him," said Margo.

"Or the maintenance crew went on strike." Beth laughed. "I have a question for you two. Ronda called and invited me to Thanksgiving dinner at their house. Paul and Andrea are coming and staying with me, but Ronda wanted them to come to dinner at her house. She's inviting Sky, too, and she said why didn't I just come and bring Mom. Think I should go?"

"You get to see Sky, you don't have to cook," said Margo.

"Where's the downside?" Vanessa pointed out.

"I don't know. I worry about being a fifth wheel."

"Beth, how can you be a fifth wheel?" Margo protested.

"Hell, yeah, I'd go," Vanessa said.

"I think they also invited Steven Novak. And, who knows, maybe Julie and her husband, too."

"Listen, show up with flowers, a positive attitude, and a sweet potato casserole. It sounds damn civilized to me. And . . . did I hear that Barry is coming down to stay with Buddy and his wife again?"

"Yes, he is."

"Did he . . .?" prodded Vanessa.

"Call me? Yes, he did."

"And did you . . .?" prodded Margo.

"Take the call? Yes, I did indeed."

Margo and Vanessa started to hoot and holler, and Beth felt her face go hot in the midst of laughing so hard.

When Barry called, Beth had just settled into bed with a good book. Beth answered, expecting that this late at night it would certainly be Paul or her mother.

"You probably thought you'd never hear from me again, but you're not going to be that lucky," Barry said.

Beth tried not to let the surprise show in her voice. "No, it's great to hear from you," she said, trying to calm her nerves. "How are you? How's Aaron?"

"We're hanging in there. My sister invited us down for Thanksgiving. We're coming." He hesitated. "I was wondering if you were up for a rematch."

"Just a rematch?" She held her breath.

"Yes. I mean no. I'd love to take you for dinner afterwards."

"Sure." She felt a slight shiver as she remembered their night together. "And, by the way, I finally remembered the name of the author whose name I'd forgotten. Anne Tyler."

"Oh!" he said. "*The Accidental Tourist*. That weird guy that used to take showers with his clothes on to clean the clothes and himself at the same time."

"Yeah! You read it?'

"No." He hesitated, then went on. "My wife loved that book. She read me parts of it, and then dragged me to the movie."

In the ensuing moment of silence, Beth reflected with pleasure that she and Barry's wife had had Anne Tyler in common. Then he went on.

"So, Thanksgiving weekend, is it a date?"

"It's a date," Beth had said. This time, she was getting her hair done. And wearing cologne.

Now she tightened her grip on her club and proceeded to hit a low screamer directly into the woods. "Shit, I haven't been in the woods all day. Thinking about Barry must have messed me up."

"Well, you need to mess up more often," Vanessa said.

"Ha ha." Beth trudged after it.

Margo hit a wild shot that bonked a tree limb and bounced miraculously onto the green.

"Member's bounce!" Beth yelled. She'd heard from Vanessa that Margo's partner Jean had taken a leave of absence from her firm and had signed up for a mission trip to South America, and that Margo was going with her, but that was an after-the-round subject, like Julie.

Beth crunched through pine needles and dead leaves, and found her ball nestled near a dried-up clump of poison ivy. Above her, puzzle pieces of brilliant blue peeked between half-bare branches.

"Come on, Beth," Margo yelled from the fairway.

"Knock it out of there," Vanessa echoed.

"See what I can do." She took her stance a few times, waggled, tested the angles. Dammit, no shot. Well, that was, unless she could cut it between those two dogwoods. The opening was extremely narrow but what the heck, it was worth a shot.

"Where the hell are you aiming?" Margo shouted. "Are you out of your mind?"

"I guess so," Beth said. She closed her eyes and let Sky rise up behind her lids.

She swung. The ball nipped sweetly between the narrow trunks of the two dogwoods, just below the cascade of tear-shaped, reddish-brown leaves, then flashed like a shooting star as it soared over the trap and rolled to the edge of the green.

"What a shot!" Margo yelled, raising her arms.

"You're on the dance floor, girl!" Vanessa did a little dance right on the fairway.

Beth felt an elusive spark of excitement rekindle. She threaded her way through the changing leaves and out of the woods, into the bright, angled autumn light.

ACKNOWLEDGMENTS

I probably would never have written about golf if my husband Jeff had not been such a passionate fan of the game and encouraged me to play. It's been a joy playing golf with him for many years. Once Jeff taught me how to play, I was able to also play with my beloved father, brother, and uncle, and those memories are pristine. There have also been many rounds filled with hilarity with my dear friends Cathy Crouch, Deb Waldron, and Betty Lou Washburn.

To be clear, I'm a mediocre golfer. But that doesn't mean I don't enjoy it. The seed of this novel was born when I thought, "Would I have to be great at golf to try to write about it?" I decided the answer was no.

I followed Hayley Hammond, who played college golf at Radford University, on several high school tournament rounds to write the girls' competitive golf scenes. Thanks to Hayley and her parents, dear friends Deb Waldron and Kevin Hammond, for giving me that opportunity.

This novel is also about much more than golf. It's about many versions of love—love for children and grandchildren, love for parents, married love, single love, divorced love, love for friends, and even love for pets. For that constant inspiration I must thank my beloved family and friends.

I wrote the first draft of *Ladies' Day* in the MFA program at Queens University. Thanks to the teachers and fellow students who patiently read and commented on those early chapters, probably hoping for something more literary. After that, superb freelance editor Betsy Thorpe gave me excellent feedback and I undertook a major revision. Then editor Karen Alley went over the manuscript with a fine-toothed comb, and really helped me bring it to the next level.

I joined the Women's Fiction Writers' Association and had several helpful critiquers encourage me with the opening pages, including Kathryn Daugherty, Tiffany Hawk, and Falguni Kothari.

Many thanks to Amy Sue Nathan for very helpful feedback on this novel.

My colleagues and writers' groups have been pillars of support. Ann Campanella, Liz Hatley, Michelle Moore, Emily Pearce, and Betsy Thorpe—I treasure you all.

From the moment Sue Arroyo called me and said, "I want to buy your book!" working with CamCat has been a dream. Sue asked Allyson Williams, a competitive golfer, to read the manuscript, and I am indebted to her for her expertise. Any mistakes that remain are mine. Helga Schier is an incredibly astute editor and I feel lucky to have had her helping me hone this manuscript. Thank you to copy editor Penni Askew for her precise attention to detail and for her delightful sense of humor. I love the way the cover, designed by Maryann Appel, captures the emotion of the story. Heartfelt thanks to the whole CamCat team for a wonderful publishing experience.

ABOUT THE AUTHOR

L adies' Day (CamCat Books) is Lisa Williams Kline's second novel for adults. She is also the author of historical fiction *Between the Sky and the Sea* (Dragonblade), an essay collection called *The Ruby Mirror* (The Bridge), and a short story collection called *Take Me* (Main Street Rag). Her stories and essays have appeared in *Literary Mama, Skirt, Sasee, Carolina Woman, moonShine review, The Press 53 Awards Anthology, Sand Hills Literary Magazine,* and *Idol Talk,* among others. She is also the author of ten novels and a novella for young readers. She lives in Davidson, North Carolina with her veterinarian husband, a cat who can open doors, and a sweet chihuahua who has played Bruiser Woods in *Legally Blonde: The Musical.* Lisa treasures frequent visits with her grown daughters and their husbands.

Please visit her website at www.lisawilliamskline.com or follow her at IG: @lisawilliamskline and on FB: @lisa.kline.566.

If you liked
Lisa Williams Kline's *Ladies' Day*,
we hope you will consider leaving a
review to help our authors.

Also check out
Haleigh Wenger's *Managing the Matthews*.

— • —

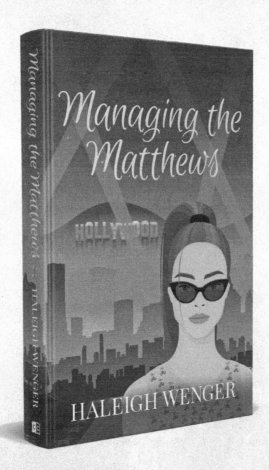

CHAPTER ONE

Kell

Being the manager for a trio of hot celebrity brothers sounds amazing until you're the one thing standing in the way of their sleep.

Between the three of them—Ash, Jonah, and Ryan—I don't get days off. Someone always ends up needing to be on set at eight a.m. sharp, no matter the day.

Never mind that wake-up calls are most definitely not in my job description.

Today, I have the unparalleled pleasure of knocking loudly on Ash Matthew's bedroom door, waiting outside of it for an appropriate amount of time, and then beating on the door some more. It's a blast. "Ashley! I know you're in there! You have a photoshoot in fifteen! Fifteen minutes!"

There's not a single sound from inside his room. When yelling doesn't work, I pull my cell phone from my purse and call him over and over and over. He doesn't answer. Instead, a banging sound comes from inside his bedroom and the door swings open.

Ash looks me over through half-open eyes and then flops back onto the enormous California King in the center of his room. I toss my phone back into the bag on my arm and follow him in. "I don't have work today," he says, his words obscured by the pillow he's planted his face into. His dark-brown hair splays out to the sides, curling slightly at the ends. I tried to talk him into a haircut a few months ago, but it turns out he was right. Annoying, but right, that the longer hair suits him.

I put a hand on my hip. "You do have work."

Despite the text I received at 2:00 a.m. letting me know that he didn't think he'd make it in, I'm not letting Ash off this easily. As his manager, it's my job to keep on top of him about these kinds of things.

He grumbles something else unintelligible into his pillow. I sigh and lower myself to his bed, swaying slightly at the too-soft mattress underneath me. "You're contracted. The movie is almost done. Just promo and then you're off the hook for this one. And, come on, it wasn't that bad. From what I saw of it, there were some really funny scenes."

Ash lifts his head and glares at me, daring me to keep going with the lie. "I want out. I don't want to be the romance guy anymore. Not for movies like this."

"What if I promise to buy you pizza afterward?"

He scoffs. "Bribery doesn't work on me anymore. I can buy my own pizza."

I nudge his foot with my hand, but he swats at me. "It's not gonna happen. I'm not doing the photo shoot."

The dejection in his voice hits me, stalling me for a quick second. It sounds like he needs a vacation. I'll have to check his calendar. Ash and I were friends in college and when he told me that he was going into acting, it felt like fate: platonic, career-oriented fate. I was nearly done with my public relations degree and had a healthy obsession with Hollywood. He got cast in a handful of quirky indie films, one of them took off, and he's scored half a dozen romantic comedy roles since then. But lately, something has shifted and more and more often I find myself here, trying to talk him into putting on pants and getting his ass to work. Things were simpler before fame.

I flip open my phone and scroll through the online calendar while I talk. "I don't know what to tell you, Ash. Ryan does action movies, you do romantic comedies, and Jonah does sports. I can put feelers out for more serious auditions, but for now—you signed the contract. You have to finish this out."

"You'll tell people I'm looking for different stuff?" He arches an eyebrow. He rolls to sitting and leans forward to balance on the edge of the bed. His gray eyes, just the tiniest tinge of blue at the edges, study me.

None of the producers we work with will be very happy with me, but I'll let them know. I'm not going to make him lose himself over movies he hates. When we first decided to work together we agreed: friendship before business. It may not be a motto that works for everyone, but it's always served us well.

"Fine." He winces. "But I already told them I'm pulling out. I can't go to any more promo for this. It's humiliating."

I'm too late. "You already told them? You're supposed to leave the communicating to me. I could have . . ." I trail off at the look on his face.

Whatever. It's just one more Matthew mess to clean up. "Don't worry about it. I'll deal with it." I fake an unaffected shrug as I smooth one hand over his crumpled bedsheets. I bend to pick up a stray protein bar wrapper on the floor near my feet. There's no point in getting mad when I can get the other thing I came here for: information. "Tell me about last night. How did it go?"

"You should have been there."

I arch an eyebrow, smelling a tragedy. There's something about the way he says it: You *should have* been there, because it is my job to know, after all. "What? What happened?"

Ash runs a hand over his face, messing up his hair even further. It only adds to his sex appeal, and I make a mental note to get him a new set of headshots featuring this longer, messier hairstyle. It'll kill with the casting directors, even the new ones he's looking to pursue.

He groans. "It's bad. You shouldn't hear it from me."

I almost stomp my foot with impatience. If it's as bad as his voice makes it sound, I'm surprised I haven't heard it already, no matter the early hour. "I need to hear it, period. I don't care who it comes from at this point. I'm here now, so spill."

With every emergency comes a seemingly never-ending cycle of damage control, and if I've learned anything in the past five years of managing the brothers, it's that the sooner I start on fixing their mistakes, the better.

"Talk to Ryan." Ash finally meets my eyes, and I see something there I don't expect. Is that . . . pity?

Ryan's name kicks my chest into double time, and I slap a palm over my sternum. Great. Just, honestly, great. Sure, I suspected that he was involved the moment Ash said something, but to have it confirmed sets my stomach on edge.

I grit my teeth. "Ash. Please. You're killing me here."

"We were out at the bar last night. After the fan meet and greet, remember?"

I nod. I remember because I was the one who facilitated the entire thing. Except, thanks to a major guilt trip on my parents' part, I couldn't be there. Instead, I spent the day with my GI doctor and the night hosting my out-of-town parents before they caught a late flight. I was forced to listen to Mom bemoan that fact that I work too much for the hundredth time.

"Ryan spent all night with this one fangirl. She was sitting in his lap, and they were all over each other. Out of nowhere he proposed. It was bizarre. I've never seen him act like that. I don't even think he had that many drinks. It was like he pulled a diamond ring from thin air."

I flinch but cover it as I stand. Maybe we can work out a deal if Ryan agrees to let her keep the ring. I lick my lips and half turn, nodding. "Thanks for the heads up. I'll go find the girl and take care of this. We probably should keep Ryan away from fans for the next few weeks, or they'll all be expecting proposals."

Ryan has done worse, like the fan's husband he got into a bloody bar fight with last month. I'm not supposed to get my feelings hurt about him going out and doing things like this. Still, as his manager, it's a nuisance.

But as just me, Kell, it feels like a betrayal.

Ash doesn't laugh at my dumb attempt at humor. The space between his eyebrows furrows, forming a sharp V. "I doubt they will. Now that, you know, he's engaged and all."

The room freezes around us. "What do you mean?"

Ash gives his head a slow shake. "I told you. He proposed to this girl at the thing last night. Which means ... Ryan is engaged. He says they're getting married. Having an actual wedding. The whole big thing. He seems serious for once."

"Serious about some woman? Who even is she?" My body flushes hot and then cold as a mixture of emotions hits me at once. I stutter but nothing comes out. I'm completely out of words.

"Just some fan who he's been out with a few times. I don't think anyone saw this coming."

A hysterical laugh nearly chokes out of me. "This is ridiculous. Ryan wouldn't ... Ryan's not ... ."

"I'm sorry, Kell." Ash's voice is soft but out of focus. "I don't know what he's thinking. But yeah, it seems real."

"How could it be real?" Somehow, I find the doorknob, and I prop myself up on it with one hand. I thought that this was another one of Ryan's stunts. He does over-the-top public displays and then sends me in to clean up the ensuing chaos. None of the tabloid-worthy escapades are real, though. Not wedding-planning real.

The floor spins beneath me as I try to gather my thoughts because this can't be happening. Ryan getting engaged without so much as a heads up is a PR nightmare, but I can deal with it.

Normally, I can deal with anything. But with Ryan things are different, and there's no way I'm letting him do this without having a serious conversation for once. Given our history, it's way overdue.

CHAPTER TWO

Ash

After Kell leaves, I crawl from bed and look at my phone. It really sucked having to be the one to tell her about Ryan. Especially since I don't think I'm supposed to know, but— I know.

Kell isn't exactly subtle. Not about the way she gapes at my brother. I knew even before I walked in on them getting hot and heavy a few weeks back. Unfortunately, I've known for years. Never worried about it because I thought we had an unspoken agreement that Kell was off-limits. She's our manager for crying out loud. But my brother wouldn't understand that. Nothing is off-limits to Ryan.

Seeing them together was something. Believe me, I still wish I could purge it from my mind. We'd just gotten back from going out to dinner. It was all of us, which is rare. Jonah took a call and started spouting football stats into the phone. I took a shower to scrub off the makeup they caked on me during filming. And Ryan and Kell stayed behind in the living room. Not out of the ordinary since Kell is the one we all go to when we need someone to talk to. Just how it's always been. I figured that Ryan wanted to whine about his latest career drama.

I came back to them sucking each other's faces off. I'd never wanted to un-see something so badly.

And now he's engaged to some fan he's met a handful of times. I could see right away that it hit Kell. But it's also none of my business.

I get out of bed and practically sleepwalk into the kitchen. Hunger wins out, or else I'd stay in my room all day since I don't have work. Might never work again after the way I blew off movie promo. I'm just about to open the fridge and stare at the contents when someone dashes past me. I turn just in time to see a flash of Kell's light brown hair swinging behind her. Her head is ducked and her face not visible, but I can tell from the sounds that she's crying. The back door bangs shut.

Damn it.

I slap a palm against the cool stainless steel of the fridge door. And then I go find Ryan. He's lounging on our leather couch, his legs outstretched and spread wide. He's not wearing a shirt.

"What did you say to her?"

He turns his head slowly to face me, his eyes wide. Oh yeah, here comes Ryan Matthew's famous innocent act. "What are you talking about? You mean Kell? I think she's stressed out, man. I didn't do anything. I didn't say a word."

He's serious. The three competing brain cells he's got left wouldn't see anything wrong with that, would they? Kell would though. Him ignoring her is the whole issue.

I glare at him until he scowls back and asks, "You got a problem, bro?"

Yeah, I have a problem. "The problem is you. You messed things up with Kell. Now you need to go fix it." I point to the door she rushed through seconds ago. She's most likely still outside trying not to cry. I've only seen her cry a handful of times in the years I've known her. She's tough. Too tough to care about my boneheaded brother, but here we are.

Ryan gives me a cool look. "Lay off, man. Kell's a grown up. She knew what the deal was. I never promised her anything."

My finger is still outstretched so I step closer and jab it into his chest. "Go. Talk. To. Her. Now." I'm dangerously close to doing more than poking him. Maybe he can sense it, and for once Ryan gives in. If I had to guess I'd say it's the guilt.

He knows what he did.

He holds up his hands. "Okay. We'll talk. Calm down, Hulk." Ryan laughs, knowing his use of my childhood nickname is the perfect revenge. I was a chubby kid with a propensity for temper tantrums. Call yourself the Hulk once and your older brother will never let you live it down. I follow him to the back door. Slam it shut behind him before walking to the kitchen. On the counter I find a paper bag. The outside is labeled muffins in curly handwriting. Kell. I open it and am hit by the smell of warm blueberries.

Exhibit A in my reasoning of why she is too good for us. There's no polite way to tell her that she has to stop taking care of everyone in this house. No way that won't hurt her feelings. I reach for a muffin and stuff it into my mouth, sighing around the warm, buttery goodness. I'm going to kill my brother.

The back door swings open and Kell bursts in followed by Ryan. Her face is the shade of a tomato.

"Kell—"

Ryan reaches for her like he might try to hug her. But he stops short and pats her shoulder instead.

I should disappear or give them some space. Can't bring myself to do either though so I just stand here as unwitting witness to their drama once again.

She sniffs and looks up at him with watery eyes. "Please just tell me that this is some kind of stupid prank."

Ryan winces. His head ducks down. "You'd really like Samantha. I've already told her all about you."

"Samantha." Her mouth forms silently around the name. "I don't understand how this happened. When did you even meet her?"

It can't have been very long. They kissed sometime last month. Or maybe it was more than a kiss. I left as soon as I saw them on the couch. Whatever it was clearly led Kell to think something was happening. Ryan glances at me like I'm supposed to help him. No way in hell am I getting involved in this. I have my brother's back, but I draw the line at relationships. Especially when we both know he's in the wrong.

"I don't know. A few weeks." He scratches his chin. "I think it was a month ago."

The look on Kell's face says it all. She makes a small choking noise and shakes her head. "I—I can't do this right now."

She pivots and turns down the hall where the front door slams shut seconds later.

Ryan sighs. "You happy?"

I set down the last bite of my muffin and resist the urge to throw it at him. "No."

"Are you jealous or something? If you wanted to go for Kell you should have told me." He cracks a half-smile. "All those romantic movies are turning you soft."

I grit my teeth so hard Ryan can probably hear the sound of bone on bone. Exactly the reaction he wants from me. "And you're a jerk. Maybe all your movies are messing with your head. No one thinks you're James Bond in real life. It's not cool to play with people's feelings like this." If Dad were still alive he'd lay into Ryan. But maybe he'd do the same to me. I haven't been doing so hot lately either.

Ryan scoffs and reaches around me for a muffin. "Relax. Kell will get over it. It's not like we were actually dating." He stalks back to his spot on the couch with his muffin. "Blueberry. My fave."

Ryan is either oblivious or heartless. Not sure which would be better. It makes hanging out with him that much harder when he's like this though.

What I should do is go find Kell and talk her down myself. But if I were her I wouldn't want to see a Matthew brother face for at least a few good hours. Instead, I take a shower and get ready for the day. Then I wander down the long hall to Jonah's side of the house. As often as we piss each other off, I guess it says something that we all choose to live together.

Those movies I've grown sick of making pay well enough that I could have my own house far away from Ryan's exploits. Hell, I could probably have my own street. But there's something about living with both of my brothers that grounds me. I feel more like Ashley Matthew, middle child, than Ash Matthew, movie star. Not exactly great for my ego, but that's the point.

I knock once on his closed bedroom door. "It's Ash."

He's wearing gray sweatpants and a UCLA hoodie, but his muscles still show through. All the hours Ryan and I spend sleeping in, our youngest brother uses at the home gym set up in his spare bedroom. "Hey." He notices me looking around. "Jessie's at work."

I nod. His live-in girlfriend is often either gone at work or gone because they're in a fight. "So Ryan is going through with the engagement thing, apparently. Kell's upset." I don't say any more because I haven't told anyone, not even Jonah, about seeing Kell and Ryan together.

"I thought she might be," Jonah says thoughtfully. His phone buzzes and he picks it up. While he looks at the notification on his screen, my phone buzzes too.

A group text from Kell.

Emergency meeting tonight at your place. 7. Someone order pizza.
This has to be about Ryan. And based on how upset she was, it can
only mean one thing. One thing I'm worried about anyway.

"You don't think she'd quit on us?" Jonah's eyes match the worry
I'm starting to feel.

I know I'm always saying that we don't deserve her, but that
doesn't mean I think I can make it for a second without her.

WHILE WE WAIT for Kell's meeting, Jonah, Ryan, and I are in the home
gym watching as Jonah goes for his personal record on the weight
machine. He grunts out each rep and Jessie, who's just gotten back,
cheers him on after each one.

Ryan is holding an ice pack to each side of his face. He's puffy
and dotted with multicolored bruises from needles. Dermal fillers.
Apparently he spent half the day letting a plastic surgeon experiment
on him with the newest technique for a toned facial structure.

Meanwhile, I'm trying to make sure we're all on track for
convincing Kell not to leave us high and dry at this surprise meeting
she's set up.

"Why are you so worried about this?" Ryan slaps me on the back
and then winces with the movement. "You think Kell would ever
leave us? She loves us, man."

"Kell does love us," Jonah agrees, but he's only half listening.
Half concentrating. He prefers to walk the thin line in between our
disagreements. Likes waiting it out until things blow over. This time
I wish he'd tell Ryan he's being a dick. Coming from Jonah it might
be harder to ignore. The way I see it, Kell's love for us is the problem.

I shake my head at my brother. "If she does quit, it's your fault.
You know that, right? We'd lose all the connections she's made for
us. We'd be back at square one without Kell."

Ryan shrugs and changes the subject. "We're making her good money. I don't see her complaining about that."

I almost flick one of Jessie's resistance bands at his head. "Money isn't the problem."

Ryan rolls his eyes. "I'm going to call Judith and grab a fresh ice pack. I have auditions to prep for tomorrow."

Jonah grunts and sets down his barbell. "We ordered pizza. It's already on the way."

"I'll be quick." Ryan wanders off and Jonah gives me a look but goes back to his reps.

"Jonah. You've got to talk to him. Tell him to stay away from Kell until she cools off at least."

My younger brother doesn't look back as he focuses on the weights. "I tried last week," he says around heavy breaths. "Not about Kell. But his whole . . . thing. His attitude lately. Didn't listen."

"He's obsessed with taking on more projects," Jonah adds.

"Yeah, I've noticed." Last week when I tried to ask him how he had the time to star in a commercial for a brand deal and shoot two movies back to back, he almost bit my head off.

"He told me that he's not going to stop auditioning for stuff until he's the most recognizable name across the board. Not just movies. I don't know what set this off."

"Well, no one can control Ryan, but Kell deserves to be heard," Jessie says, looking at me. She keeps one eye on Jonah as he lifts. "Why don't you talk to her before the meeting? You're closest with her and it sounds like she might need someone to talk to."

"We don't talk about relationships," I say, exhaling. Our friendship has always been solid. No point in ruining things by bringing either of our love lives into it.

"Maybe you should start." Jessie raises her eyebrows at me pointedly.

She might be right.

I'm capable of talking if that's what Kell needs to stay. Like I said—leaving might be what's best for her but I'm going to have to be selfish. I can't do my job without her. Especially not the new projects I'm pursuing. Yeah, we need to talk about it. Maybe I'll be the one to convince her that Ryan isn't worth her time. I hope so.

"I'll go call her before she gets here. Your girlfriend is smart," I tell Jonah. He looks up at her and they both smile. It's a private moment and I've disappeared to them. My gut twists and I don't even know why. Maybe because no one has ever looked at me like that. And all of this drama is messing with my head. I'm going to go ahead and blame that on Ryan too.

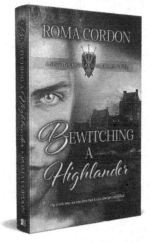
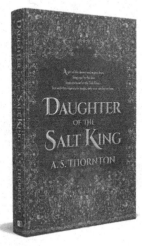
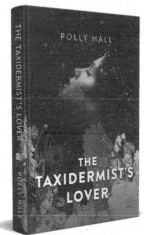

CamCat
Books

VISIT US ONLINE FOR MORE BOOKS TO LIVE IN:
CAMCATBOOKS.COM

SIGN UP FOR CAMCAT'S FICTION NEWSLETTER FOR
COVER REVEALS, EBOOK DEALS, AND MORE EXCLUSIVE CONTENT.

CamCatBooks   @CamCatBooks   @CamCat_Books   @CamCatBooks